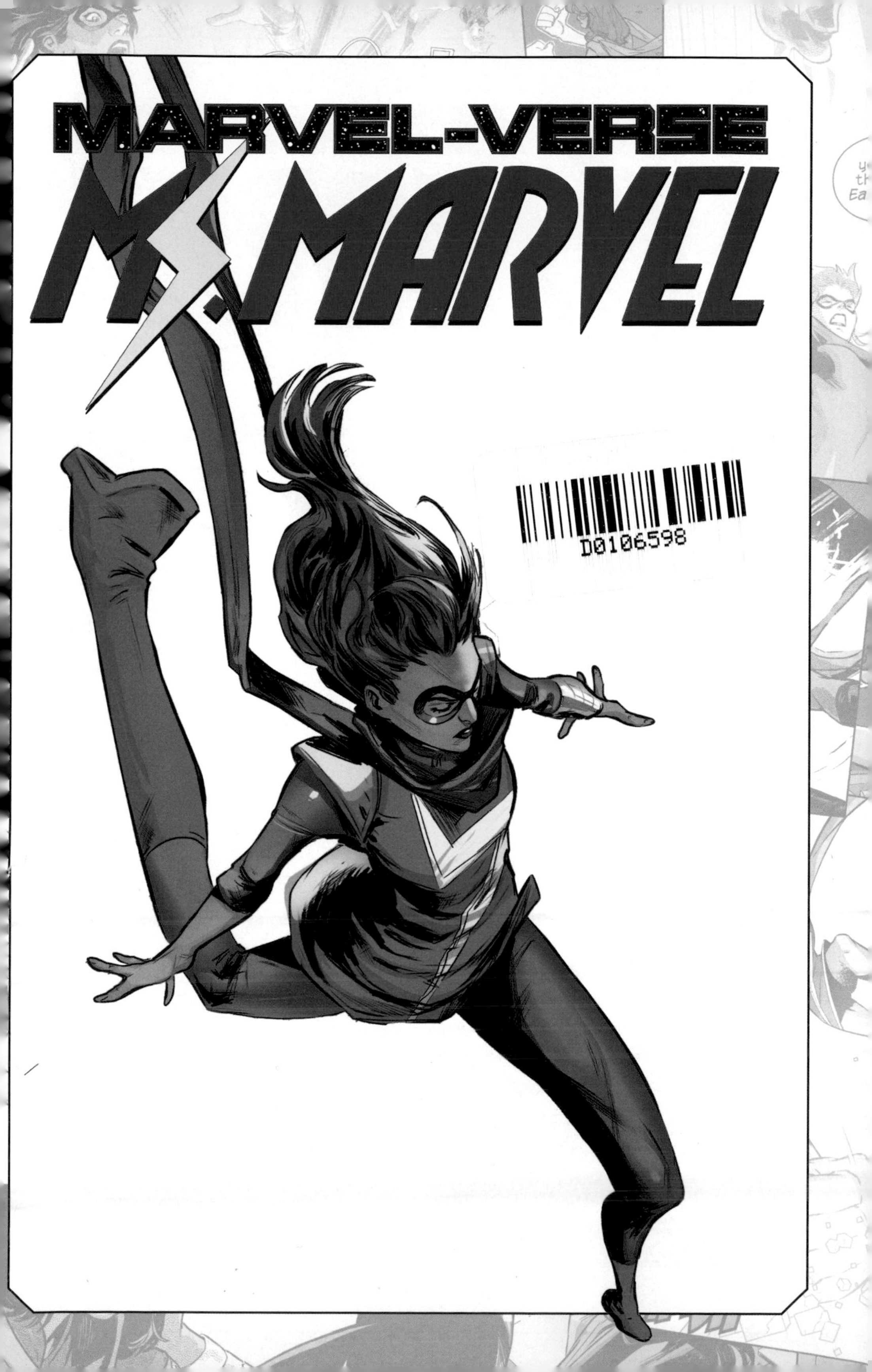
MARVEL-VERSE
MS. MARVEL

MARVEL-VERSE
MS. MARVEL

MS. MARVEL: MARVEL LEGACY PRIMER

WRITER: **ROBBIE THOMPSON**
ARTIST: **DIEGO OLORTEGUI**
COLOR ARTIST: **IAN HERRING**
LETTERER: VC's **JOE CARAMAGNA**
ASSISTANT EDITOR: **KATHLEEN WISNESKI**
EDITOR: **DARREN SHAN**

MS. MARVEL (2014) #12

WRITER: **G. WILLOW WILSON**
ARTIST: **ELMO BONDOC**
COLOR ARTIST: **IAN HERRING**
LETTERER: VC's **JOE CARAMAGNA**
COVER ART: **KRIS ANKA**
ASSISTANT EDITORS: **CHARLES BEACHAM & DEVIN LEWIS**
EDITOR: **SANA AMANAT**
SENIOR EDITOR: **NICK LOWE**

GENERATIONS: MS. MARVEL & MS. MARVEL

WRITER: **G. WILLOW WILSON**
ARTIST: **PAOLO VILLANELLI**
COLOR ARTIST: **IAN HERRING**
LETTERER: VC's **JOE CARAMAGNA**
COVER ART: **NELSON BLAKE II & RACHELLE ROSENBERG**
EDITOR: **CHARLES BEACHAM**
SUPERVISING EDITOR: **SANA AMANAT**

MS. MARVEL (2015) #38

STORY: **G. WILLOW WILSON**

WRITERS: **G. WILLOW WILSON** (PP. 1-9),
DEVIN GRAYSON (PP. 10-12),
EVE L. EWING (PP. 13-15),
JIM ZUB (PP. 16-18) &
SALADIN AHMED (PP. 19-21)

ARTISTS: **NICO LEON** (PP. 1-9),
TAKESHI MIYAZAWA (PP. 10-12),
JOEY VAZQUEZ (PP. 13-15),
KEVIN LIBRANDA (PP. 16-18) AND
MINKYU JUNG & JUAN VLASCO (PP. 19-21)

COLOR ARTIST & BONUS PAGE: **IAN HERRING**

LETTERER: **VC's JOE CARAMAGNA**

COVER ART: **SARA PICHELLI & JUSTIN PONSOR**

EDITORS: **SANA AMANAT & ALANNA SMITH**

MILES MORALES: SPIDER-MAN #24

WRITER: **SALADIN AHMED**

ARTIST: **CARMEN CARNERO**

COLOR ARTIST: **DAVID CURIEL**

LETTERER: **VC's CORY PETIT**

COVER ART: **TAURIN CLARKE**

ASSISTANT EDITOR: **LINDSEY COHICK**

EXECUTIVE EDITOR: **NICK LOWE**

COLLECTION EDITOR: **JENNIFER GRÜNWALD** ASSISTANT EDITOR: **DANIEL KIRCHHOFFER**
ASSISTANT MANAGING EDITOR: **MAIA LOY** ASSOCIATE MANAGER, TALENT RELATIONS: **LISA MONTALBANO**
VP PRODUCTION & SPECIAL PROJECTS: **JEFF YOUNGQUIST** RESEARCH: **JESS HARROLD**
BOOK DESIGNERS: **STACIE ZUCKER & JAY BOWEN** SENIOR DESIGNER: **ADAM DEL RE**
SVP PRINT, SALES & MARKETING: **DAVID GABRIEL** EDITOR IN CHIEF: **C.B. CEBULSKI**

MARVEL-VERSE: MS. MARVEL GN-TPB. Contains material originally published in magazine form as MS. MARVEL (2014) #12, GENERATIONS: MS. MARVEL & MS. MARVEL (2017) #1, MS. MARVEL (2015) #38 and MILES MORALES: SPIDER-MAN (2018) #24. First printing 2022. ISBN 978-1-302-94781-1. Published by MARVEL WORLDWIDE, INC., a subsidiary of MARVEL ENTERTAINMENT, LLC. OFFICE OF PUBLICATION: 1290 Avenue of the Americas, New York, NY 10104. © 2022 MARVEL No similarity between any of the names, characters, persons, and/ or institutions in this book with those of any living or dead person or institution is intended, and any such similarity which may exist is purely coincidental. **Printed in Canada.** KEVIN FEIGE, Chief Creative Officer; DAN BUCKLEY, President, Marvel Entertainment; JOE QUESADA, EVP & Creative Director; DAVID BOGART, Associate Publisher & SVP of Talent Affairs; TOM BREVOORT, VP, Executive Editor; NICK LOWE, Executive Editor, VP of Content, Digital Publishing; DAVID GABRIEL, VP of Print & Digital Publishing; SVEN LARSEN, VP of Licensed Publishing; MARK ANNUNZIATO, VP of Planning & Forecasting; JEFF YOUNGQUIST, VP of Production & Special Projects; ALEX MORALES, Director of Publishing Operations; DAN EDINGTON, Director of Editorial Operations; RICKEY PURDIN, Director of Talent Relations; JENNIFER GRÜNWALD, Director of Production & Special Projects; SUSAN CRESPI, Production Manager; STAN LEE, Chairman Emeritus. For information regarding advertising in Marvel Comics or on Marvel.com, please contact Vit DeBellis, Custom Solutions & Integrated Advertising Manager, at vdebellis@marvel. com. For Marvel subscription inquiries, please call 888-511-5480. **Manufactured between 6/3/2022 and 7/5/2022 by SOLISCO PRINTERS, SCOTT, QC, CANADA.**

10 9 8 7 6 5 4 3 2 1

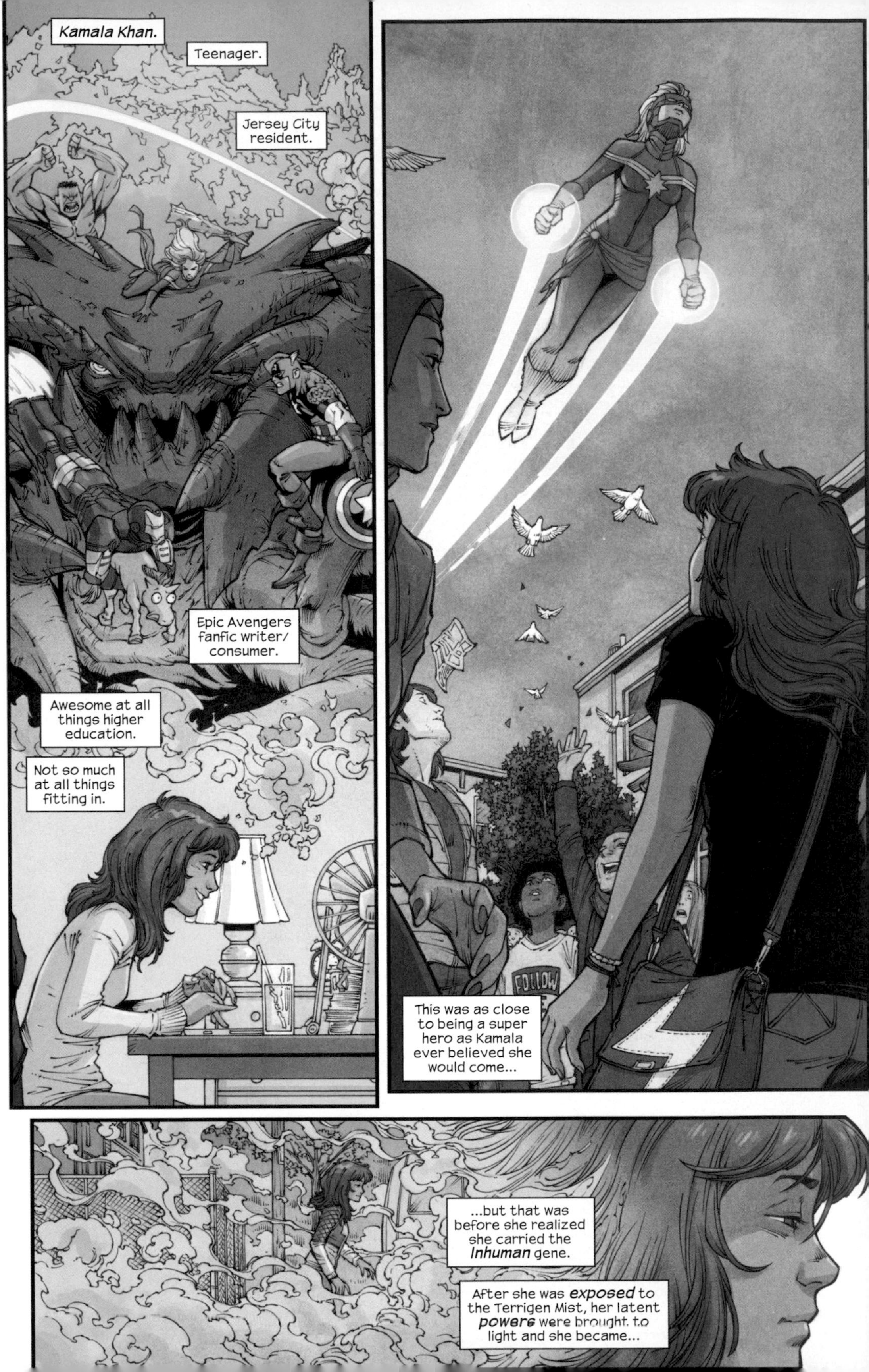
Kamala Khan.
Teenager.
Jersey City resident.
Epic Avengers fanfic writer/consumer.
Awesome at all things higher education.
Not so much at all things fitting in.
This was as close to being a super hero as Kamala ever believed she would come...
FOLLOW
...but that was before she realized she carried the *Inhuman* gene.
After she was ***exposed*** to the Terrigen Mist, her latent ***powers*** were brought to light and she became...

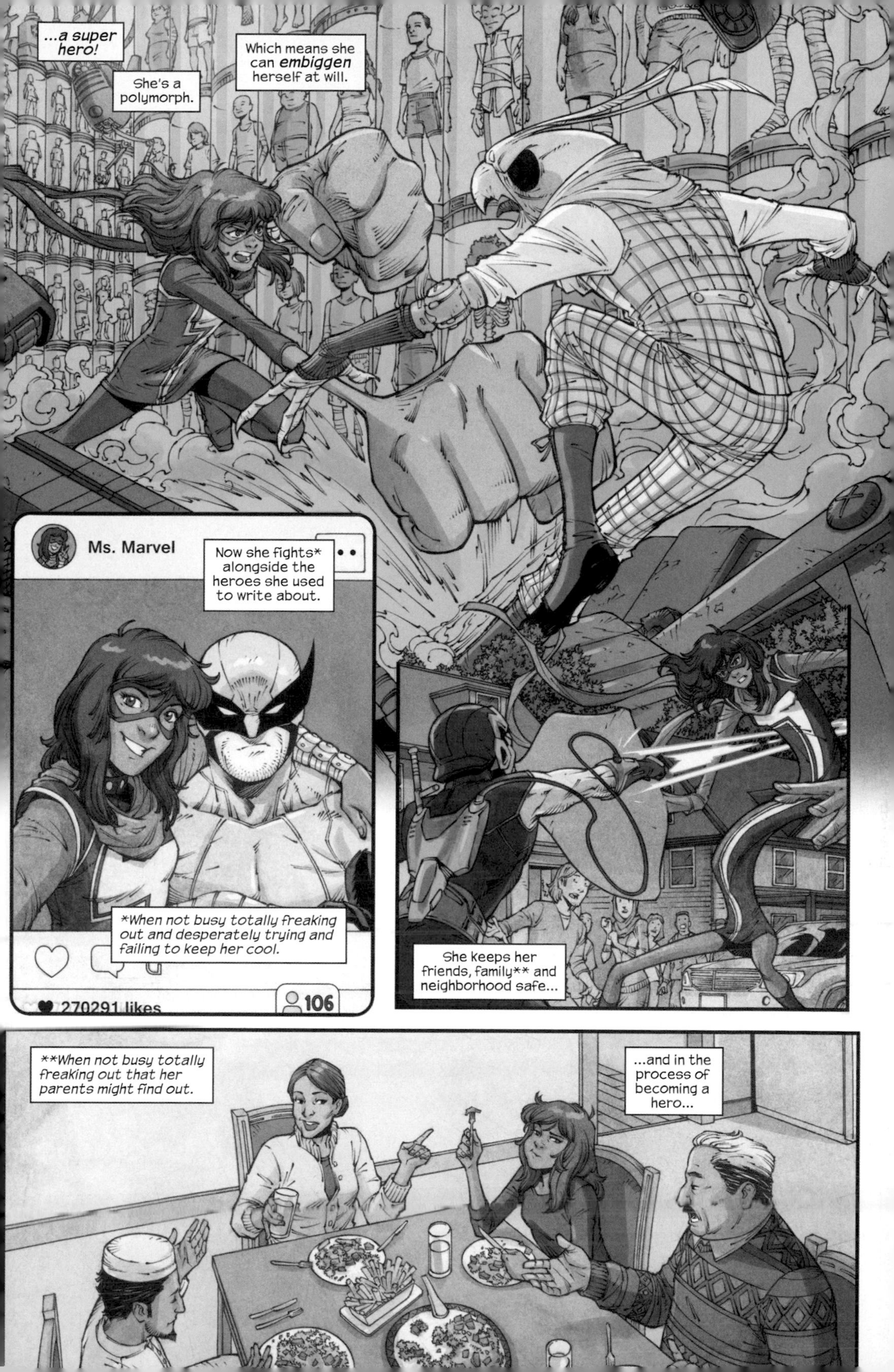

...a super hero!
She's a polymorph.
Which means she can *embiggen* herself at will.
Ms. Marvel
Now she fights* alongside the heroes she used to write about.
*When not busy totally freaking out and desperately trying and failing to keep her cool.
270291 likes
106
She keeps her friends, family** and neighborhood safe...
**When not busy totally freaking out that her parents might find out.
...and in the process of becoming a hero...

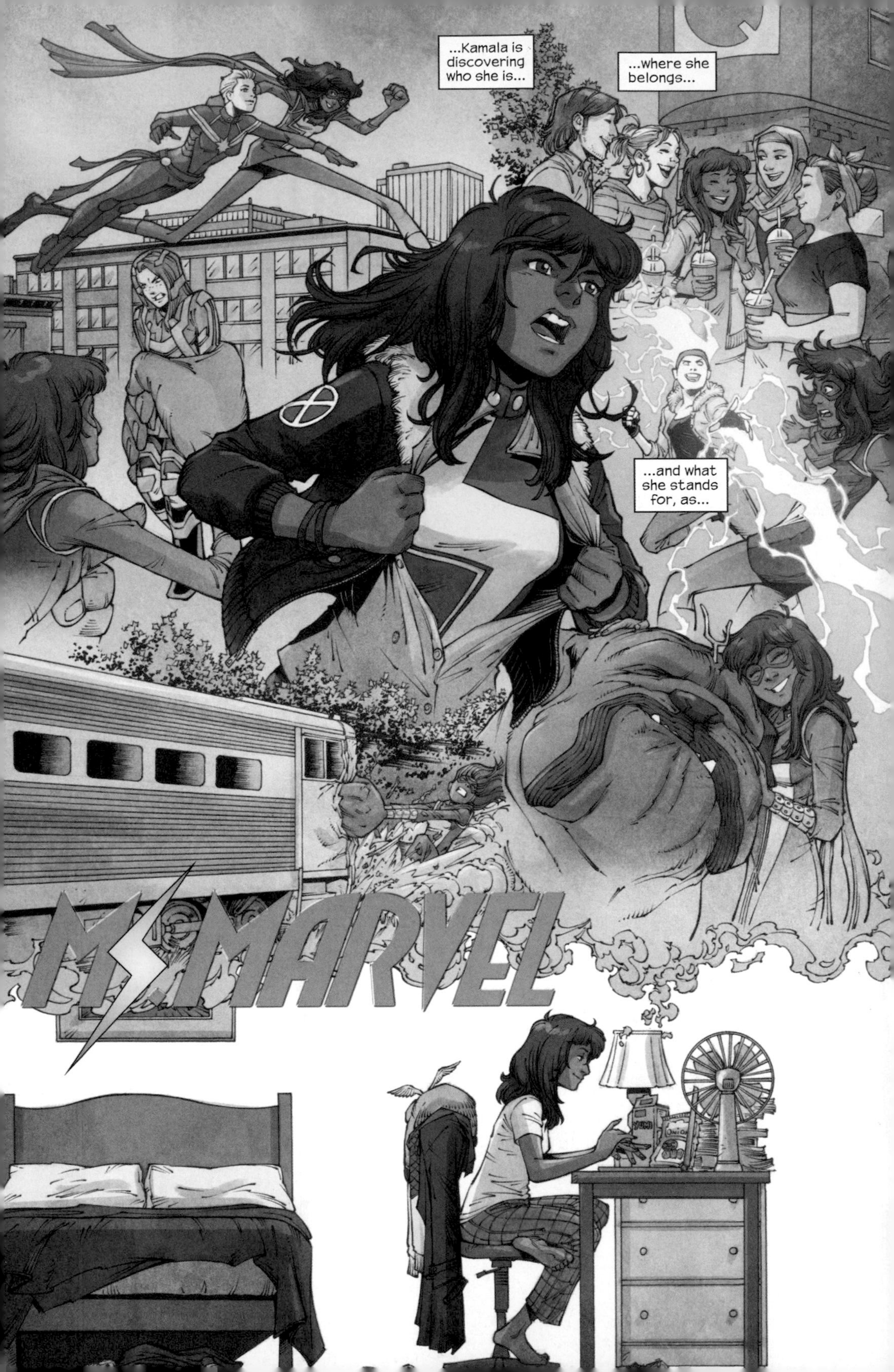

...Kamala is discovering who she is...
...where she belongs...
...and what she stands for, as...
MS. MARVEL

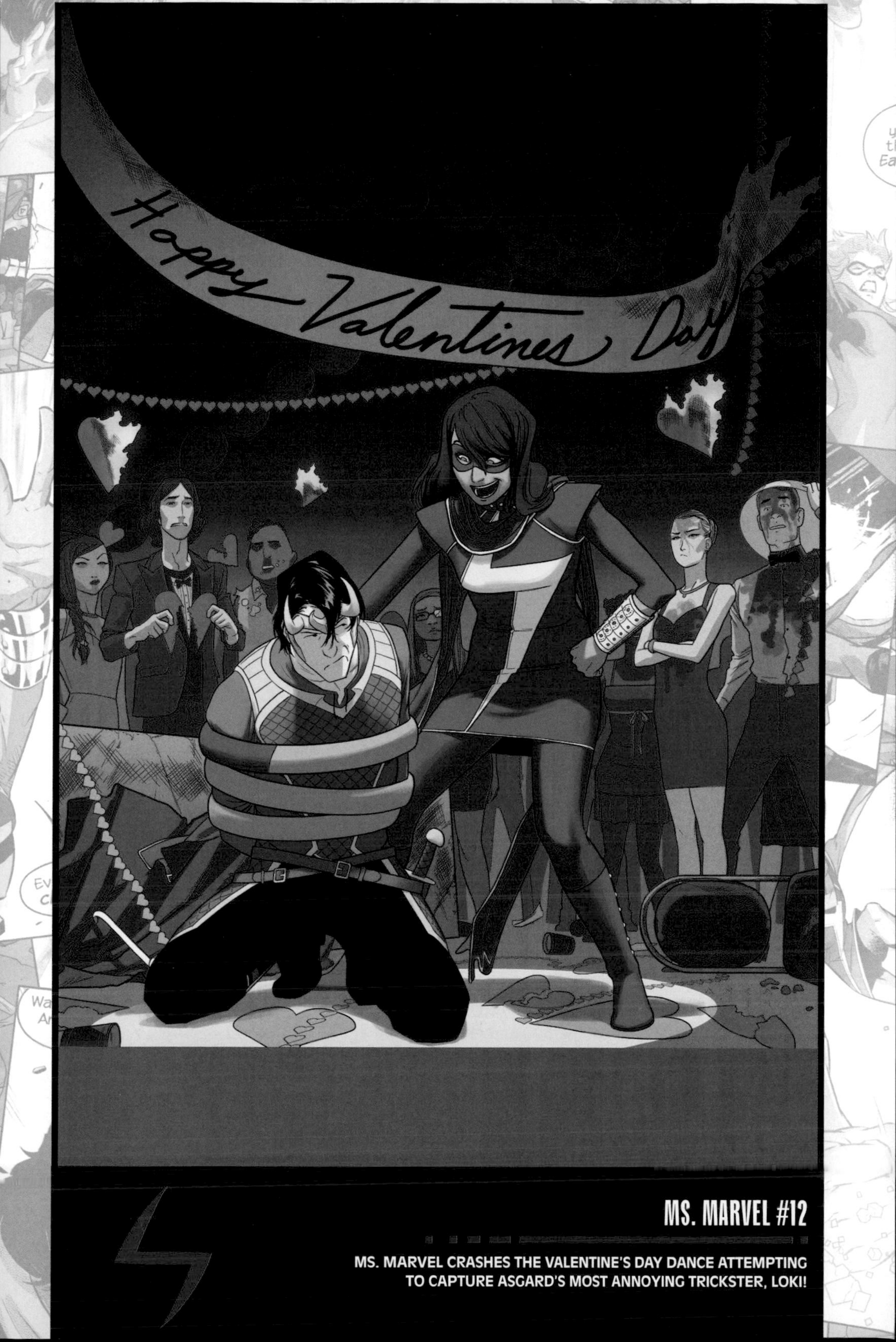
Happy Valentines Day

MS. MARVEL #12

MS. MARVEL CRASHES THE VALENTINE'S DAY DANCE ATTEMPTING TO CAPTURE ASGARD'S MOST ANNOYING TRICKSTER, LOKI!

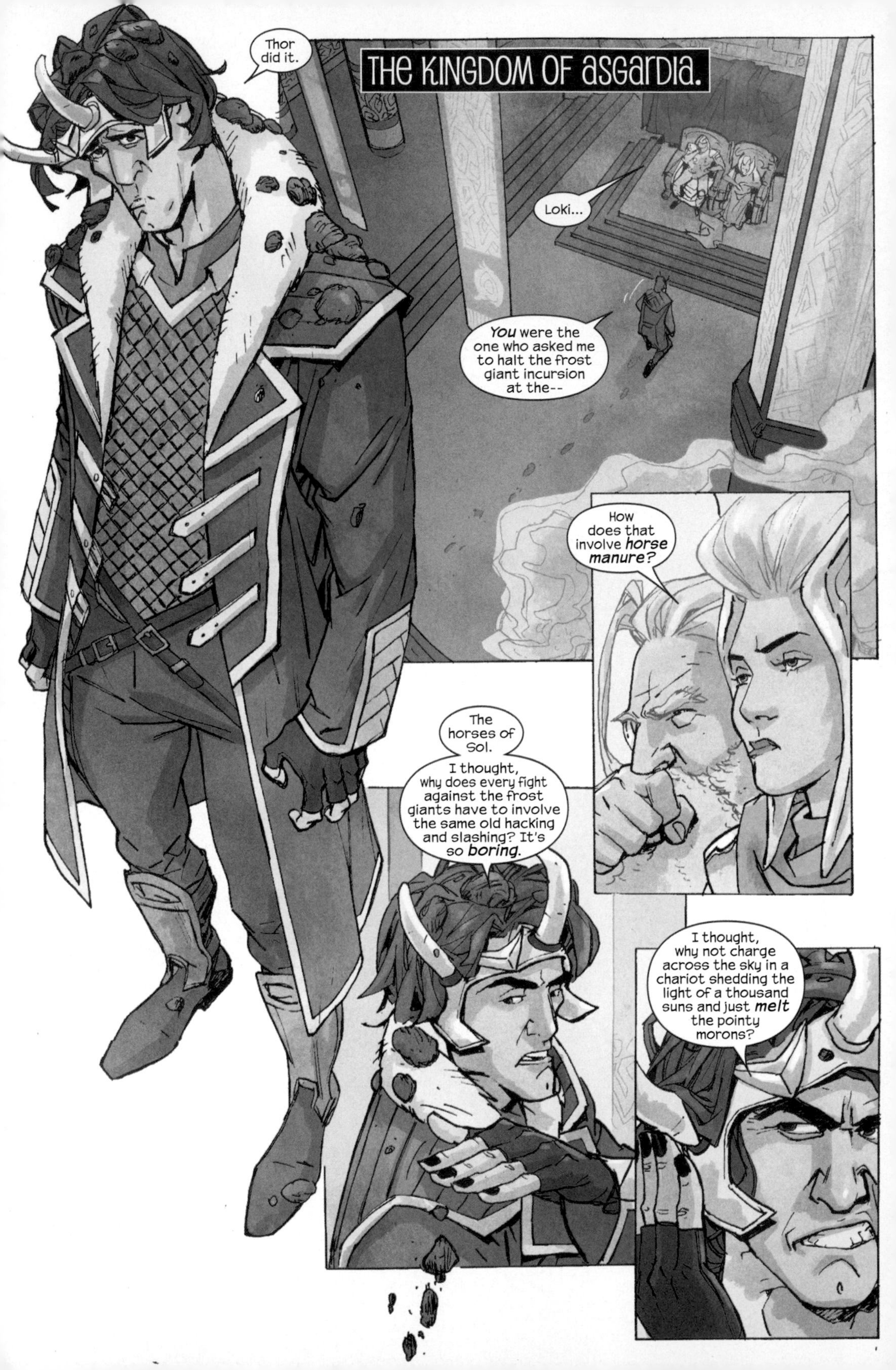
Thor did it.
THE KINGDOM OF ASGARDIA.
Loki...
You were the one who asked me to halt the frost giant incursion at the--
How does that involve horse manure?
The horses of Sol.
I thought, why does every fight against the frost giants have to involve the same old hacking and slashing? It's so boring.
I thought, why not charge across the sky in a chariot shedding the light of a thousand suns and just melt the pointy morons?

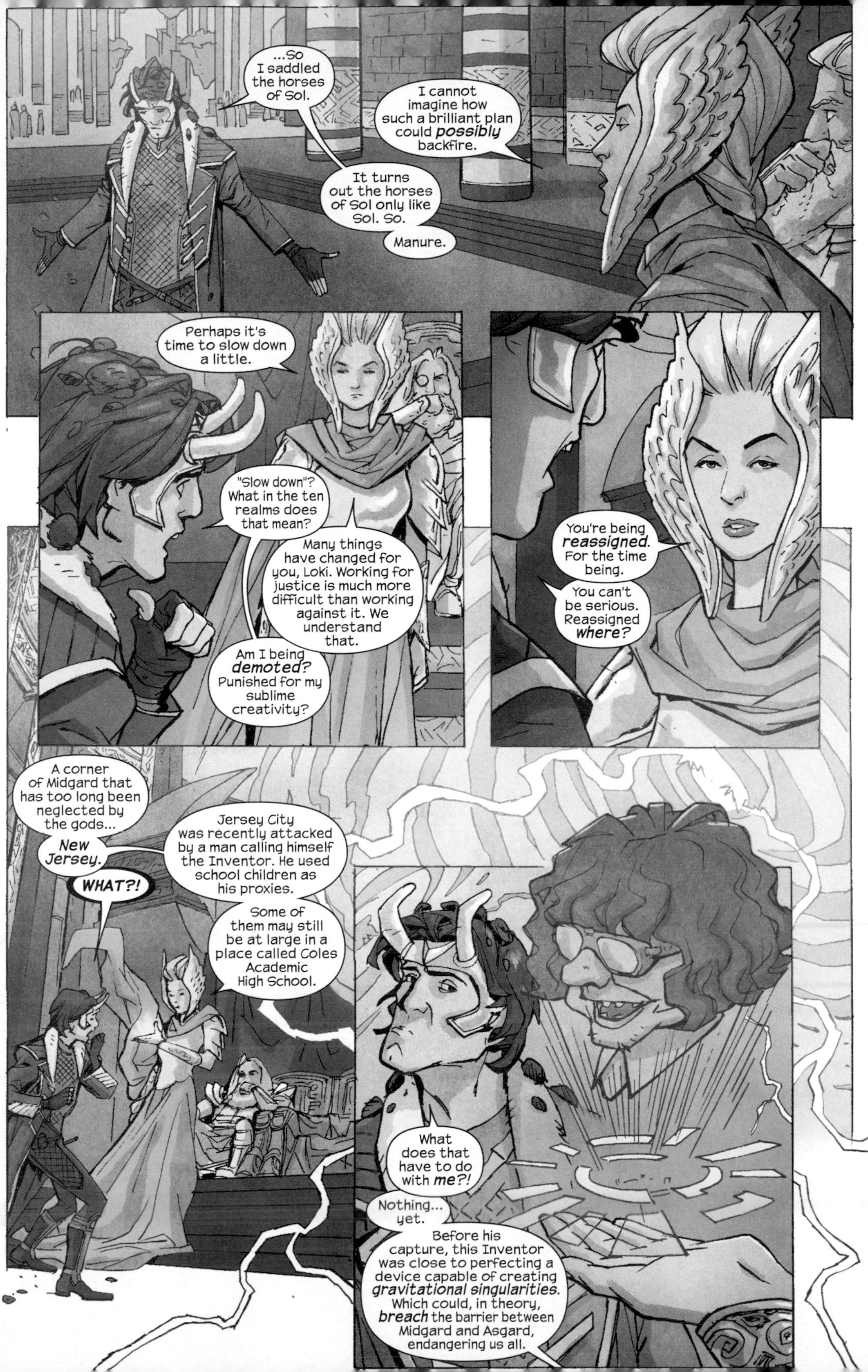

...So I saddled the horses of Sol.
I cannot imagine how such a brilliant plan could *possibly* backfire.
It turns out the horses of Sol only like Sol. So.
Manure.
Perhaps it's time to slow down a little.
"Slow down"? What in the ten realms does that mean?
Many things have changed for you, Loki. Working for justice is much more difficult than working against it. We understand that.
Am I being *demoted?* Punished for my sublime creativity?
You're being *reassigned*. For the time being.
You can't be serious. Reassigned *where?*
A corner of Midgard that has too long been neglected by the gods...
New Jersey.
WHAT?!
Jersey City was recently attacked by a man calling himself the Inventor. He used school children as his proxies.
Some of them may still be at large in a place called Coles Academic High School.
What does that have to do with *me?!*
Nothing... yet.
Before his capture, this Inventor was close to perfecting a device capable of creating *gravitational singularities*. Which could, in theory, *breach* the barrier between Midgard and Asgard, endangering us all.

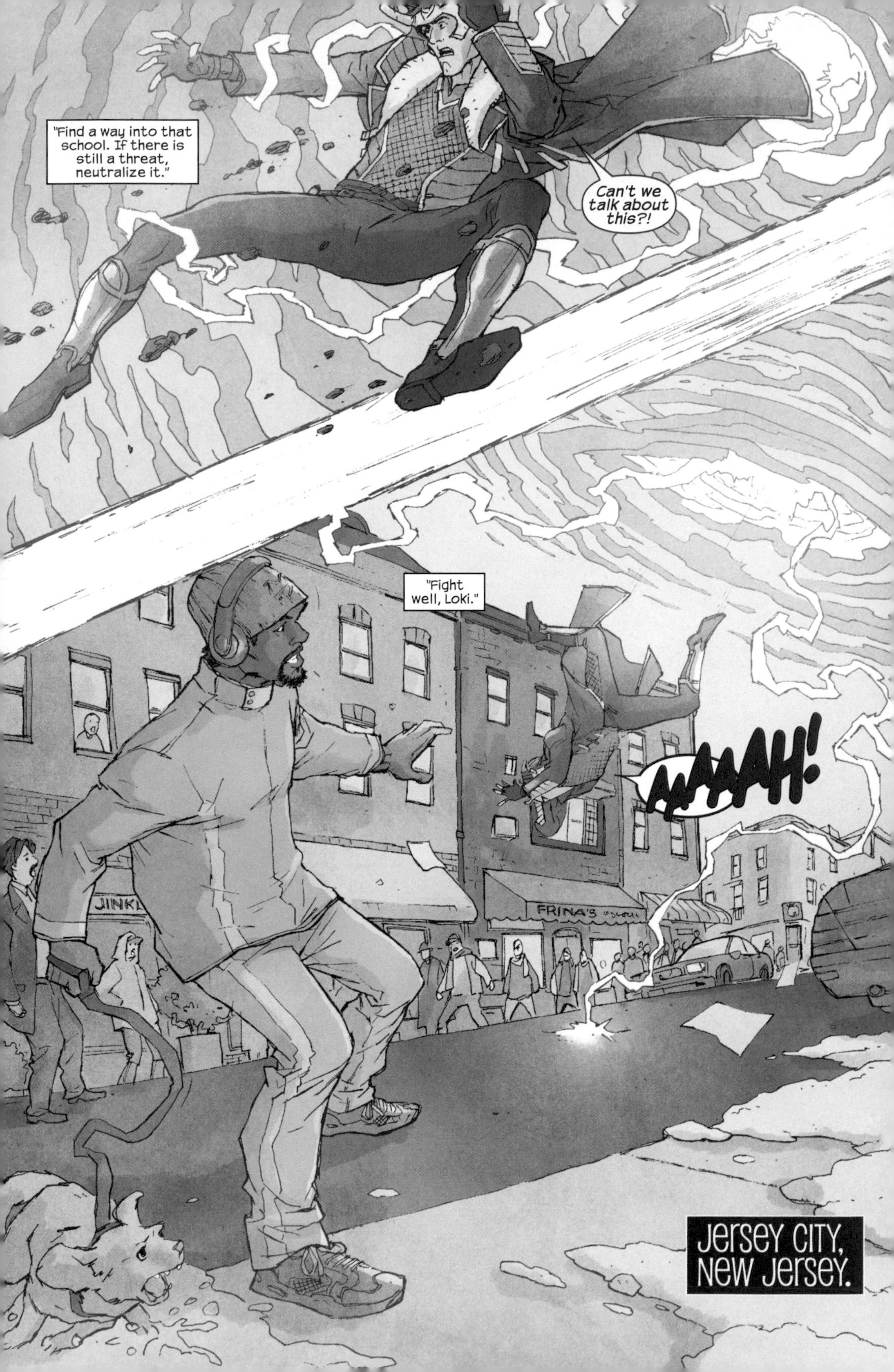
"Find a way into that school. If there is still a threat, neutralize it."
Can't we talk about this?!
"Fight well, Loki."
AAAAAH!
JINK
FRINA'S
JERSEY CITY, NEW JERSEY.

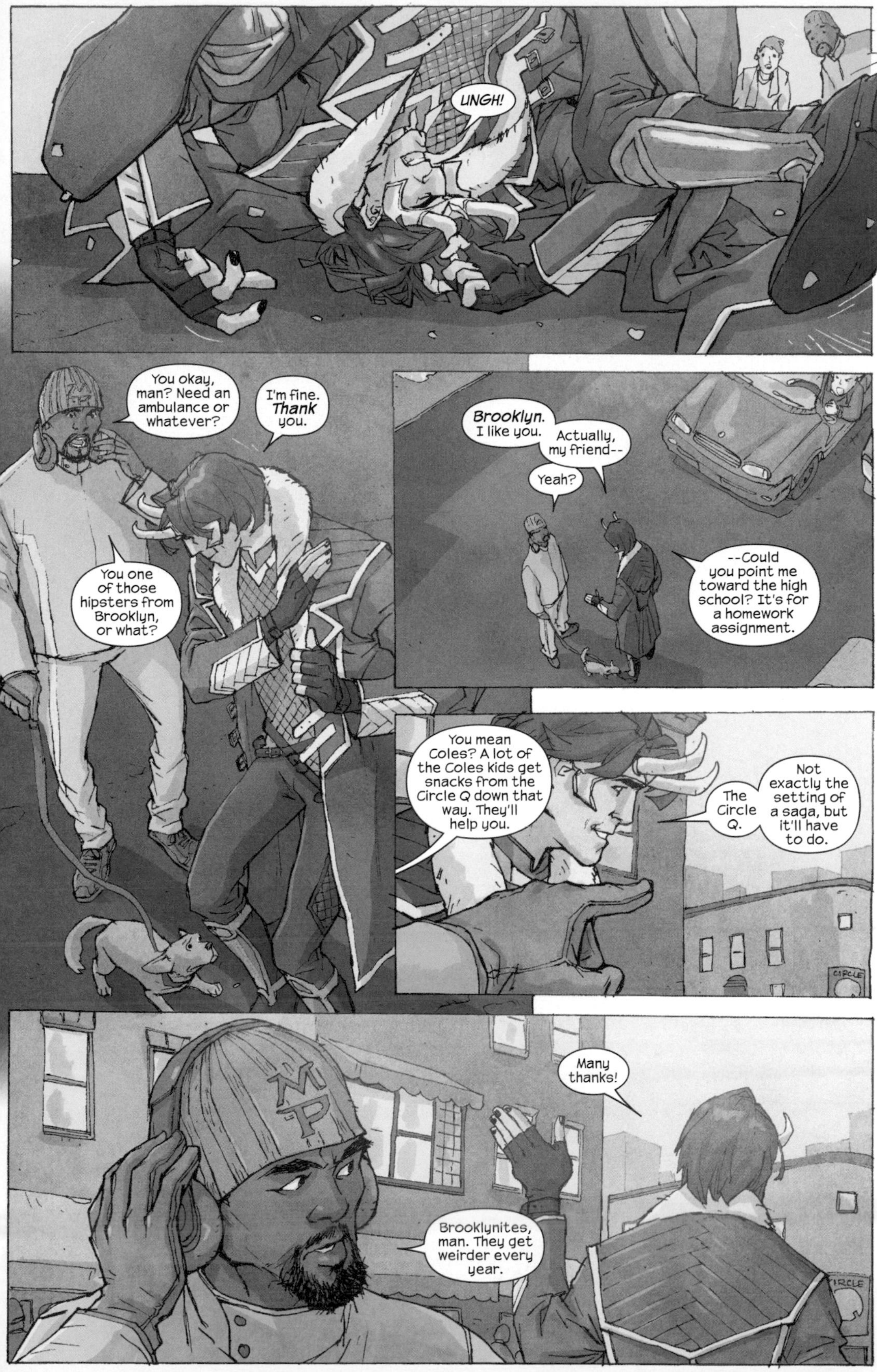
UNGH!
You okay, man? Need an ambulance or whatever?
I'm fine. *Thank* you.
You one of those hipsters from Brooklyn, or what?
Brooklyn. I like you.
Actually, my friend--
Yeah?
--Could you point me toward the high school? It's for a homework assignment.
You mean Coles? A lot of the Coles kids get snacks from the Circle Q down that way. They'll help you.
The Circle Q.
Not exactly the setting of a saga, but it'll have to do.
CIRCLE
Many thanks!
Brooklynites, man. They get weirder every year.
CIRCLE

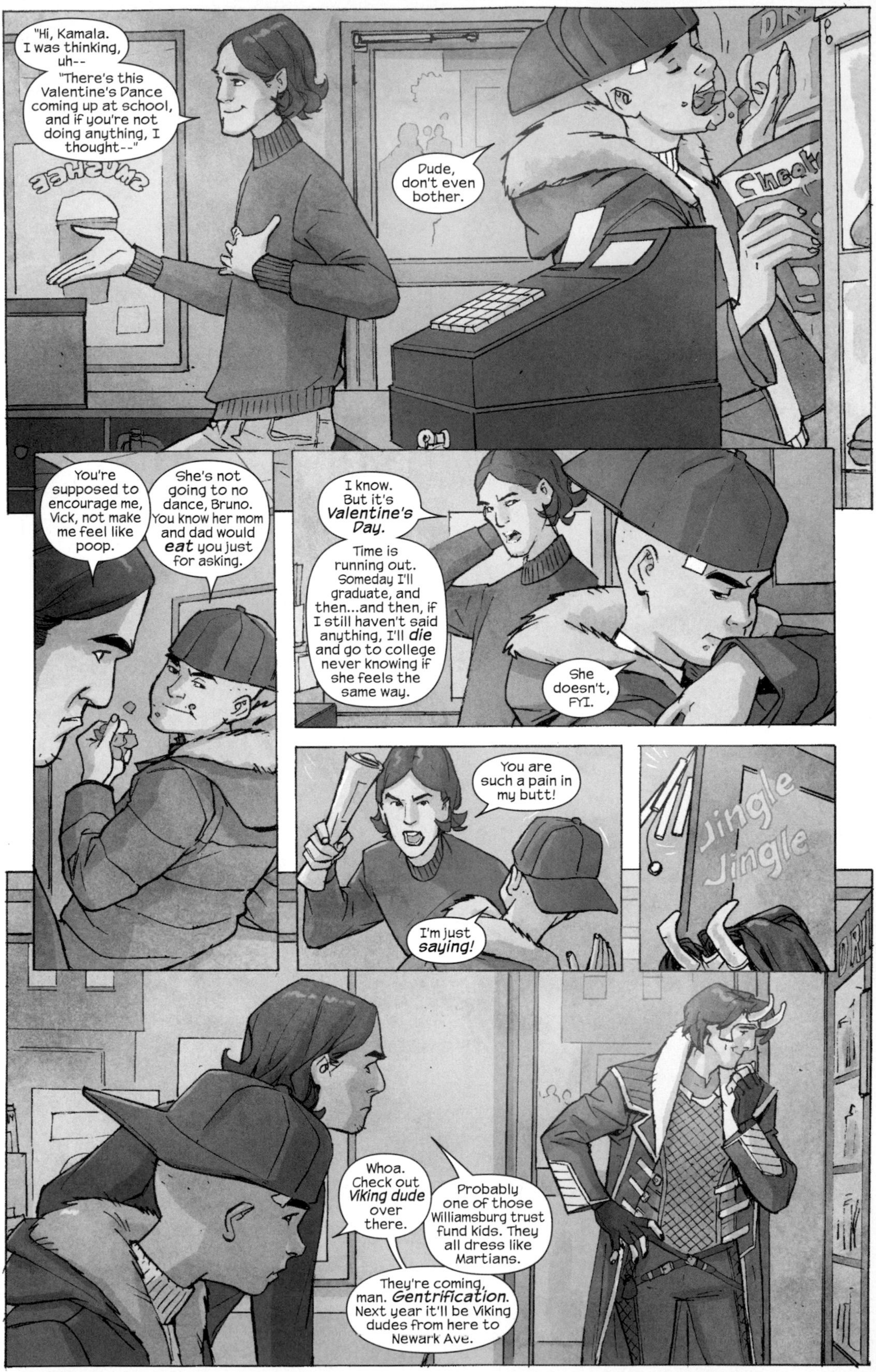

"Hi, Kamala. I was thinking, uh--
"There's this Valentine's Dance coming up at school, and if you're not doing anything, I thought--"
Dude, don't even bother.
You're supposed to encourage me, Vick, not make me feel like poop.
She's not going to no dance, Bruno. You know her mom and dad would eat you just for asking.
I know. But it's Valentine's Day.
Time is running out. Someday I'll graduate, and then...and then, if I still haven't said anything, I'll die and go to college never knowing if she feels the same way.
She doesn't, FYI.
You are such a pain in my butt!
I'm just saying!
Jingle Jingle
Whoa. Check out Viking dude over there.
Probably one of those Williamsburg trust fund kids. They all dress like Martians.
They're coming, man. Gentrification. Next year it'll be Viking dudes from here to Newark Ave.

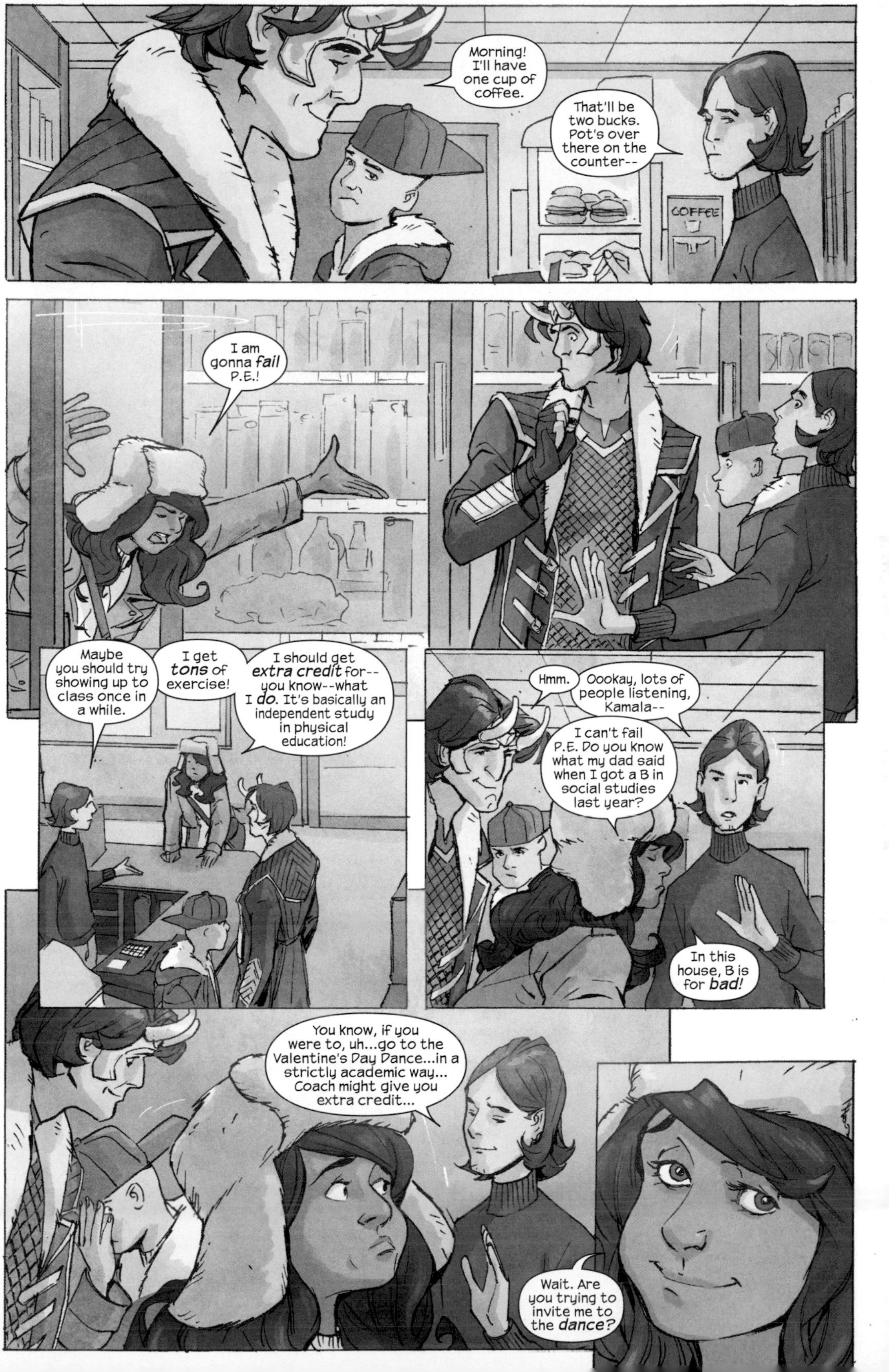
Morning! I'll have one cup of coffee.
That'll be two bucks. Pot's over there on the counter--
COFFEE
I am gonna *fail* P.E.!
Maybe you should try showing up to class once in a while.
I get **tons** of exercise!
I should get *extra credit* for--you know--what I *do*. It's basically an independent study in physical education!
Hmm.
Oookay, lots of people listening, Kamala--
I can't fail P.E. Do you know what my dad said when I got a B in social studies last year?
In this house, B is for *bad!*
You know, if you were to, uh...go to the Valentine's Day Dance...in a strictly academic way... Coach might give you extra credit...
Wait. Are you trying to invite me to the *dance?*

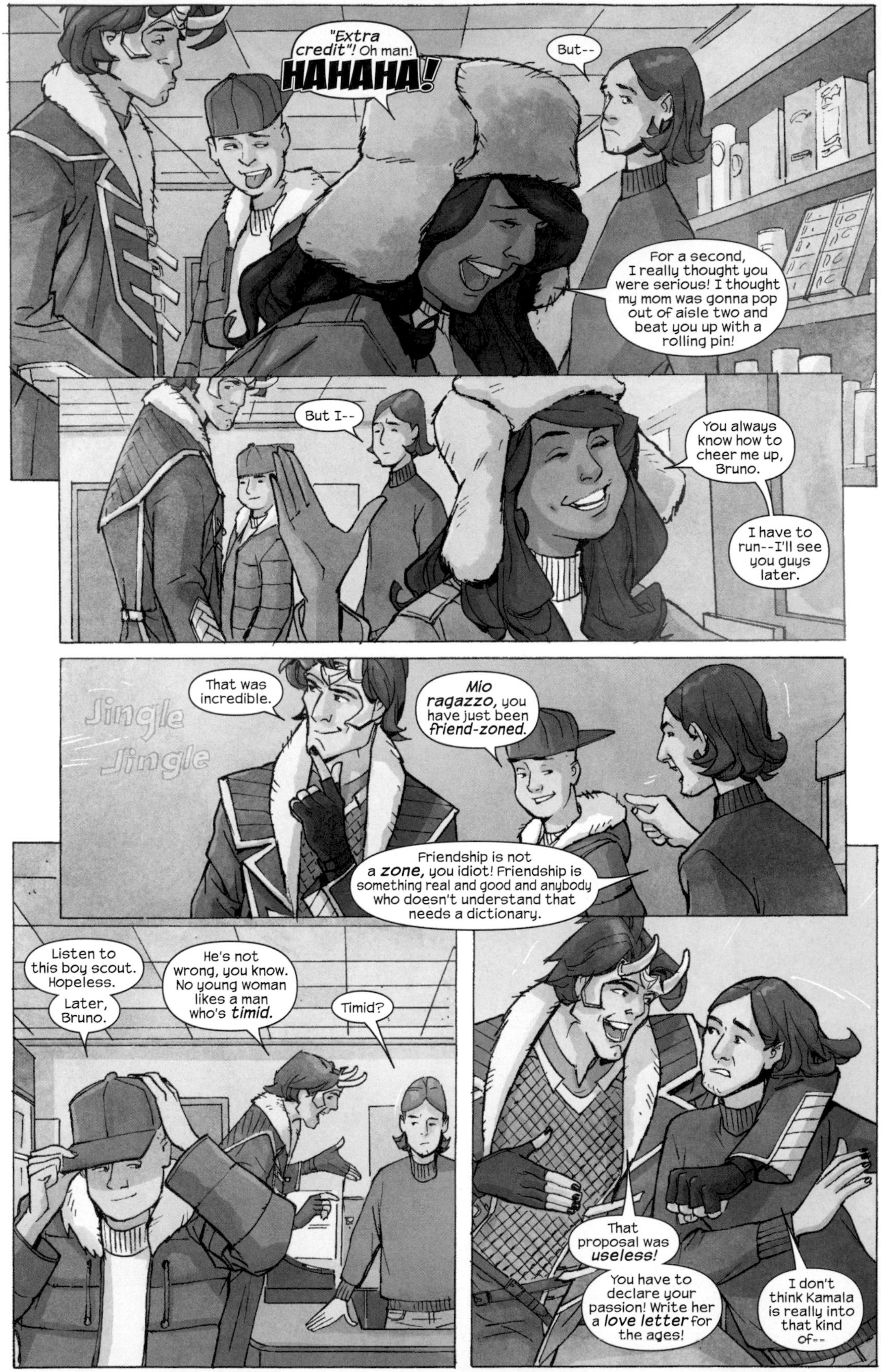
"Extra credit"! Oh man!
HAHAHA!
But--
For a second, I really thought you were serious! I thought my mom was gonna pop out of aisle two and beat you up with a rolling pin!
But I--
You always know how to cheer me up, Bruno.
I have to run--I'll see you guys later.
Jingle Jingle
That was incredible.
Mio ragazzo, you have just been friend-zoned.
Friendship is not a zone, you idiot! Friendship is something real and good and anybody who doesn't understand that needs a dictionary.
Listen to this boy scout. Hopeless.
Later, Bruno.
He's not wrong, you know. No young woman likes a man who's timid.
Timid?
That proposal was useless!
You have to declare your passion! Write her a love letter for the ages!
I don't think Kamala is really into that kind of--

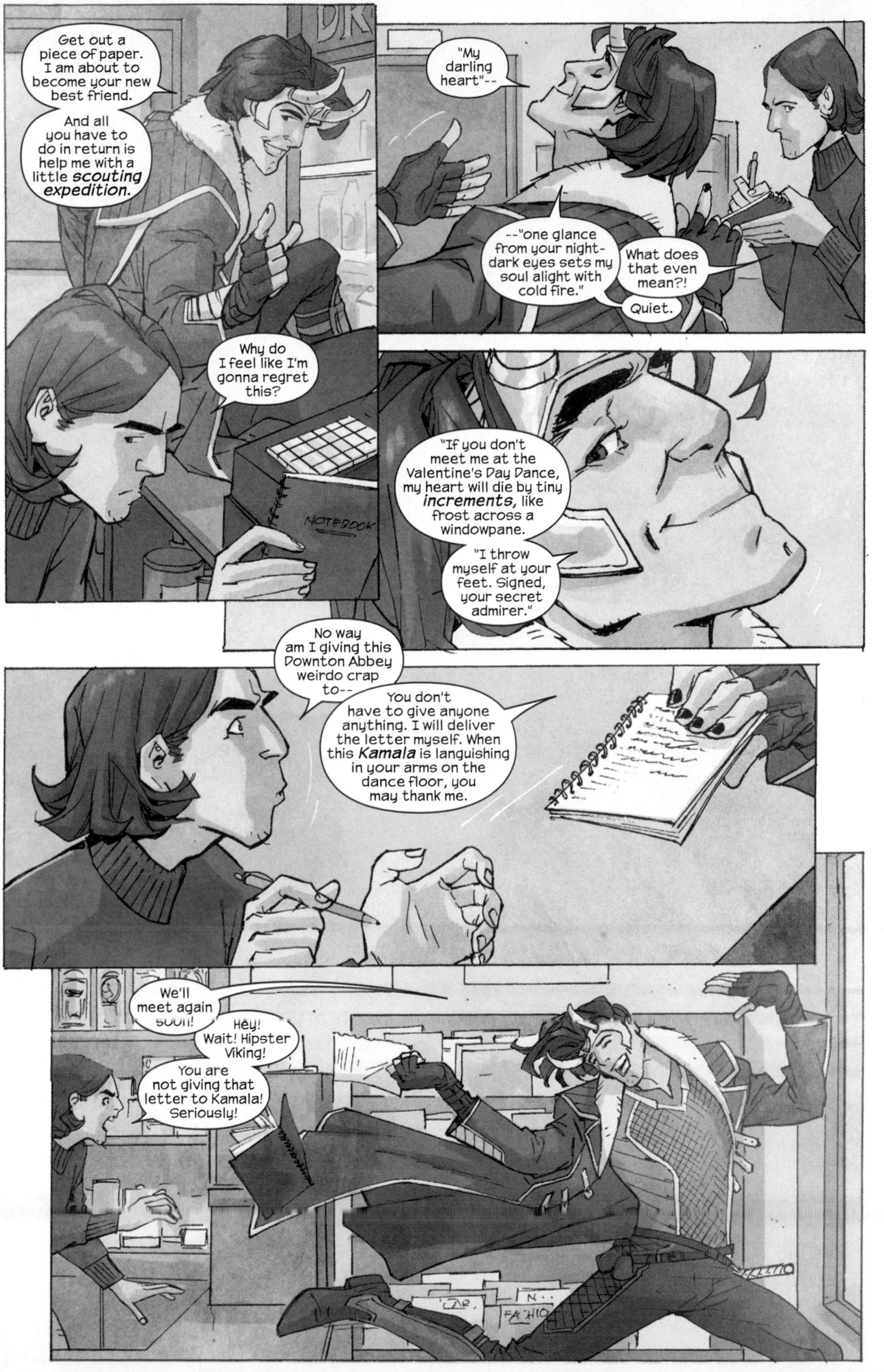

Get out a piece of paper. I am about to become your new best friend.
And all you have to do in return is help me with a little *scouting expedition.*
"My darling heart"--
--"one glance from your night-dark eyes sets my soul alight with cold fire."
What does that even mean?!
Quiet.
Why do I feel like I'm gonna regret this?
NOTEBOOK
"If you don't meet me at the Valentine's Day Dance, my heart will die by tiny *increments,* like frost across a windowpane.
"I throw myself at your feet. Signed, your secret admirer."
No way am I giving this Downton Abbey weirdo crap to--
You don't have to give anyone anything. I will deliver the letter myself. When this *Kamala* is languishing in your arms on the dance floor, you may thank me.
We'll meet again soon!
Hey! Wait! Hipster Viking!
You are not giving that letter to Kamala! Seriously!

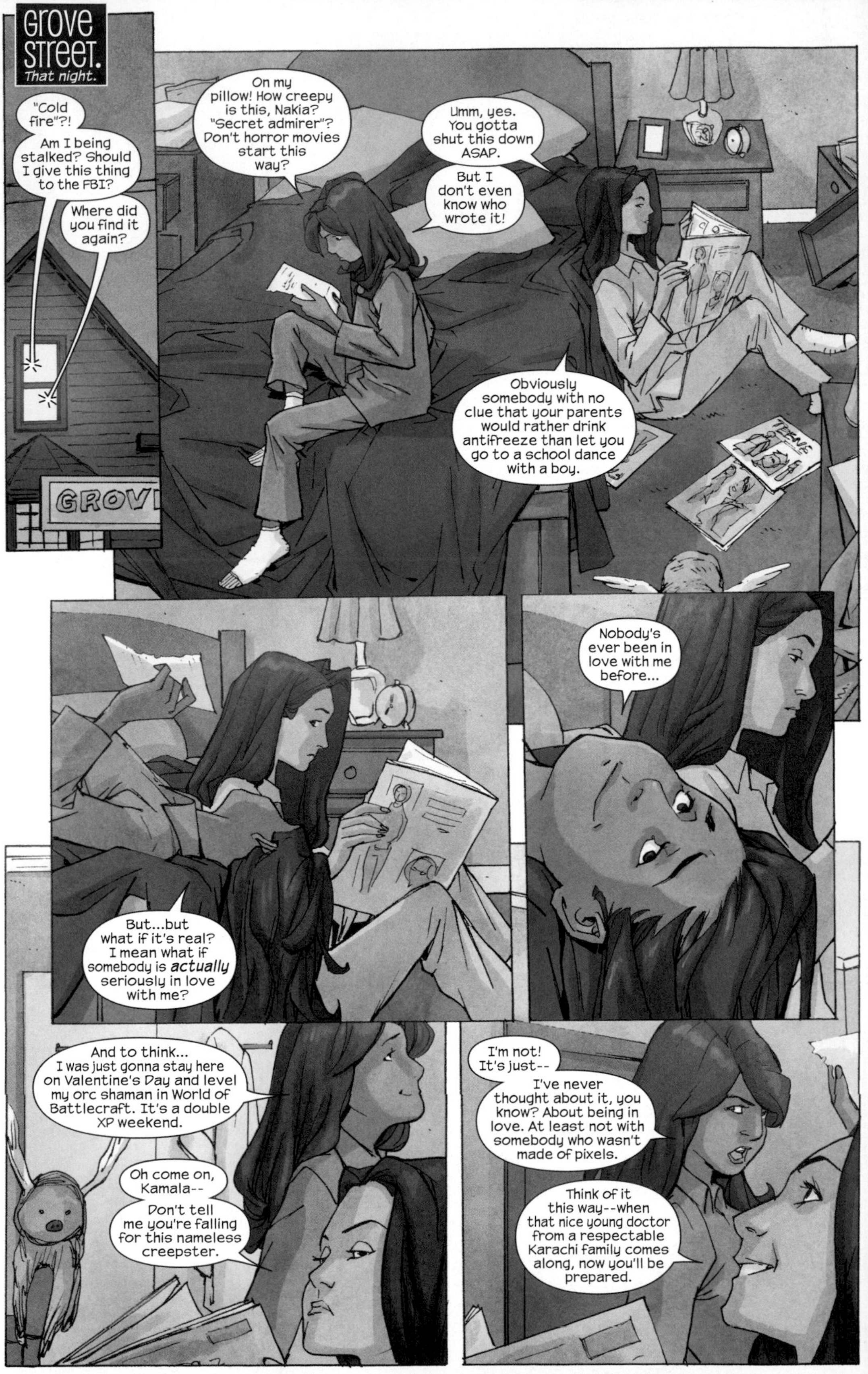
GROVE STREET.
That night.
"Cold fire"?!
Am I being stalked? Should I give this thing to the FBI?
Where did you find it again?
On my pillow! How creepy is this, Nakia? "Secret admirer"? Don't horror movies start this way?
Umm, yes. You gotta shut this down ASAP.
But I don't even know who wrote it!
Obviously somebody with no clue that your parents would rather drink antifreeze than let you go to a school dance with a boy.
GROV
TEENS
But...but what if it's real? I mean what if somebody is *actually* seriously in love with me?
Nobody's ever been in love with me before...
And to think... I was just gonna stay here on Valentine's Day and level my orc shaman in World of Battlecraft. It's a double XP weekend.
Oh come on, Kamala--
Don't tell me you're falling for this nameless creepster.
I'm not! It's just--
I've never thought about it, you know? About being in love. At least not with somebody who wasn't made of pixels.
Think of it this way--when that nice young doctor from a respectable Karachi family comes along, now you'll be prepared.

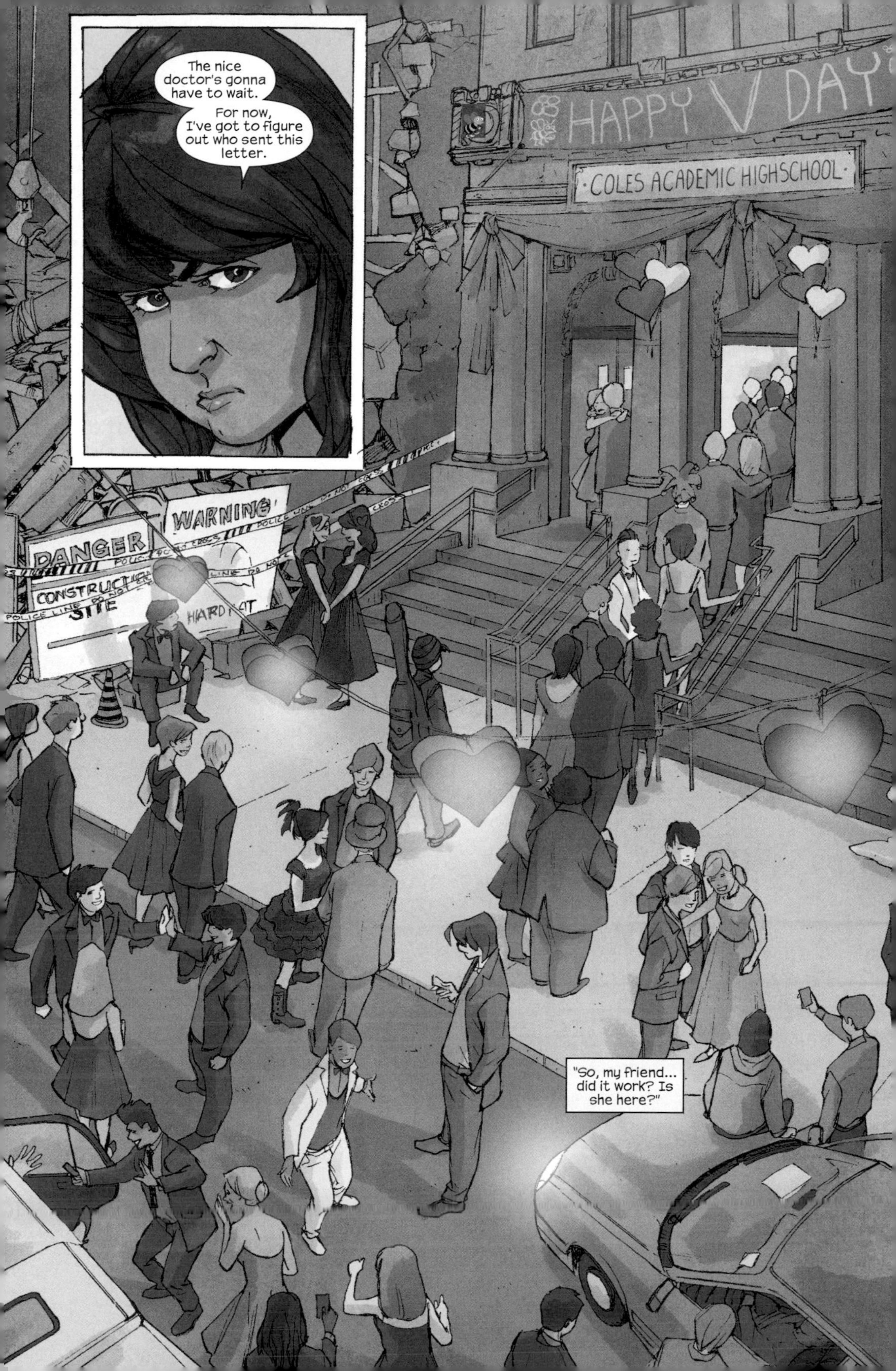
The nice doctor's gonna have to wait.
For now, I've got to figure out who sent this letter.
HAPPY V DAY
COLES ACADEMIC HIGHSCHOOL
WARNING
DANGER
CONSTRUCTION SITE
"So, my friend... did it work? Is she here?"

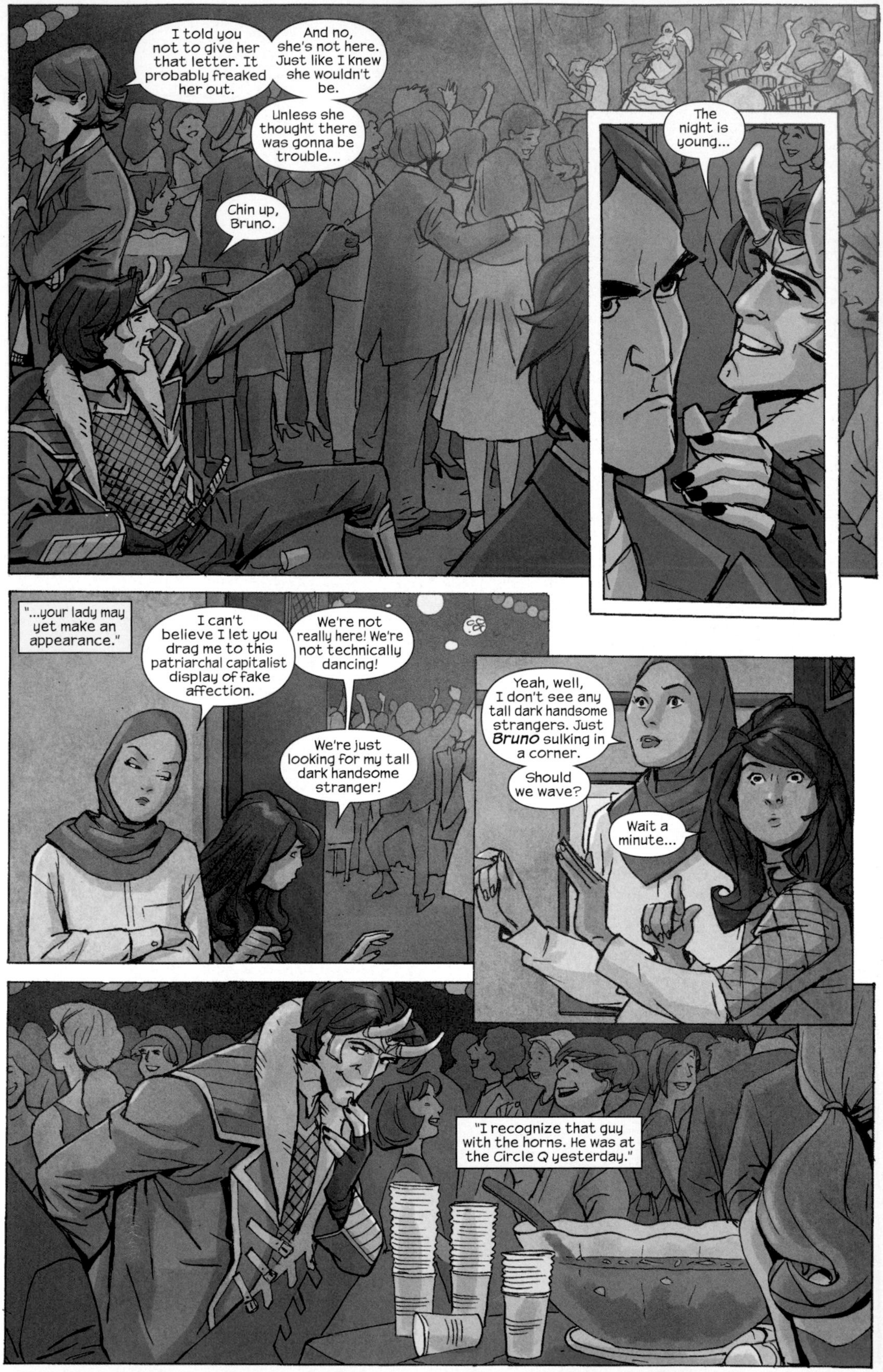
I told you not to give her that letter. It probably freaked her out.
And no, she's not here. Just like I knew she wouldn't be.
Unless she thought there was gonna be trouble...
Chin up, Bruno.
The night is young...
"...your lady may yet make an appearance."
I can't believe I let you drag me to this patriarchal capitalist display of fake affection.
We're not really here! We're not technically dancing!
We're just looking for my tall dark handsome stranger!
Yeah, well, I don't see any tall dark handsome strangers. Just *Bruno* sulking in a corner.
Should we wave?
Wait a minute...
"I recognize that guy with the horns. He was at the Circle Q yesterday."

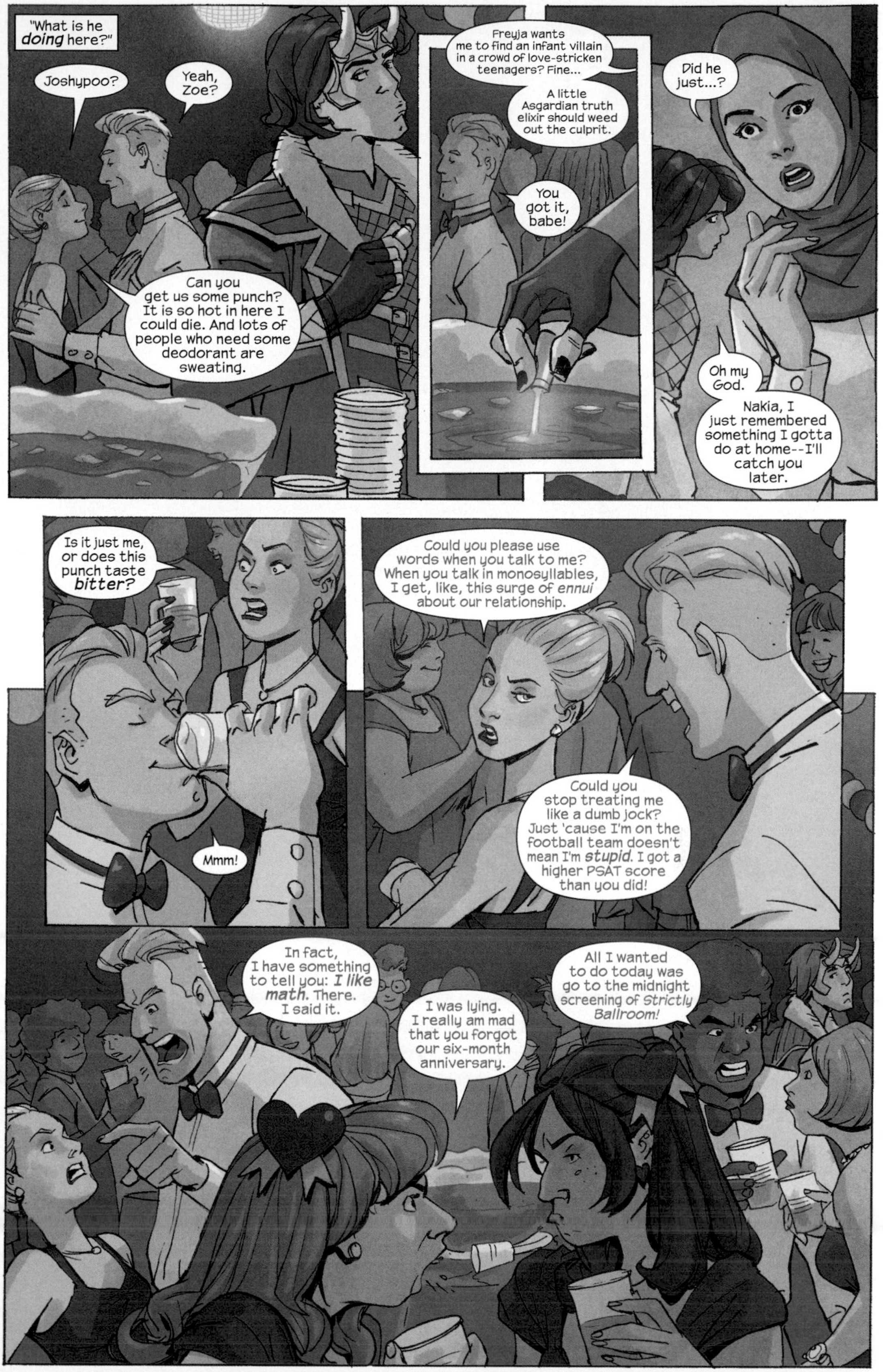

"What is he *doing* here?"
Joshypoo?
Yeah, Zoe?
Can you get us some punch? It is so hot in here I could die. And lots of people who need some deodorant are sweating.
Freyja wants me to find an infant villain in a crowd of love-stricken teenagers? Fine...
A little Asgardian truth elixir should weed out the culprit.
You got it, babe!
Did he just...?
Oh my God.
Nakia, I just remembered something I gotta do at home--I'll catch you later.
Is it just me, or does this punch taste *bitter?*
Mmm!
Could you please use words when you talk to me? When you talk in monosyllables, I get, like, this surge of *ennui* about our relationship.
Could you stop treating me like a dumb jock? Just 'cause I'm on the football team doesn't mean I'm *stupid*. I got a higher PSAT score than you did!
In fact, I have something to tell you: *I like math*. There. I said it.
I was lying. I really am mad that you forgot our six-month anniversary.
All I wanted to do today was go to the midnight screening of *Strictly Ballroom!*

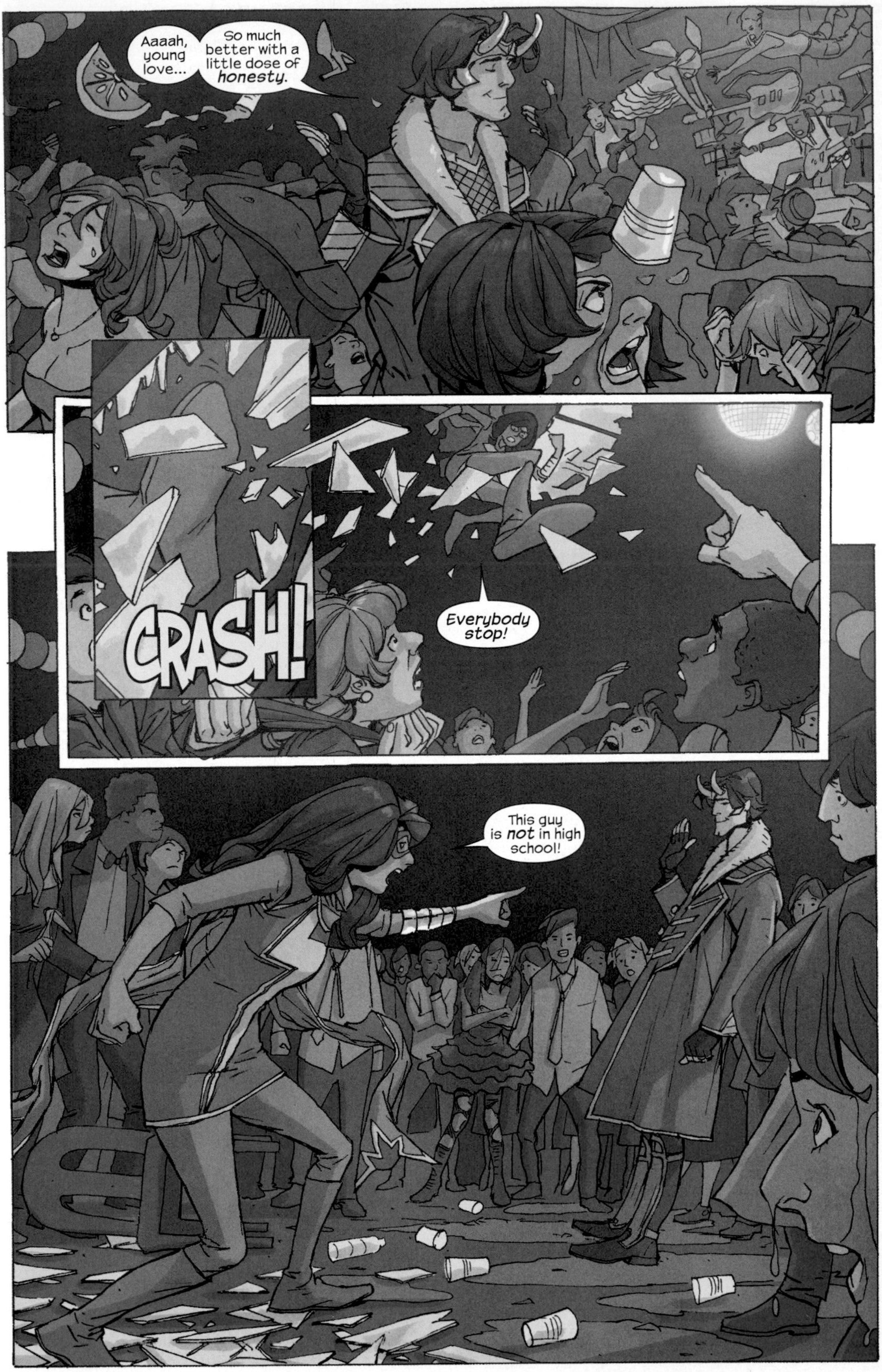
Aaaah, young love...
So much better with a little dose of *honesty*.
CRASH!
Everybody stop!
This guy is *not* in high school!

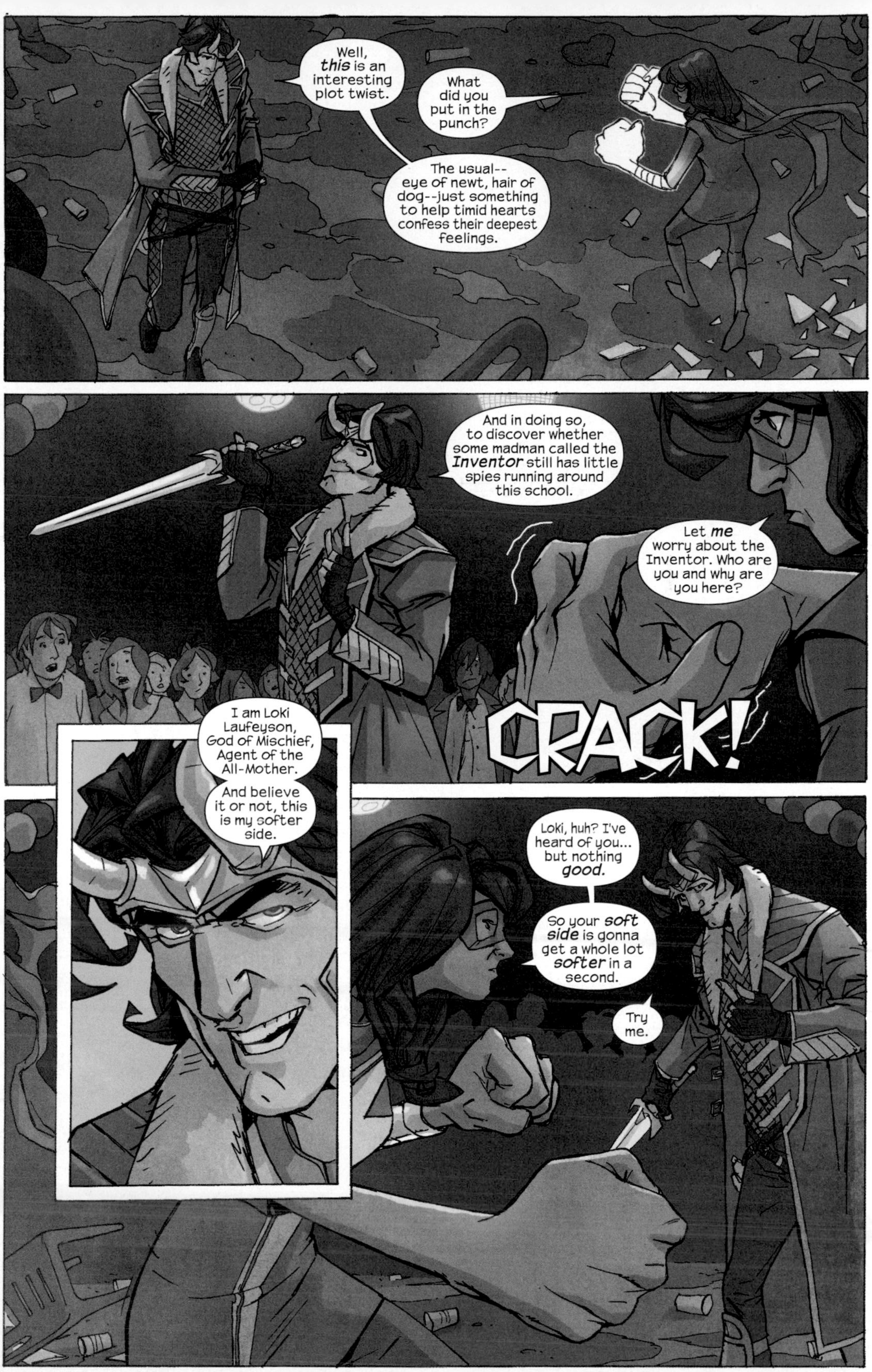

Well, *this* is an interesting plot twist.
What did you put in the punch?
The usual-- eye of newt, hair of dog--just something to help timid hearts confess their deepest feelings.
And in doing so, to discover whether some madman called the *Inventor* still has little spies running around this school.
Let *me* worry about the Inventor. Who are you and why are you here?
CRACK!
I am Loki Laufeyson, God of Mischief, Agent of the All-Mother.
And believe it or not, this is my softer side.
Loki, huh? I've heard of you... but nothing *good.*
So your *soft side* is gonna get a whole lot *softer* in a second.
Try me.

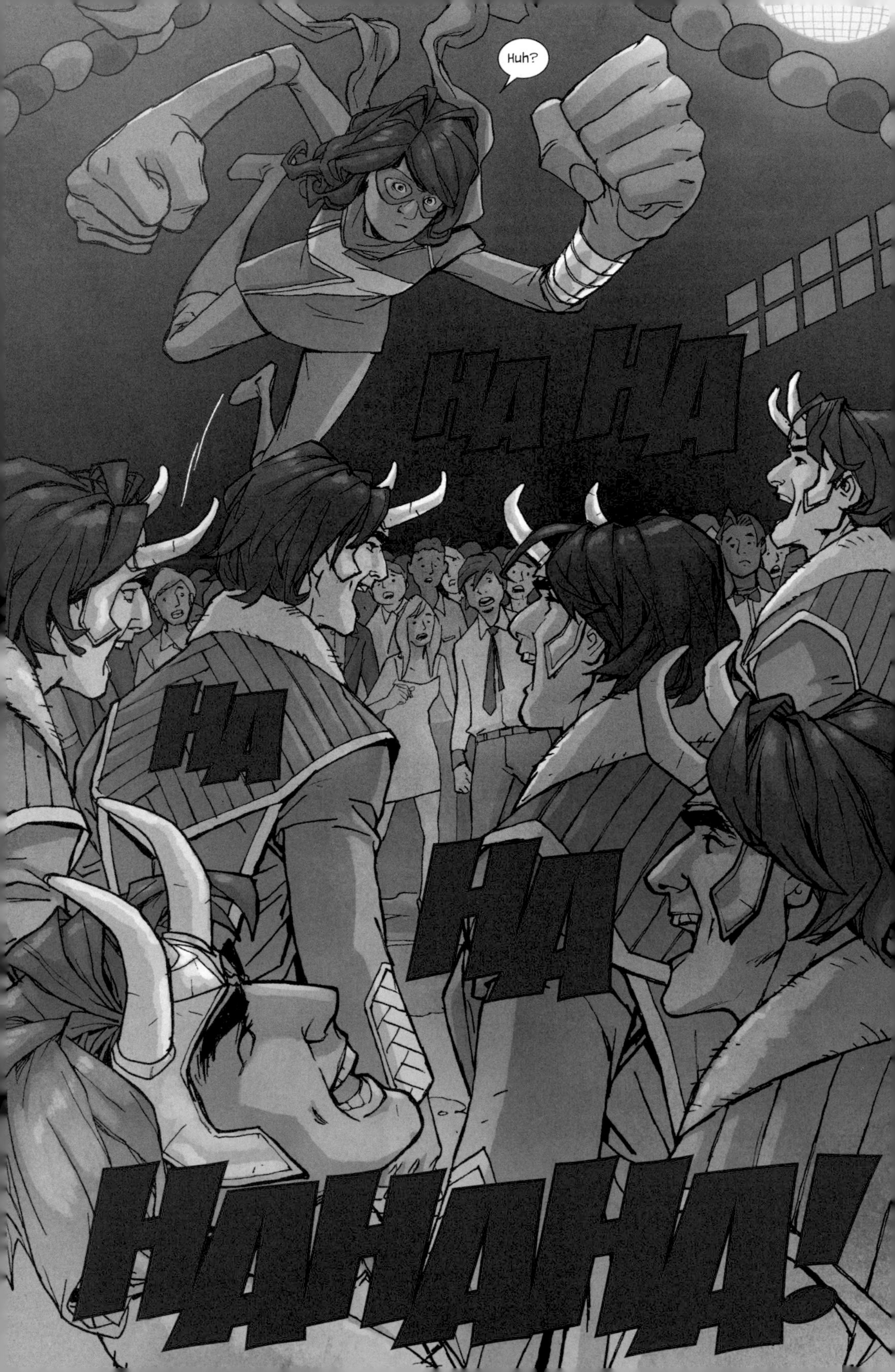
Huh?
HA HA
HA
HA
HAHAHA!

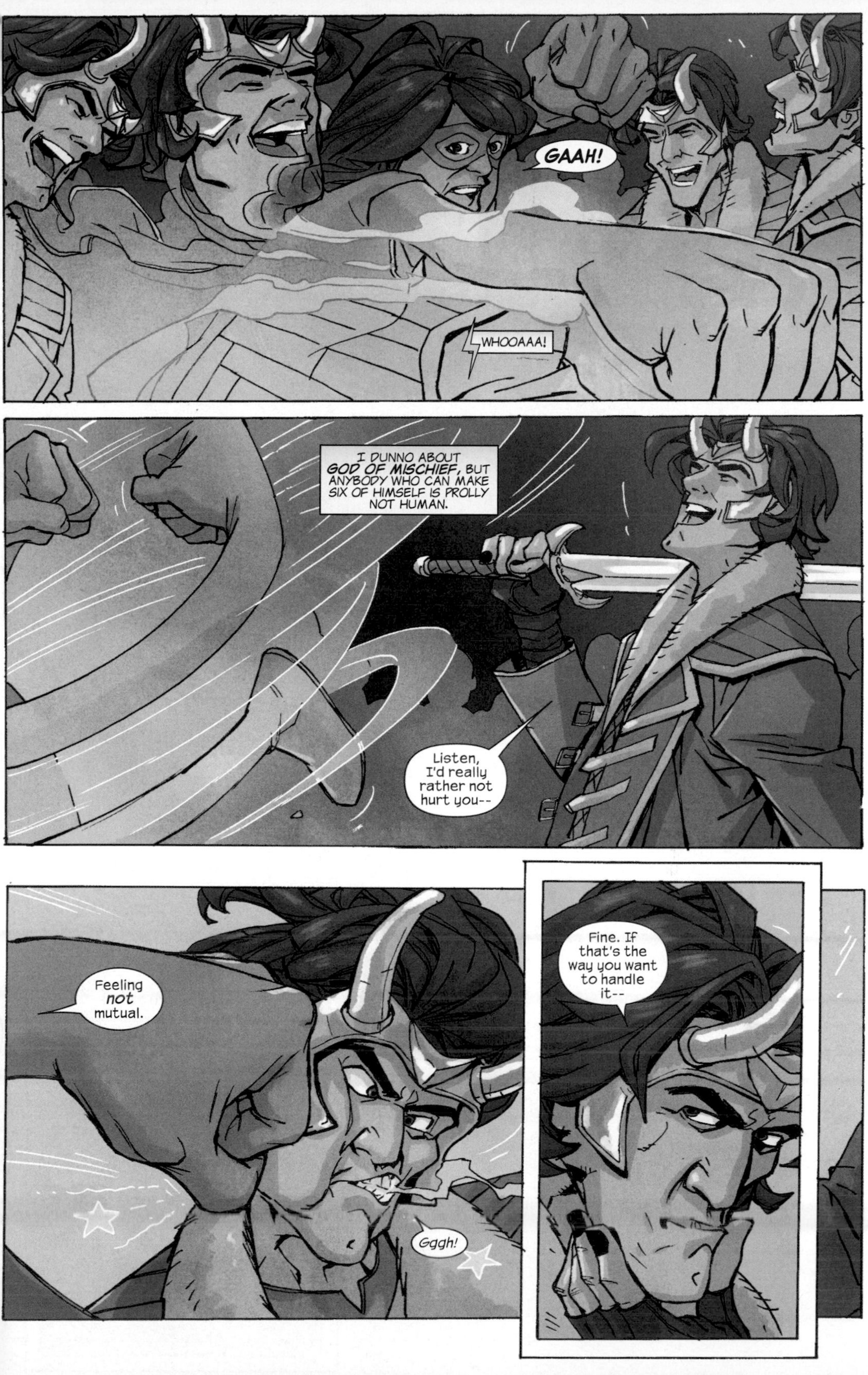
GAAH!
WHOOAAA!
I DUNNO ABOUT GOD OF MISCHIEF, BUT ANYBODY WHO CAN MAKE SIX OF HIMSELF IS PROLLY NOT HUMAN.
Listen, I'd really rather not hurt you--
Feeling not mutual.
Gggh!
Fine. If that's the way you want to handle it--

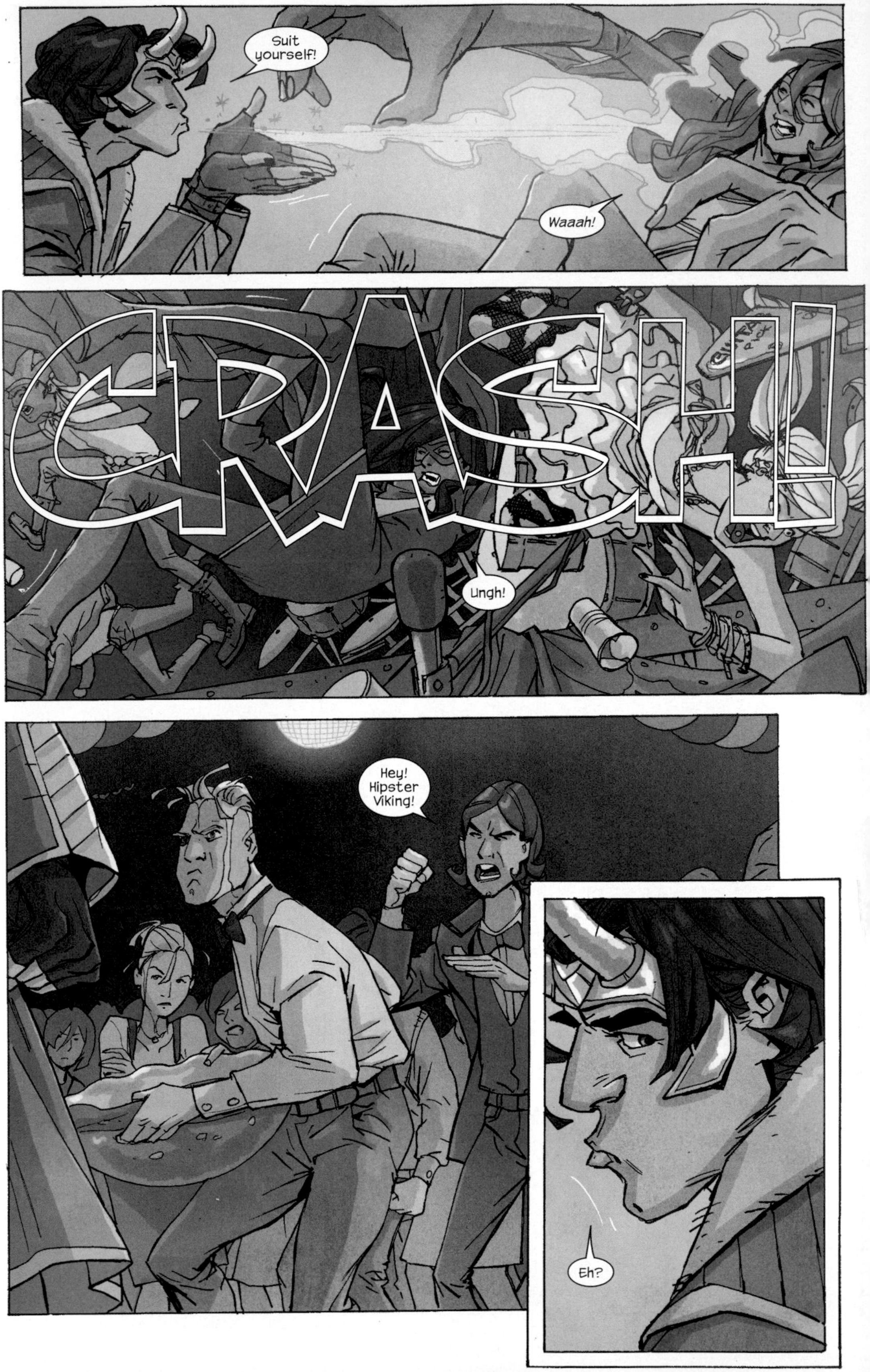
Suit yourself!
Waaah!
CRASH!
Ungh!
Hey! Hipster Viking!
Eh?

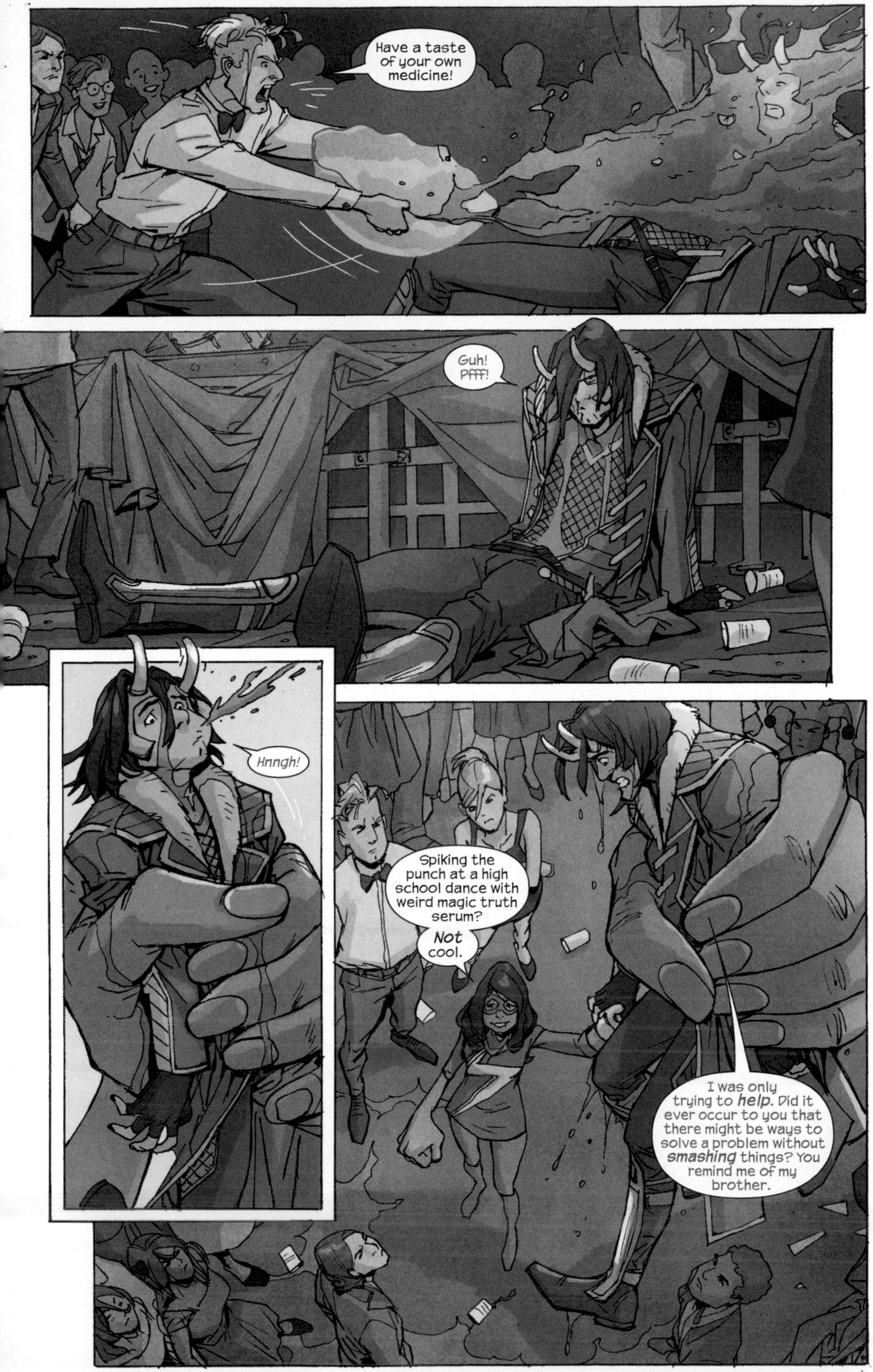
Have a taste of your own medicine!
Guh! Pfff!
Hnngh!
Spiking the punch at a high school dance with weird magic truth serum?
Not cool.
I was only trying to *help*. Did it ever occur to you that there might be ways to solve a problem without *smashing* things? You remind me of my brother.

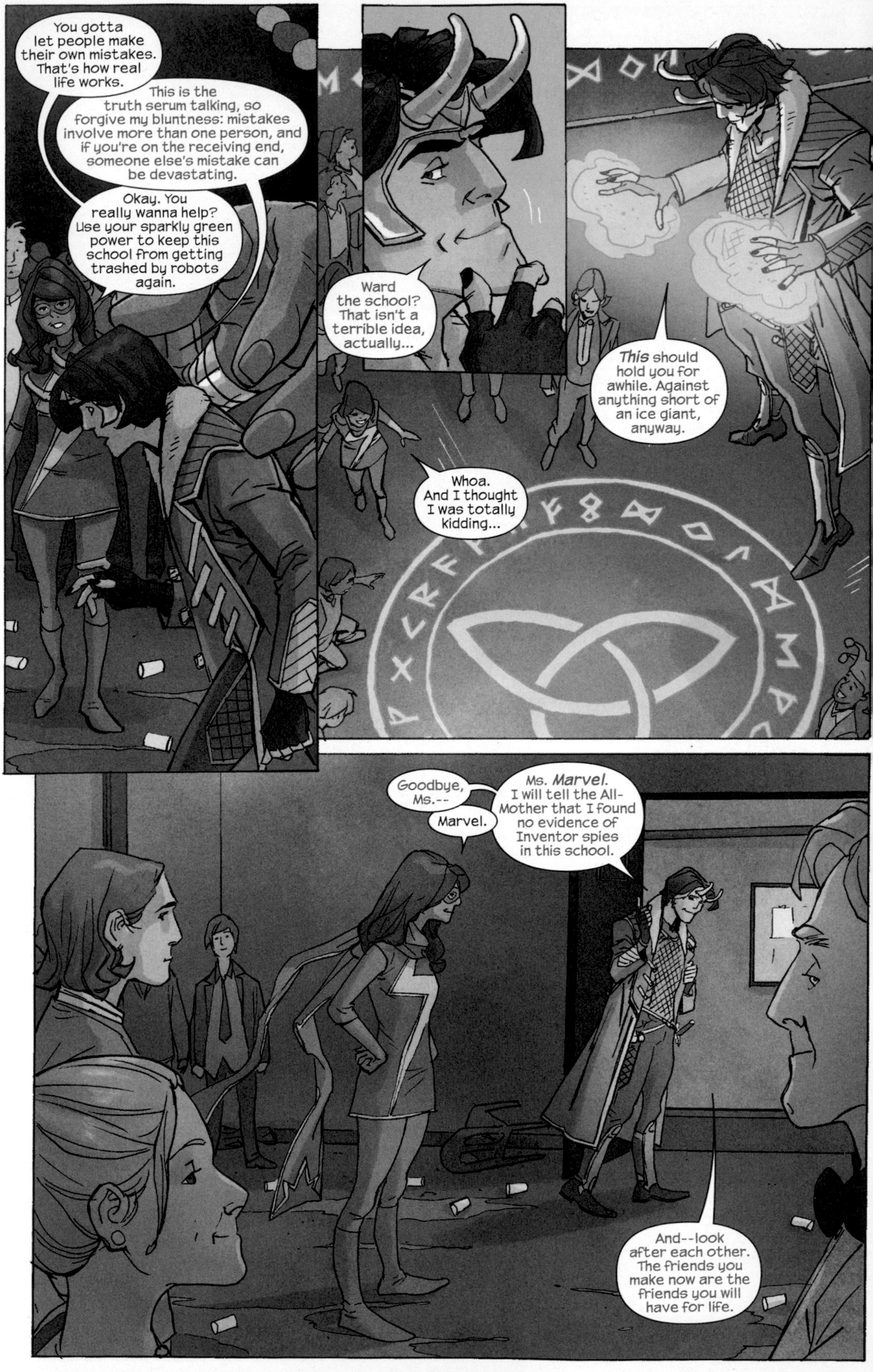
You gotta let people make their own mistakes. That's how real life works.
This is the truth serum talking, so forgive my bluntness: mistakes involve more than one person, and if you're on the receiving end, someone else's mistake can be devastating.
Okay. You really wanna help? Use your sparkly green power to keep this school from getting trashed by robots again.
Ward the school? That isn't a terrible idea, actually...
This should hold you for awhile. Against anything short of an ice giant, anyway.
Whoa. And I thought I was totally kidding...
Goodbye, Ms.--
Marvel.
Ms. *Marvel*. I will tell the All-Mother that I found no evidence of Inventor spies in this school.
And--look after each other. The friends you make now are the friends you will have for life.

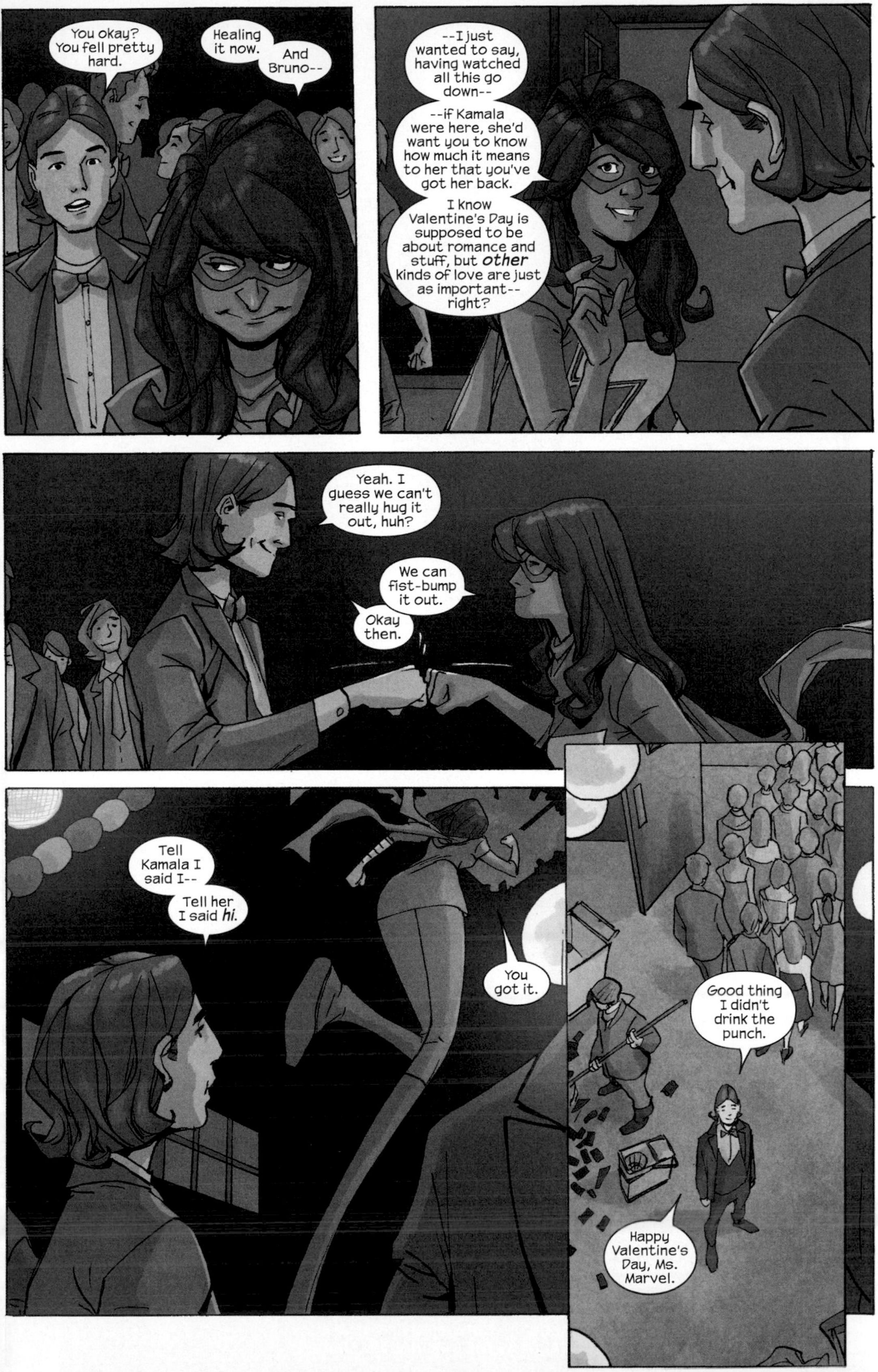
You okay? You fell pretty hard.
Healing it now.
And Bruno--
--I just wanted to say, having watched all this go down--
--if Kamala were here, she'd want you to know how much it means to her that you've got her back.
I know Valentine's Day is supposed to be about romance and stuff, but *other* kinds of love are just as important--right?
Yeah. I guess we can't really hug it out, huh?
We can fist-bump it out.
Okay then.
Tell Kamala I said I--
Tell her I said *hi*.
You got it.
Good thing I didn't drink the punch.
Happy Valentine's Day, Ms. Marvel.

GENERATIONS: MS. MARVEL & MS. MARVEL

KAMALA KHAN HAD A ROUGH FALLING OUT WITH HER IDOL,
CAROL DANVERS. AND THINGS ARE ABOUT TO GET WEIRD AS KAMALA
TRAVELS BACK IN TIME AND MEETS CAROL AS THE ORIGINAL MS. MARVEL!

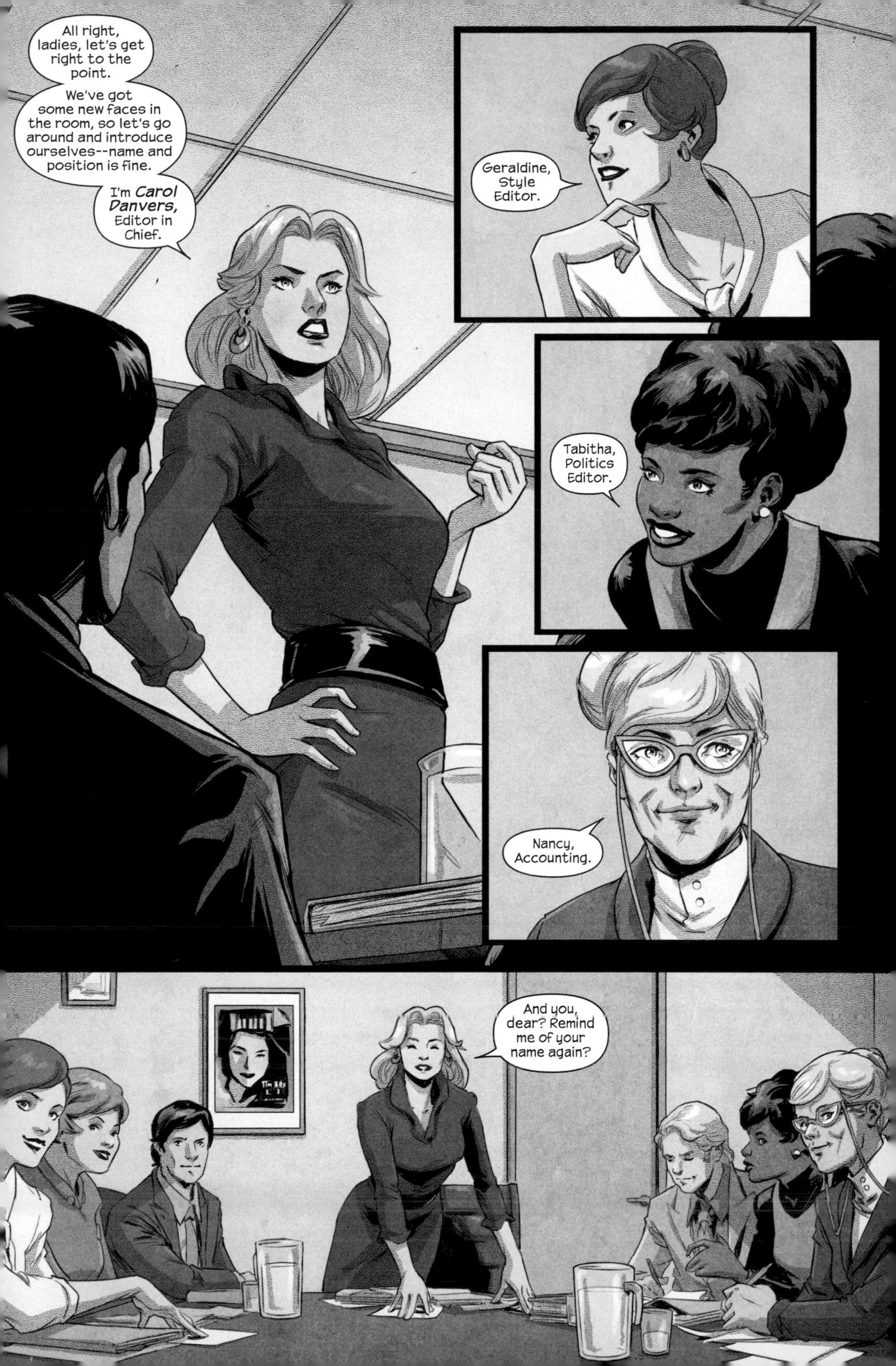
All right, ladies, let's get right to the point.
We've got some new faces in the room, so let's go around and introduce ourselves--name and position is fine.
I'm *Carol Danvers,* Editor in Chief.
Geraldine, Style Editor.
Tabitha, Politics Editor.
Nancy, Accounting.
And you, dear? Remind me of your name again?

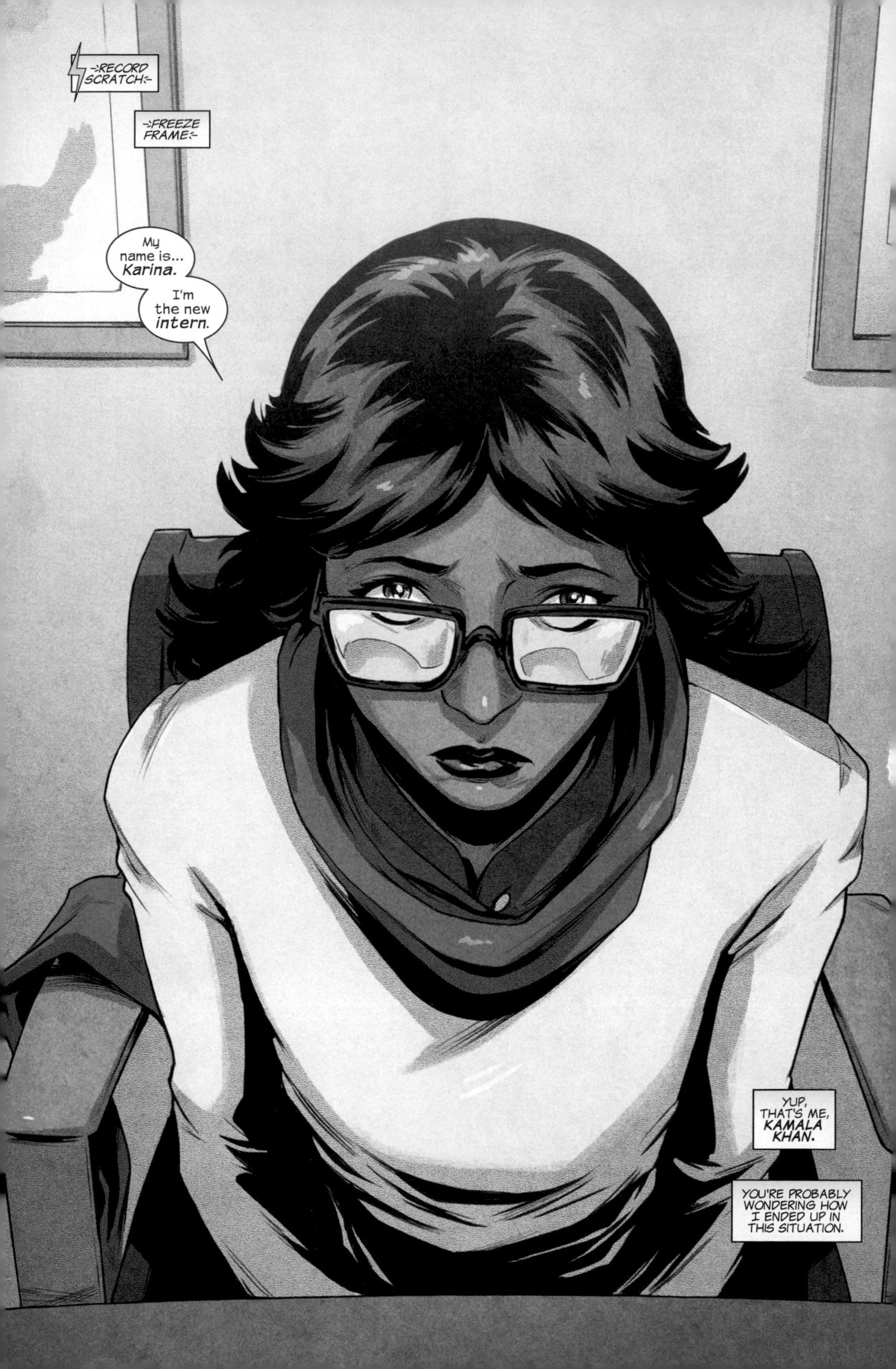
-RECORD SCRATCH-
-FREEZE FRAME-
My name is... Karina.
I'm the new intern.
YUP, THAT'S ME, KAMALA KHAN.
YOU'RE PROBABLY WONDERING HOW I ENDED UP IN THIS SITUATION.

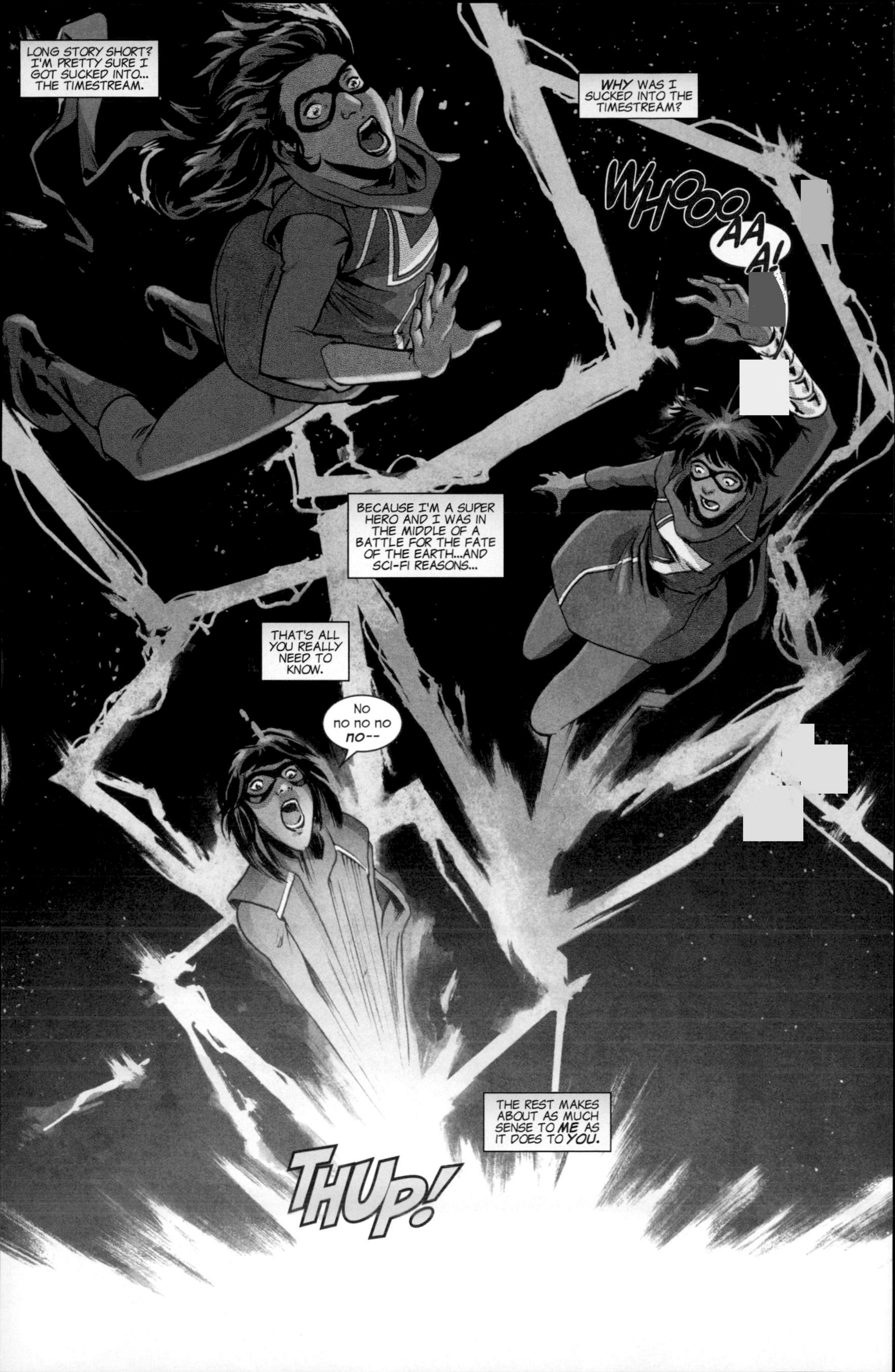
LONG STORY SHORT? I'M PRETTY SURE I GOT SUCKED INTO... THE TIMESTREAM.
WHY WAS I SUCKED INTO THE TIMESTREAM?
WHOOOAAA!
BECAUSE I'M A SUPER HERO AND I WAS IN THE MIDDLE OF A BATTLE FOR THE FATE OF THE EARTH...AND SCI-FI REASONS...
THAT'S ALL YOU REALLY NEED TO KNOW.
No no no no no--
THE REST MAKES ABOUT AS MUCH SENSE TO ME AS IT DOES TO YOU.
THUP!

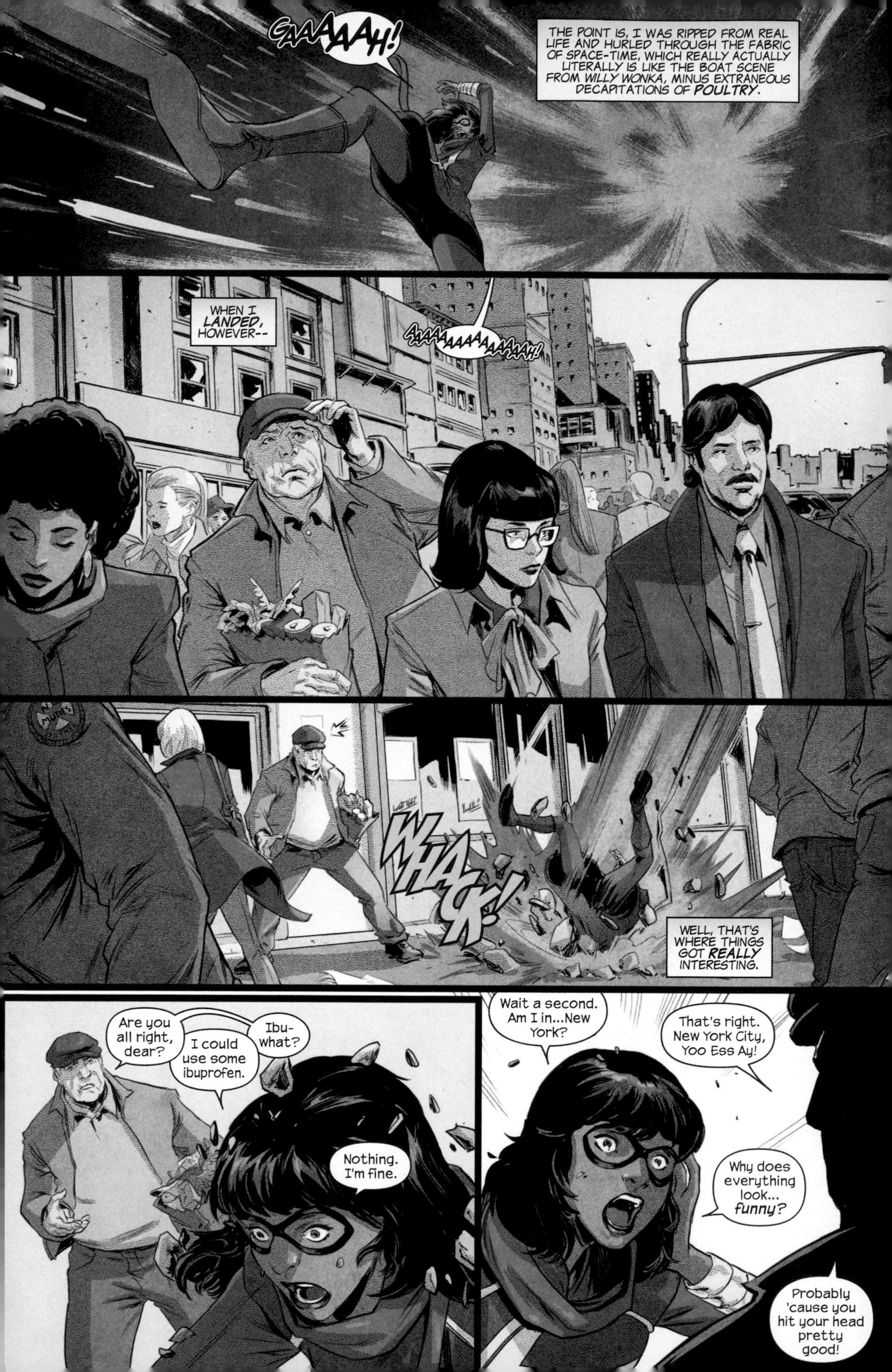
GAAAAAAH!
THE POINT IS, I WAS RIPPED FROM REAL LIFE AND HURLED THROUGH THE FABRIC OF SPACE-TIME, WHICH REALLY ACTUALLY LITERALLY IS LIKE THE BOAT SCENE FROM WILLY WONKA, MINUS EXTRANEOUS DECAPITATIONS OF POULTRY.
WHEN I LANDED, HOWEVER--
AAAAAAAAAAAAAH!
WHACK!
WELL, THAT'S WHERE THINGS GOT REALLY INTERESTING.
Are you all right, dear?
I could use some ibuprofen.
Ibu-what?
Nothing. I'm fine.
Wait a second. Am I in...New York?
That's right. New York City, Yoo Ess Ay!
Why does everything look... funny?
Probably 'cause you hit your head pretty good!

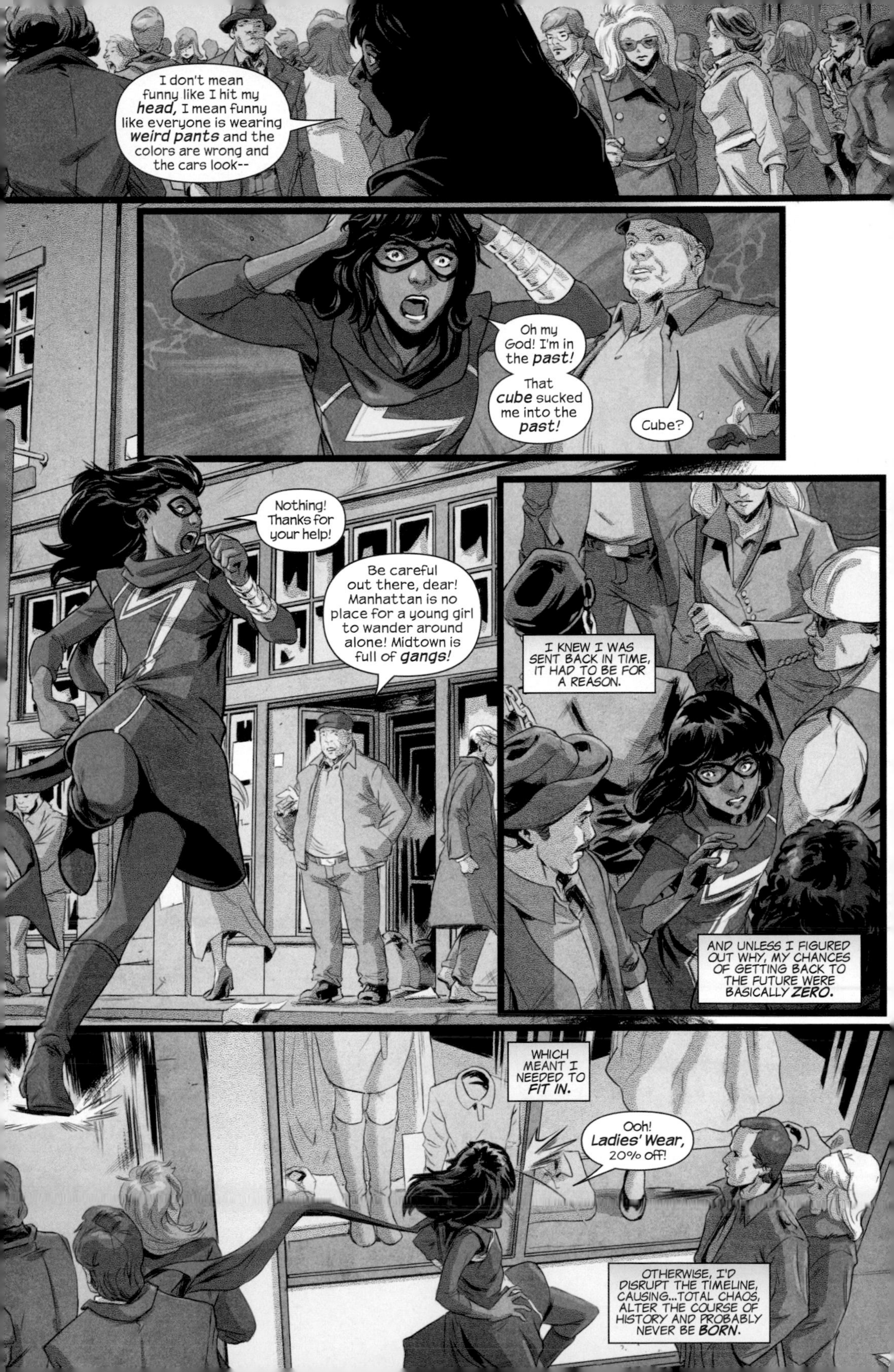
I don't mean funny like I hit my head, I mean funny like everyone is wearing weird pants and the colors are wrong and the cars look--
Oh my God! I'm in the past!
That cube sucked me into the past!
Cube?
Nothing! Thanks for your help!
Be careful out there, dear! Manhattan is no place for a young girl to wander around alone! Midtown is full of gangs!
I KNEW I WAS SENT BACK IN TIME, IT HAD TO BE FOR A REASON.
AND UNLESS I FIGURED OUT WHY, MY CHANCES OF GETTING BACK TO THE FUTURE WERE BASICALLY ZERO.
WHICH MEANT I NEEDED TO FIT IN.
Ooh! Ladies' Wear, 20% off!
OTHERWISE, I'D DISRUPT THE TIMELINE, CAUSING...TOTAL CHAOS, ALTER THE COURSE OF HISTORY AND PROBABLY NEVER BE BORN.

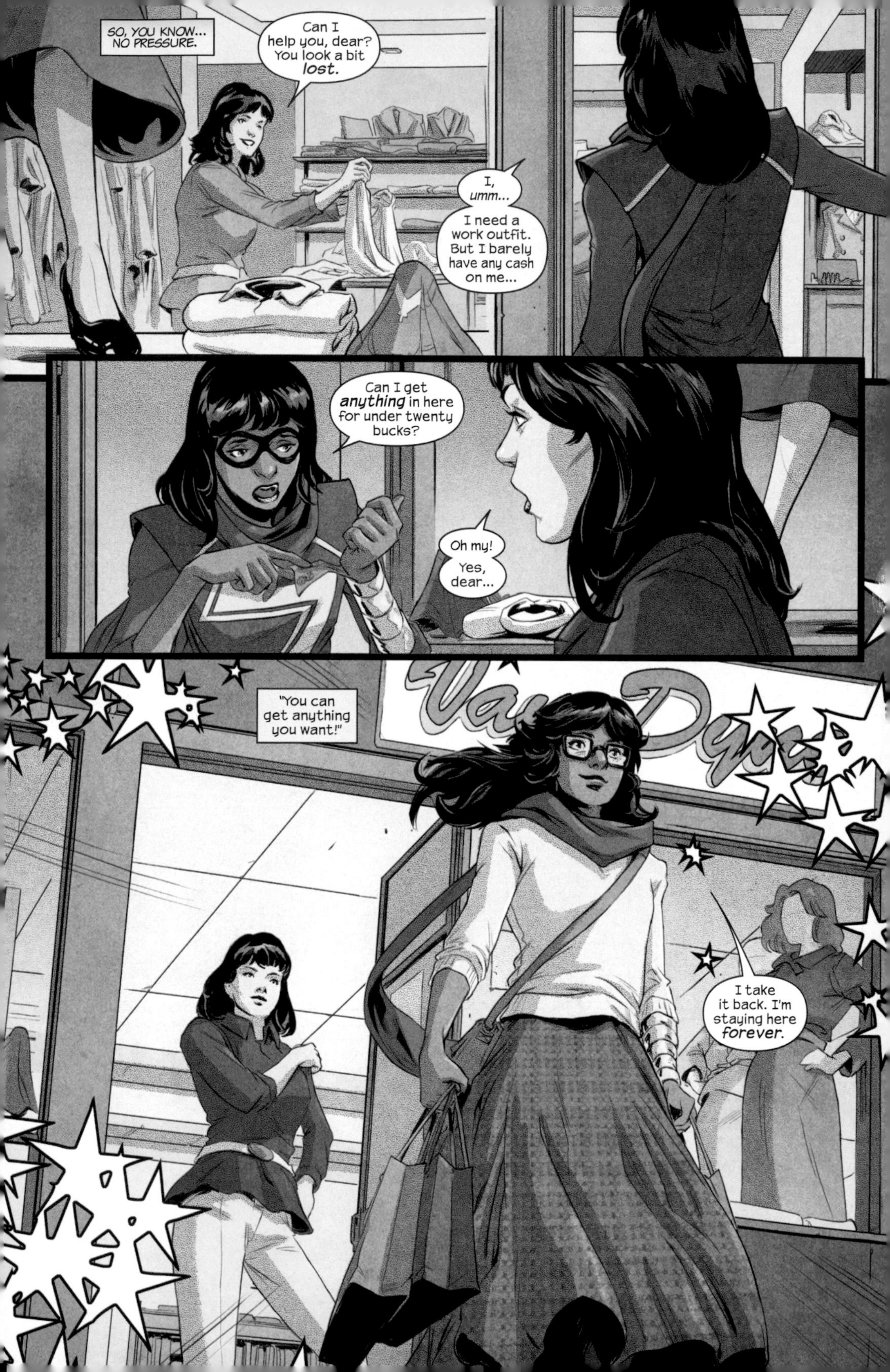

SO, YOU KNOW... NO PRESSURE.
Can I help you, dear? You look a bit *lost.*
I, umm...
I need a work outfit. But I barely have any cash on me...
Can I get *anything* in here for under twenty bucks?
Oh my!
Yes, dear...
"You can get anything you want!"
I take it back. I'm staying here *forever*.

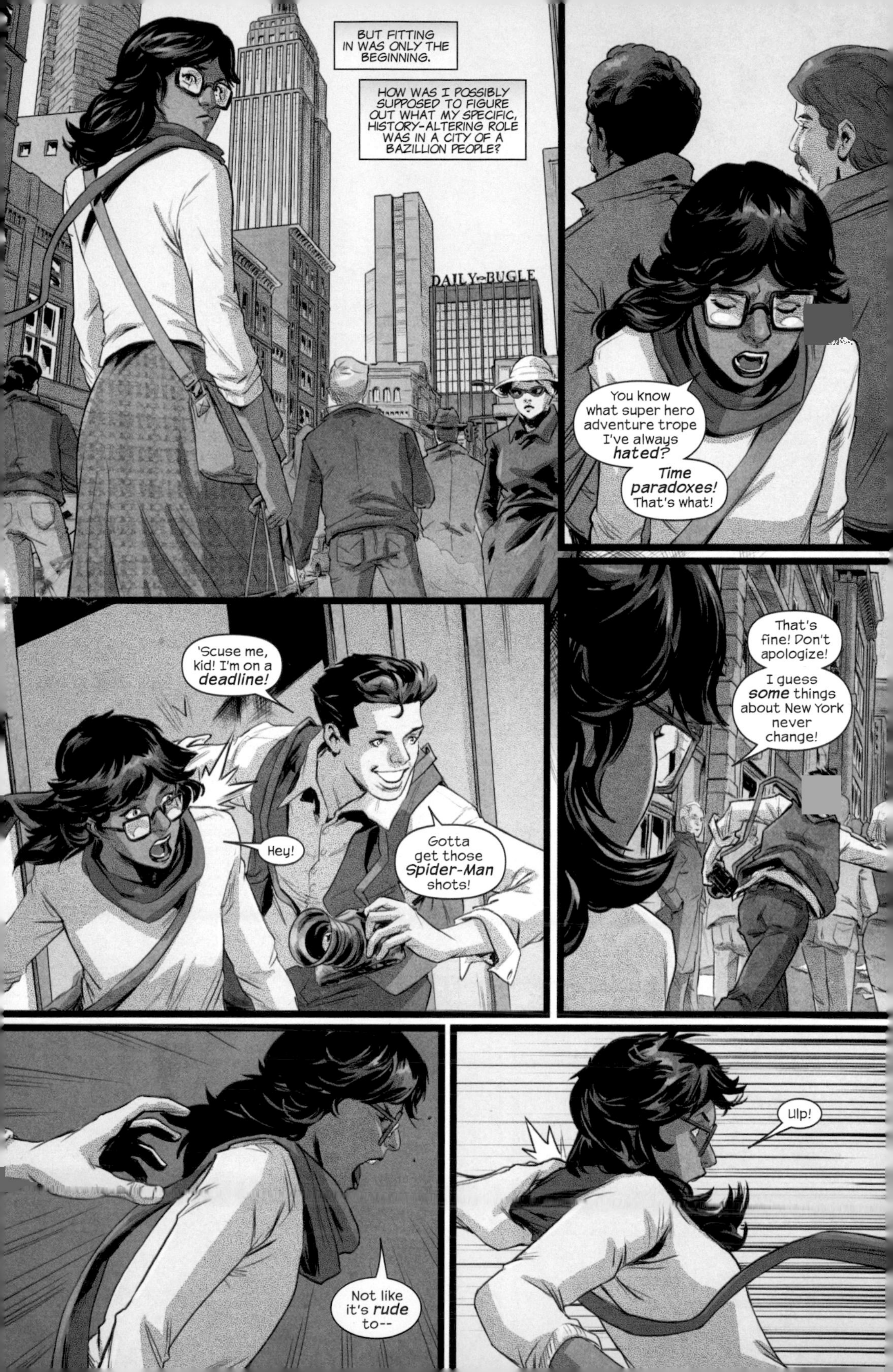
BUT FITTING IN WAS ONLY THE BEGINNING.
HOW WAS I POSSIBLY SUPPOSED TO FIGURE OUT WHAT MY SPECIFIC, HISTORY-ALTERING ROLE WAS IN A CITY OF A BAZILLION PEOPLE?
DAILY BUGLE
You know what super hero adventure trope I've always *hated?*
Time paradoxes! That's what!
'Scuse me, kid! I'm on a *deadline!*
Hey!
Gotta get those *Spider-Man* shots!
That's fine! Don't apologize!
I guess *some* things about New York never change!
Not like it's *rude* to--
Ulp!

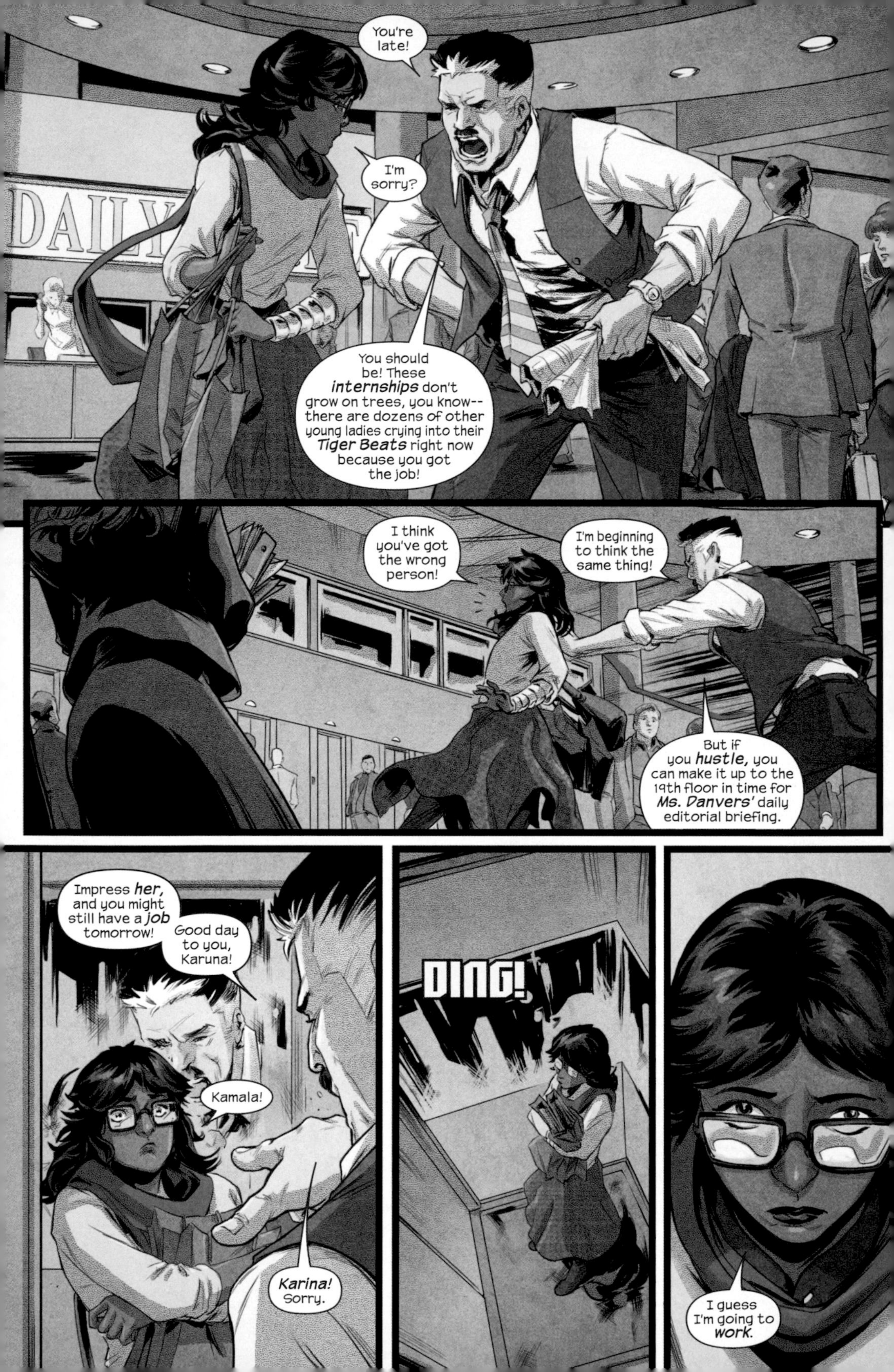

You're late!
I'm sorry?
You should be! These *internships* don't grow on trees, you know-- there are dozens of other young ladies crying into their *Tiger Beats* right now because you got the job!
I think you've got the wrong person!
I'm beginning to think the same thing!
But if you *hustle,* you can make it up to the 19th floor in time for *Ms. Danvers'* daily editorial briefing.
Impress *her,* and you might still have a *job* tomorrow!
Good day to you, Karuna!
Kamala!
Karina! Sorry.
DING!
I guess I'm going to *work.*

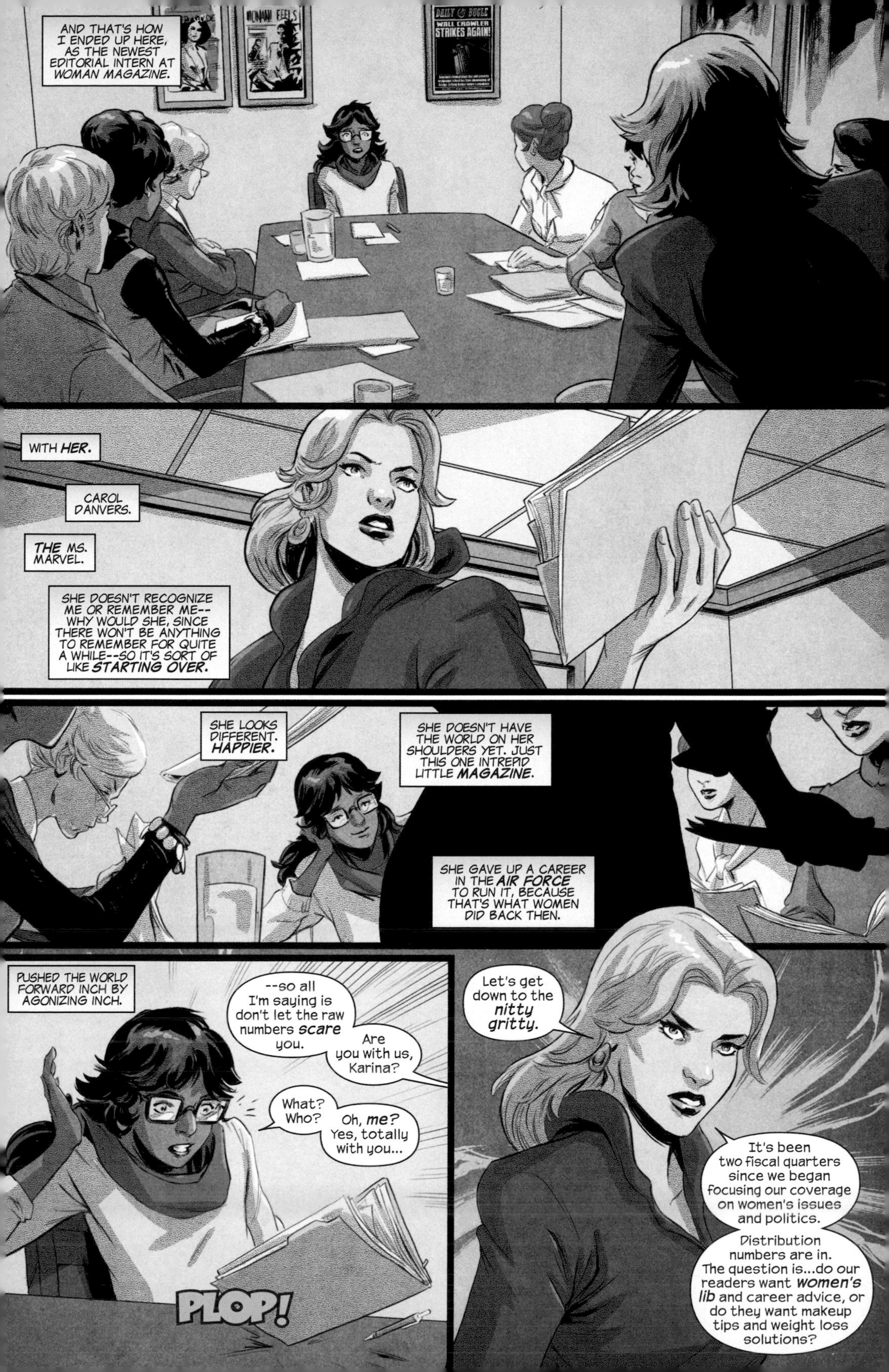

AND THAT'S HOW I ENDED UP HERE, AS THE NEWEST EDITORIAL INTERN AT WOMAN MAGAZINE.
DAILY BUGLE
WALL CRAWLER STRIKES AGAIN!
WITH HER.
CAROL DANVERS.
THE MS. MARVEL.
SHE DOESN'T RECOGNIZE ME OR REMEMBER ME--WHY WOULD SHE, SINCE THERE WON'T BE ANYTHING TO REMEMBER FOR QUITE A WHILE--SO IT'S SORT OF LIKE STARTING OVER.
SHE LOOKS DIFFERENT. HAPPIER.
SHE DOESN'T HAVE THE WORLD ON HER SHOULDERS YET. JUST THIS ONE INTREPID LITTLE MAGAZINE.
SHE GAVE UP A CAREER IN THE AIR FORCE TO RUN IT, BECAUSE THAT'S WHAT WOMEN DID BACK THEN.
PUSHED THE WORLD FORWARD INCH BY AGONIZING INCH.
--so all I'm saying is don't let the raw numbers scare you.
Are you with us, Karina?
What? Who?
Oh, me? Yes, totally with you...
PLOP!
Let's get down to the nitty gritty.
It's been two fiscal quarters since we began focusing our coverage on women's issues and politics.
Distribution numbers are in. The question is...do our readers want women's lib and career advice, or do they want makeup tips and weight loss solutions?

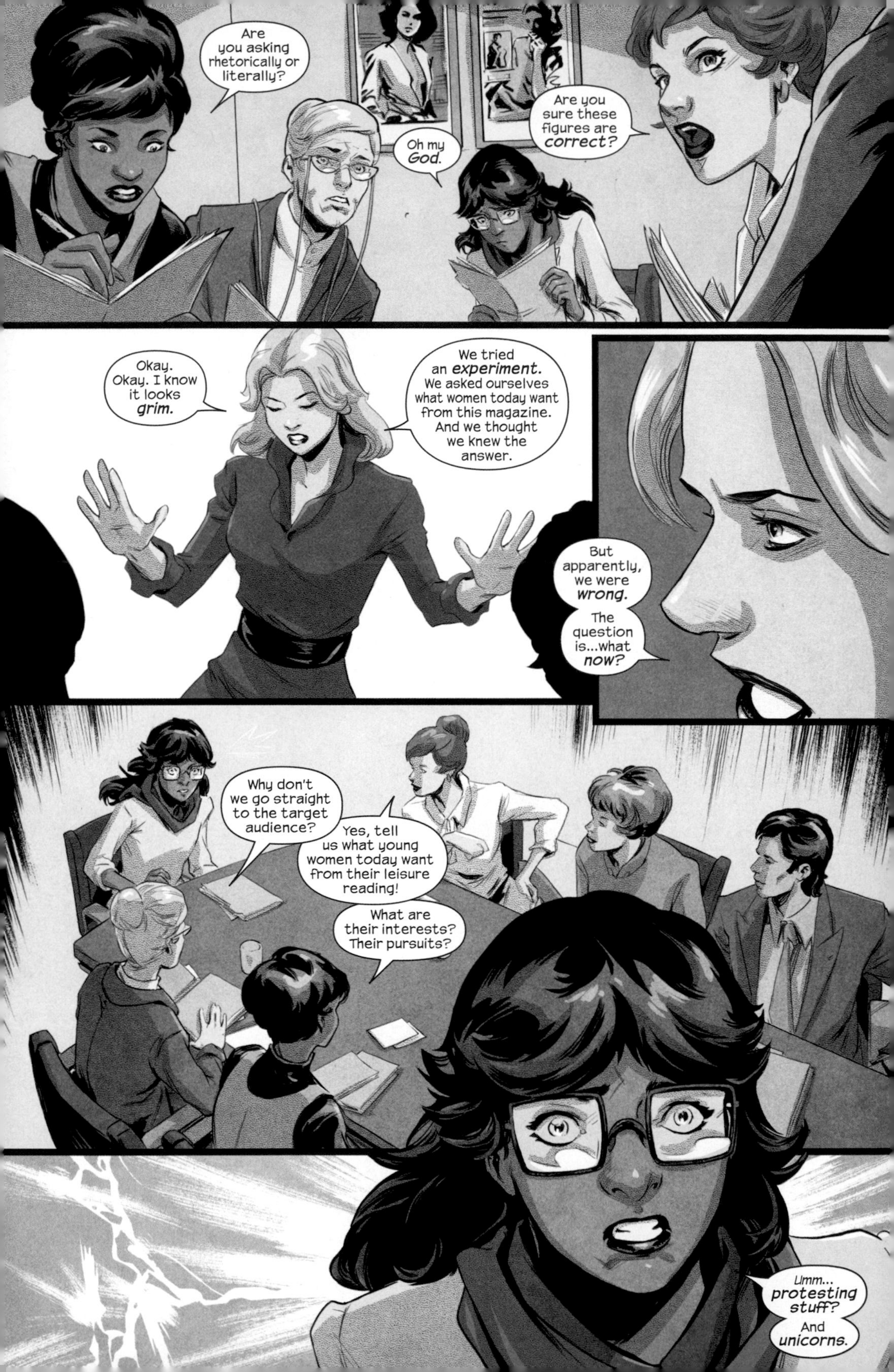

Are you asking rhetorically or literally?
Oh my God.
Are you sure these figures are correct?
Okay. Okay. I know it looks grim.
We tried an experiment. We asked ourselves what women today want from this magazine. And we thought we knew the answer.
But apparently, we were wrong.
The question is...what now?
Why don't we go straight to the target audience?
Yes, tell us what young women today want from their leisure reading!
What are their interests? Their pursuits?
Umm... protesting stuff?
And unicorns.

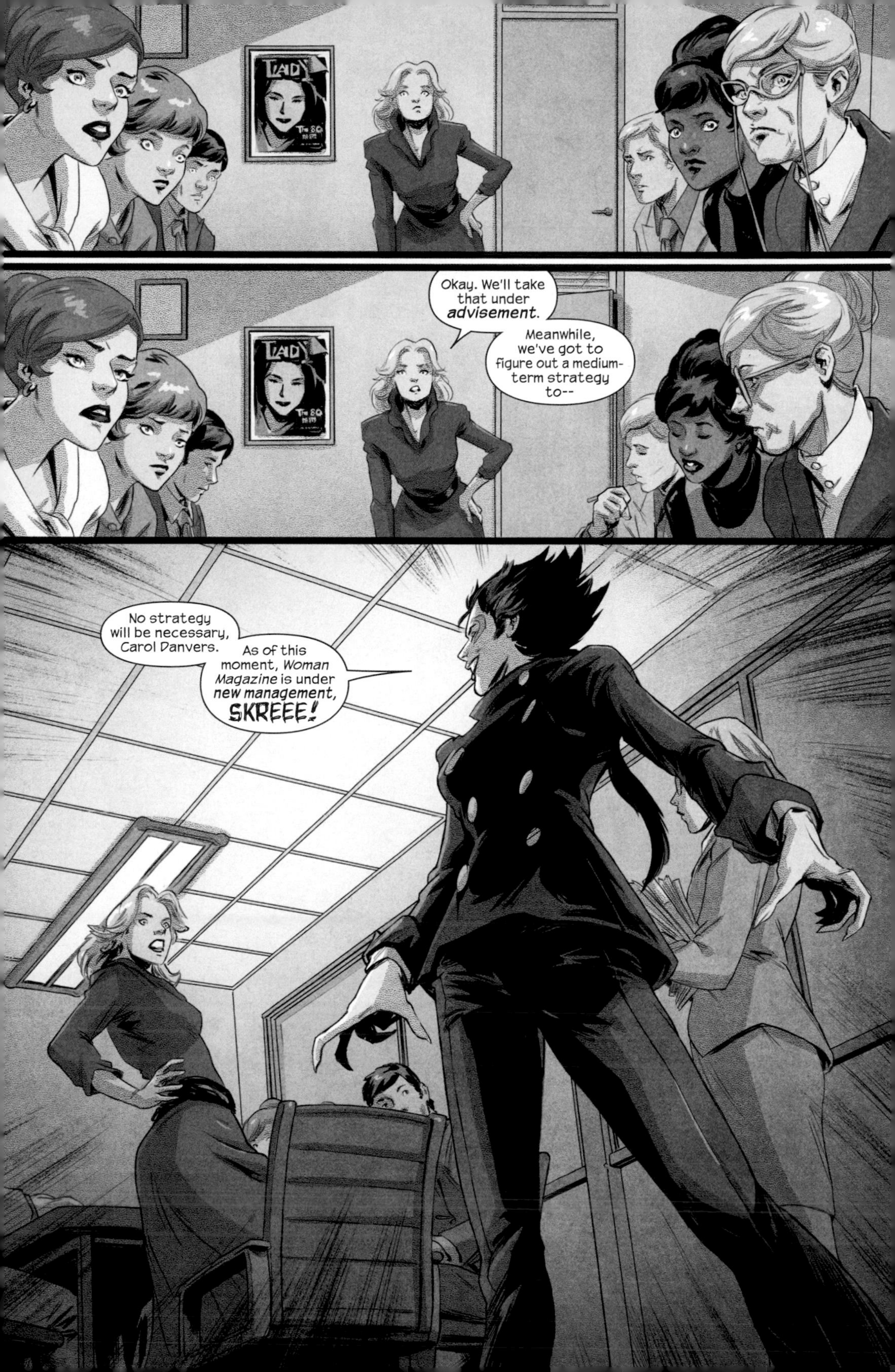
LADY
Okay. We'll take that under *advisement*.
Meanwhile, we've got to figure out a medium-term strategy to--
No strategy will be necessary, Carol Danvers.
As of this moment, *Woman Magazine* is under *new management*, SKREEE!

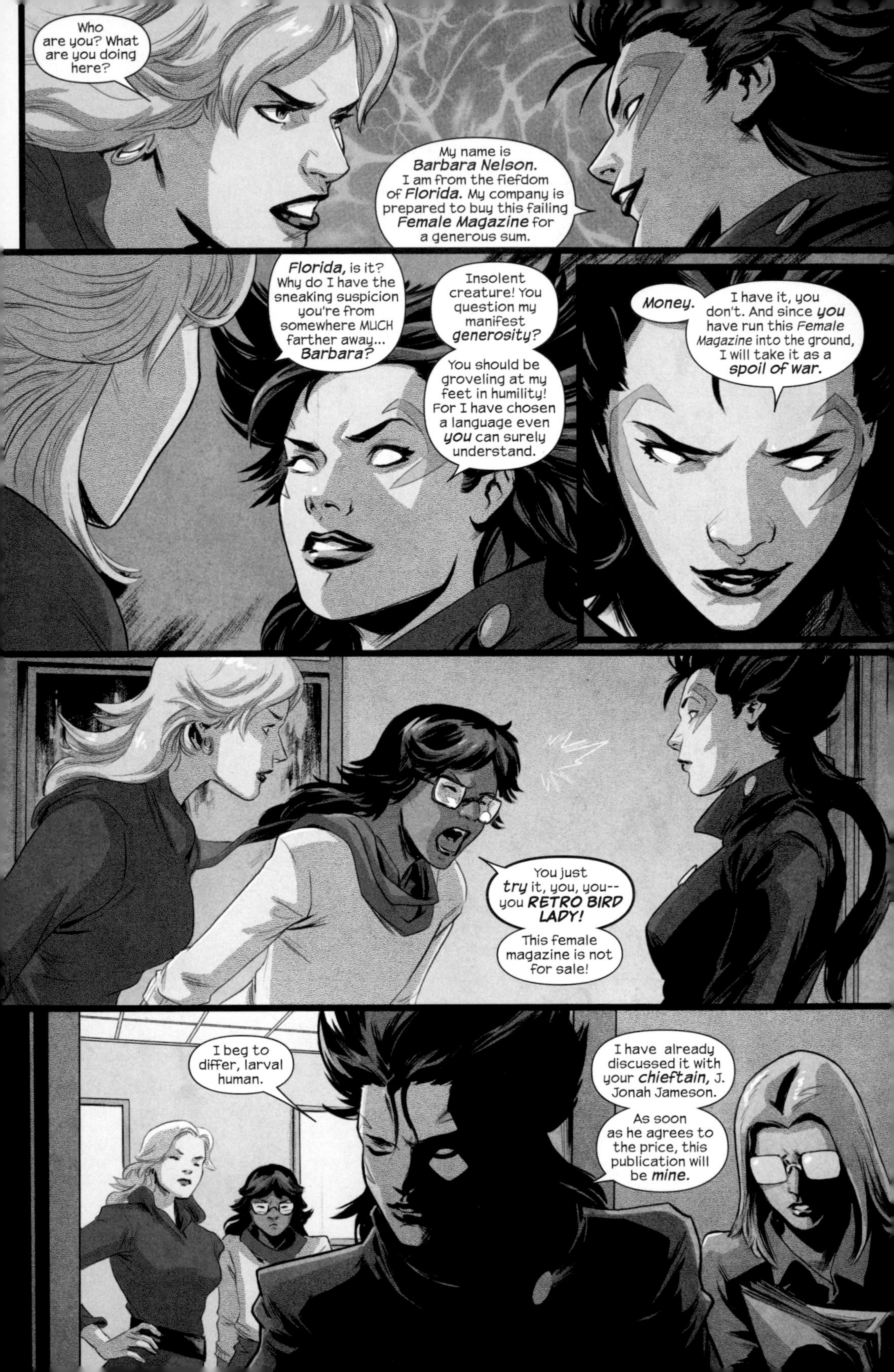
Who are you? What are you doing here?
My name is *Barbara Nelson.* I am from the fiefdom of *Florida.* My company is prepared to buy this failing *Female Magazine* for a generous sum.
Florida, is it? Why do I have the sneaking suspicion you're from somewhere MUCH farther away... *Barbara?*
Insolent creature! You question my manifest *generosity?*
You should be groveling at my feet in humility! For I have chosen a language even *you* can surely understand.
Money.
I have it, you don't. And since *you* have run this *Female Magazine* into the ground, I will take it as a *spoil of war.*
You just *try* it, you, you-- you *RETRO BIRD LADY!*
This female magazine is not for sale!
I beg to differ, larval human.
I have already discussed it with your *chieftain,* J. Jonah Jameson.
As soon as he agrees to the price, this publication will be *mine.*

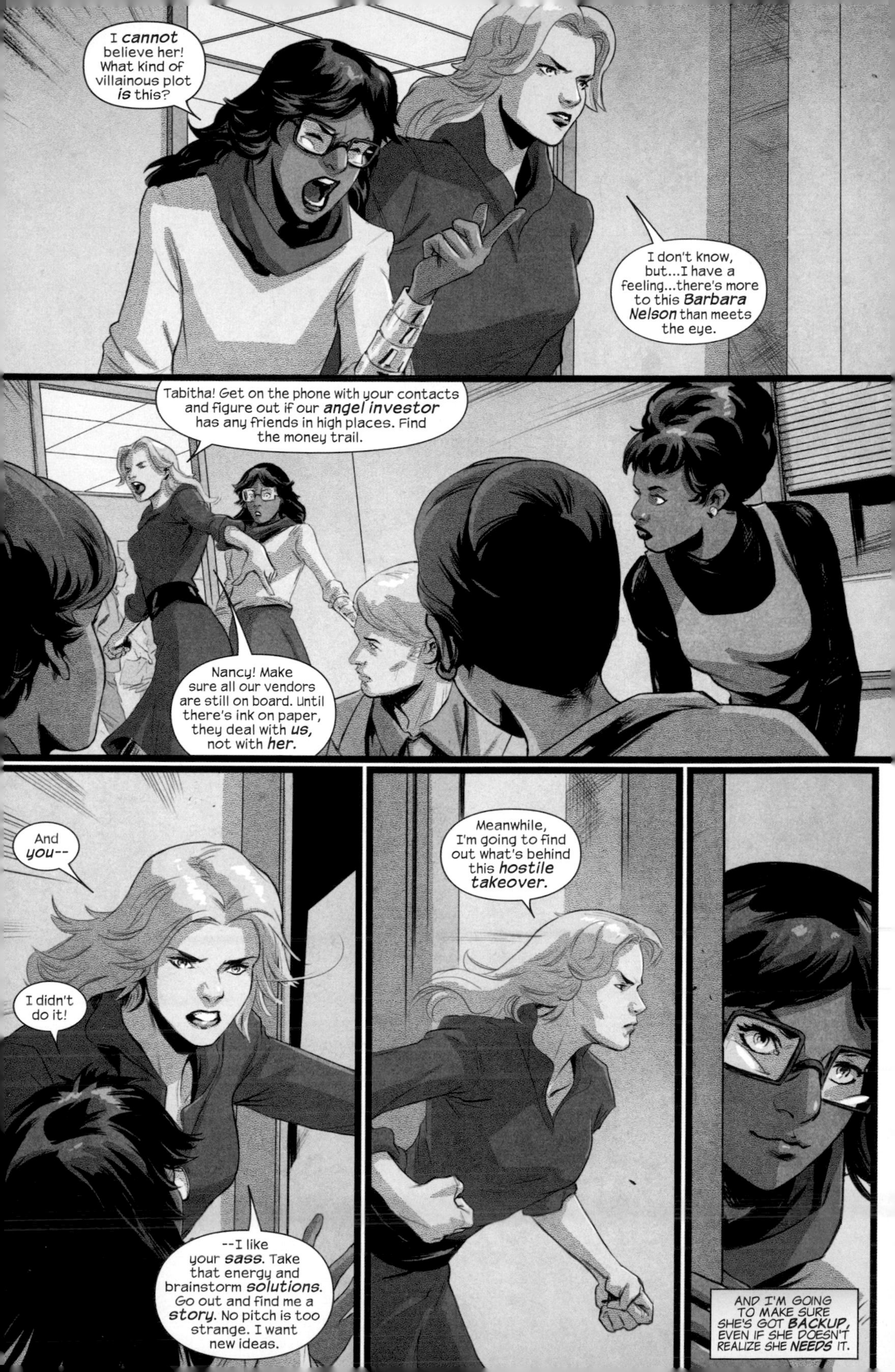

I *cannot* believe her! What kind of villainous plot *is* this?
I don't know, but...I have a feeling...there's more to this *Barbara Nelson* than meets the eye.
Tabitha! Get on the phone with your contacts and figure out if our *angel investor* has any friends in high places. Find the money trail.
Nancy! Make sure all our vendors are still on board. Until there's ink on paper, they deal with *us,* not with *her.*
And *you*--
I didn't do it!
--I like your *sass*. Take that energy and brainstorm *solutions*. Go out and find me a *story*. No pitch is too strange. I want new ideas.
Meanwhile, I'm going to find out what's behind this *hostile takeover.*
AND I'M GOING TO MAKE SURE SHE'S GOT *BACKUP,* EVEN IF SHE DOESN'T REALIZE SHE *NEEDS* IT.

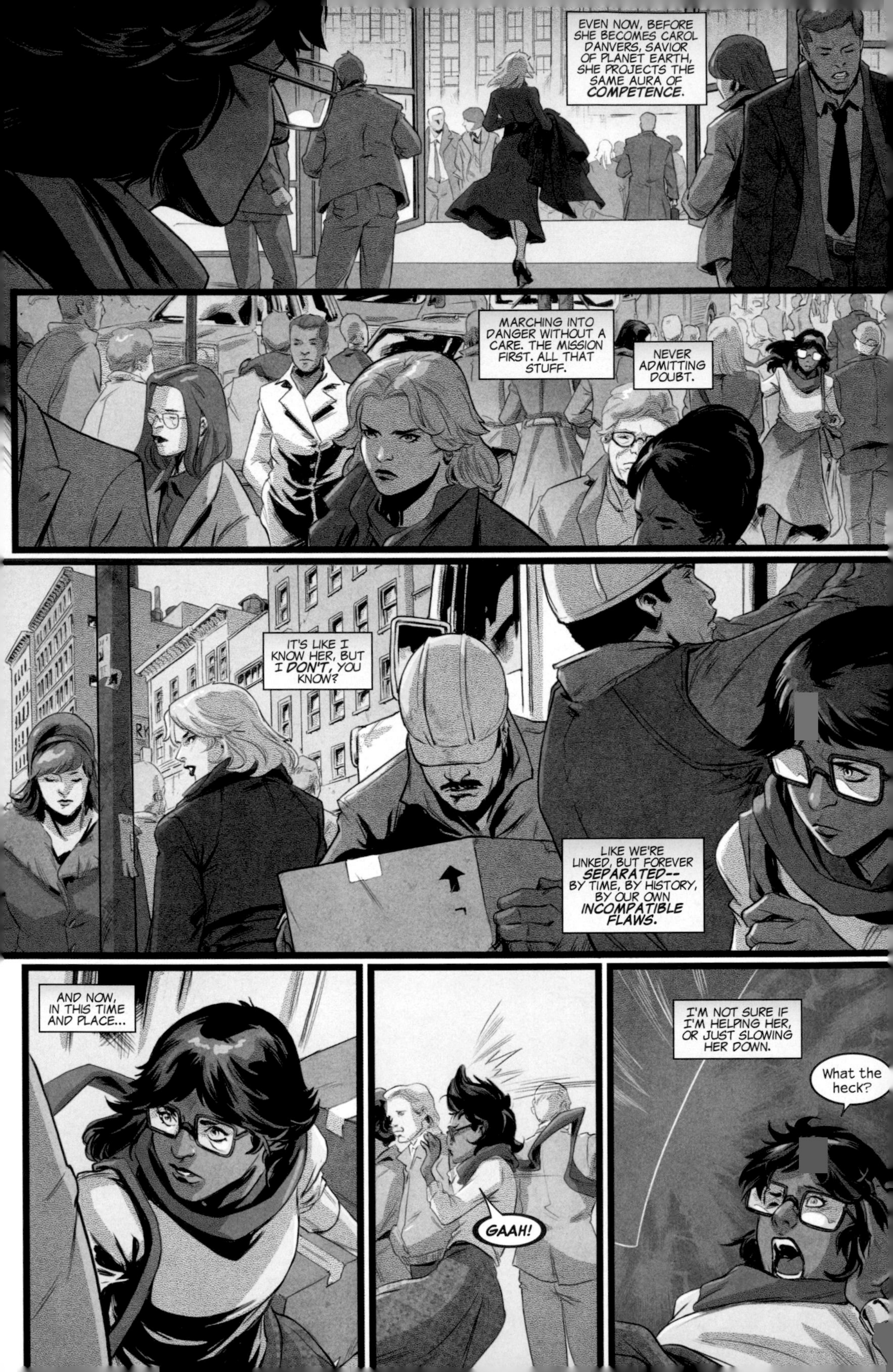
EVEN NOW, BEFORE SHE BECOMES CAROL DANVERS, SAVIOR OF PLANET EARTH, SHE PROJECTS THE SAME AURA OF COMPETENCE.
MARCHING INTO DANGER WITHOUT A CARE. THE MISSION FIRST. ALL THAT STUFF.
NEVER ADMITTING DOUBT.
IT'S LIKE I KNOW HER, BUT I DON'T, YOU KNOW?
LIKE WE'RE LINKED, BUT FOREVER SEPARATED-- BY TIME, BY HISTORY, BY OUR OWN INCOMPATIBLE FLAWS.
AND NOW, IN THIS TIME AND PLACE...
GAAH!
I'M NOT SURE IF I'M HELPING HER, OR JUST SLOWING HER DOWN.
What the heck?

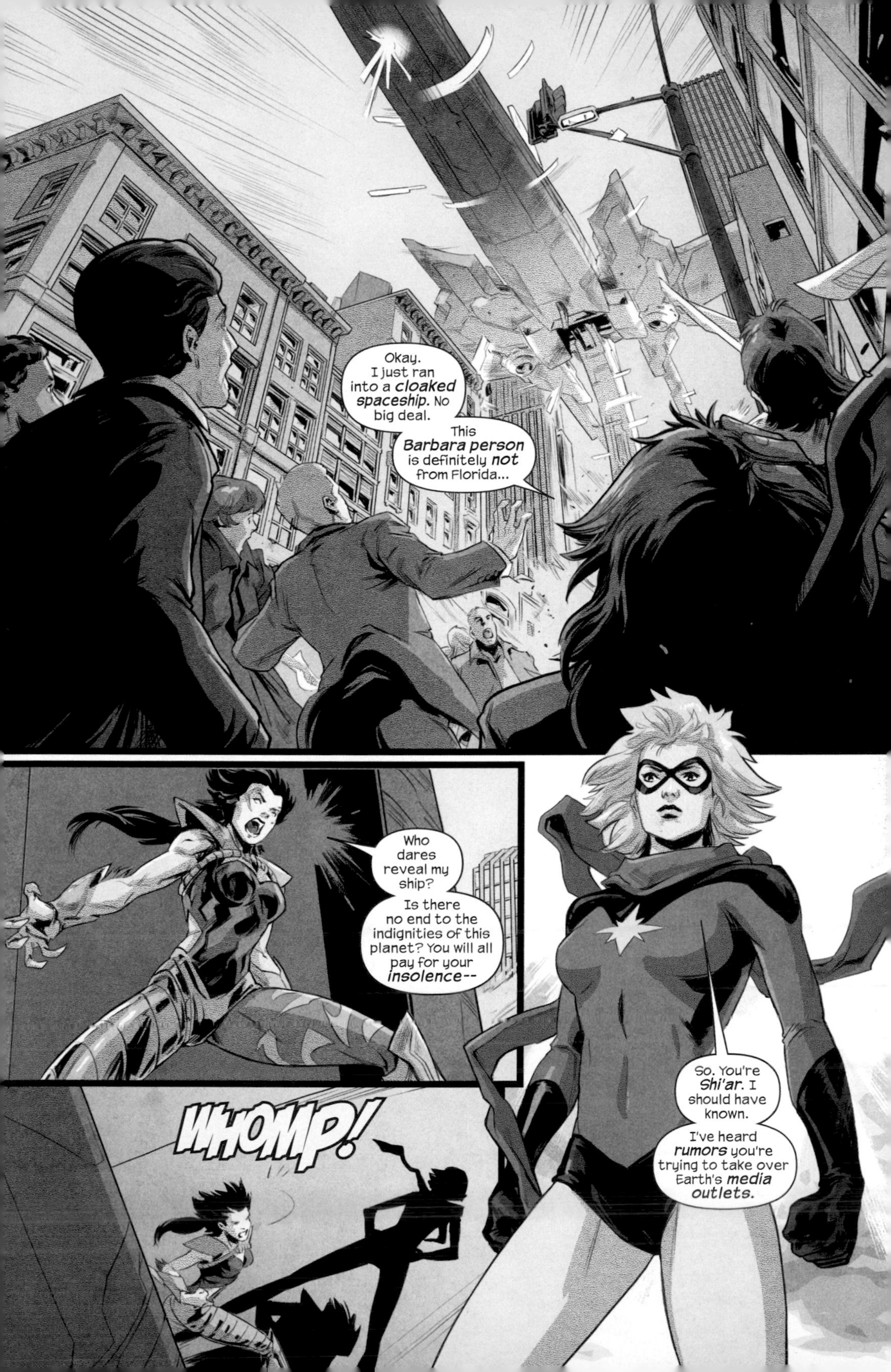
Okay. I just ran into a cloaked spaceship. No big deal.
This Barbara person is definitely not from Florida...
Who dares reveal my ship?
Is there no end to the indignities of this planet? You will all pay for your insolence--
WHOMP!
So. You're Shi'ar. I should have known.
I've heard rumors you're trying to take over Earth's media outlets.

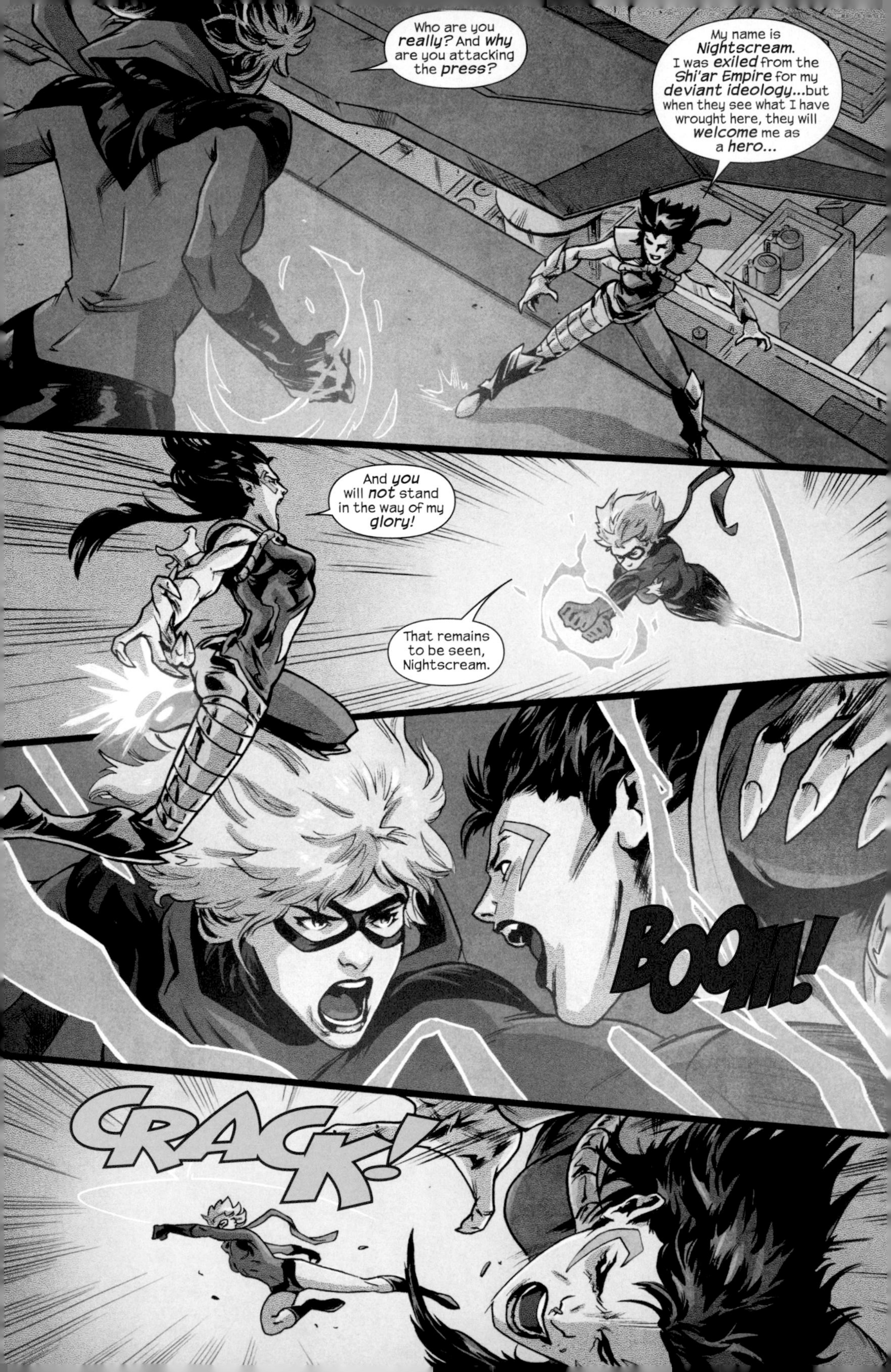
Who are you really? And why are you attacking the press?
My name is Nightscream. I was exiled from the Shi'ar Empire for my deviant ideology...but when they see what I have wrought here, they will welcome me as a hero...
And you will not stand in the way of my glory!
That remains to be seen, Nightscream.
BOOM!
CRACK!

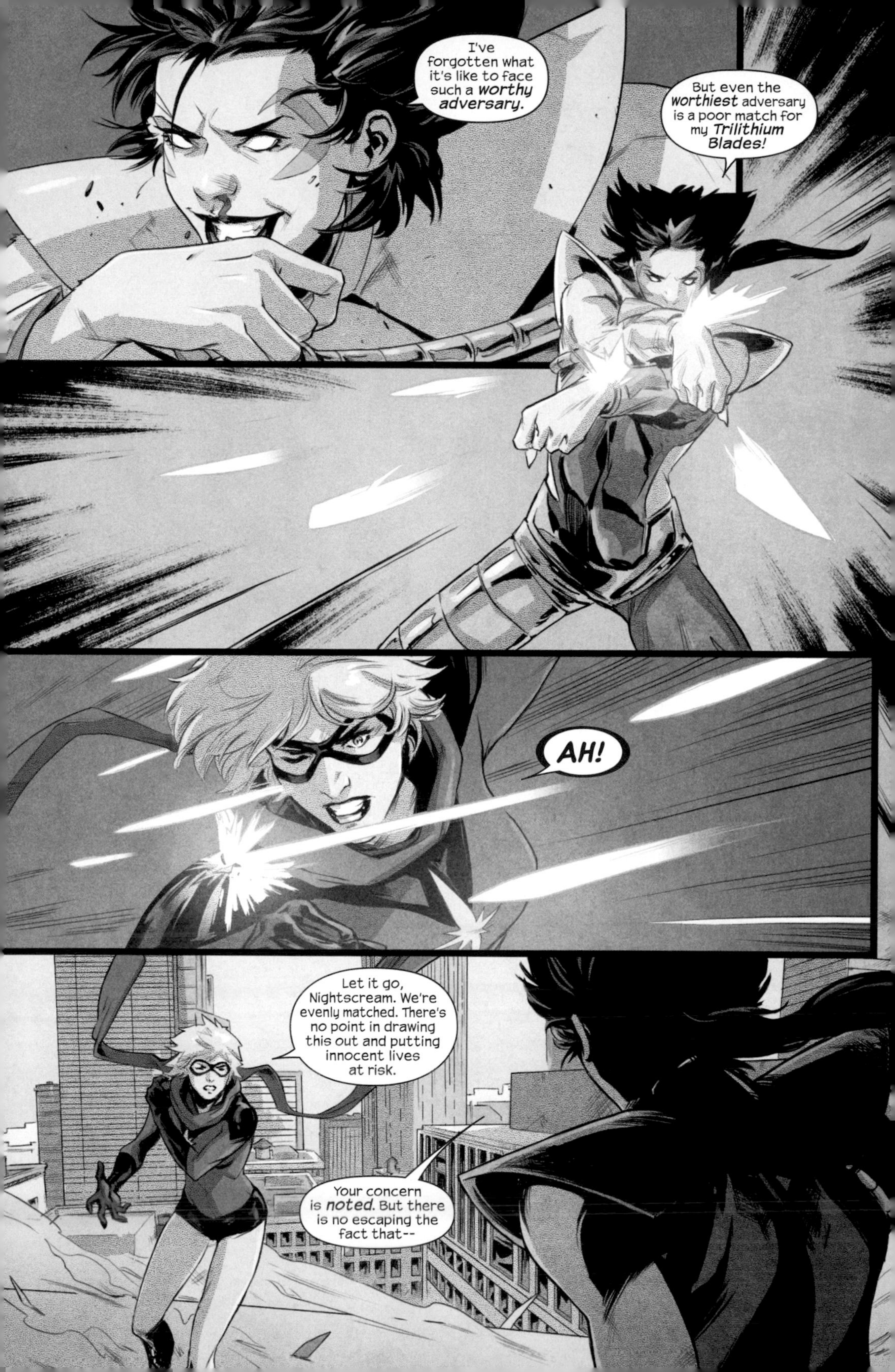
I've forgotten what it's like to face such a worthy adversary.
But even the worthiest adversary is a poor match for my Trilithium Blades!
AH!
Let it go, Nightscream. We're evenly matched. There's no point in drawing this out and putting innocent lives at risk.
Your concern is noted. But there is no escaping the fact that--

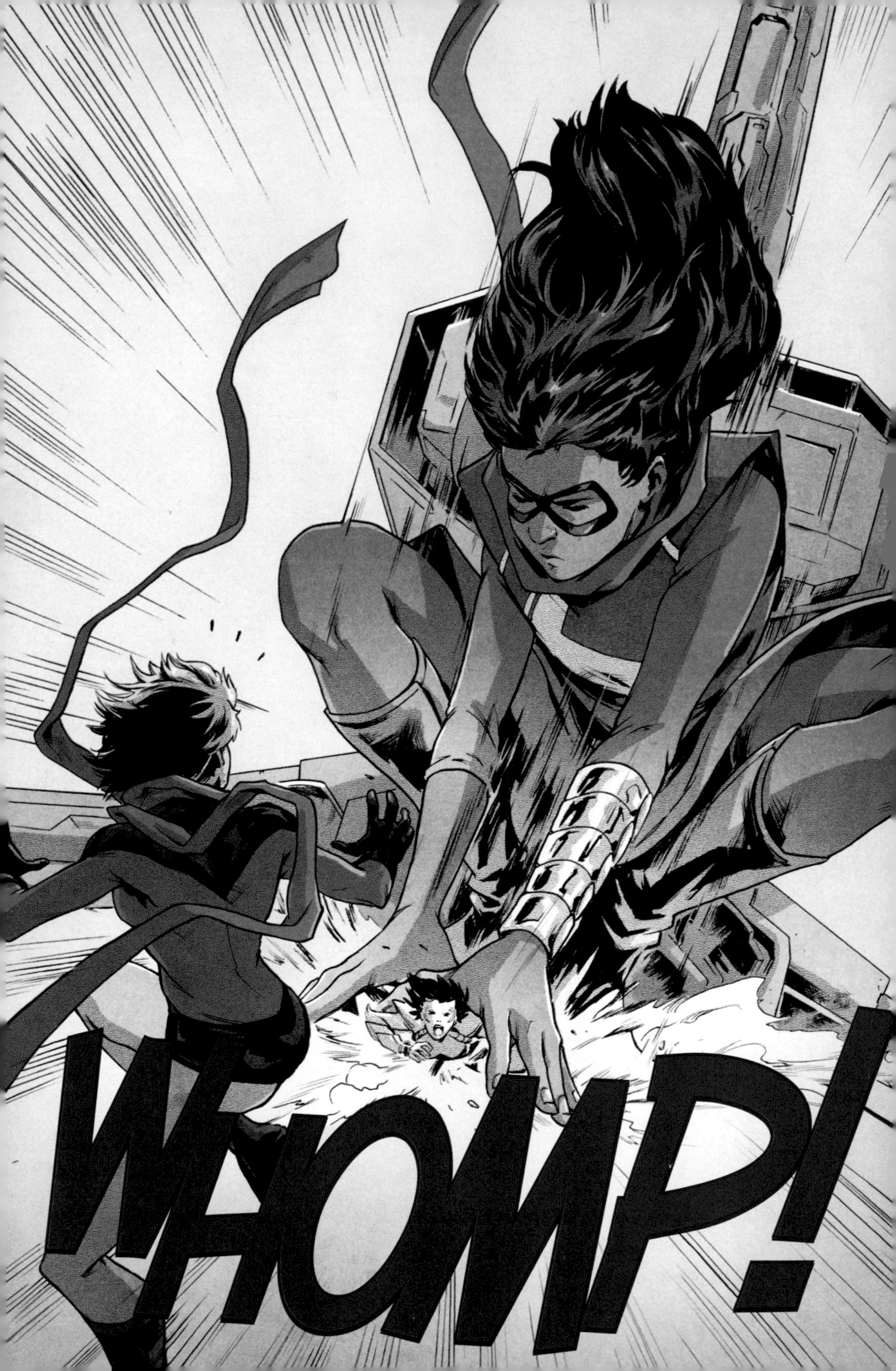
WHOMP!

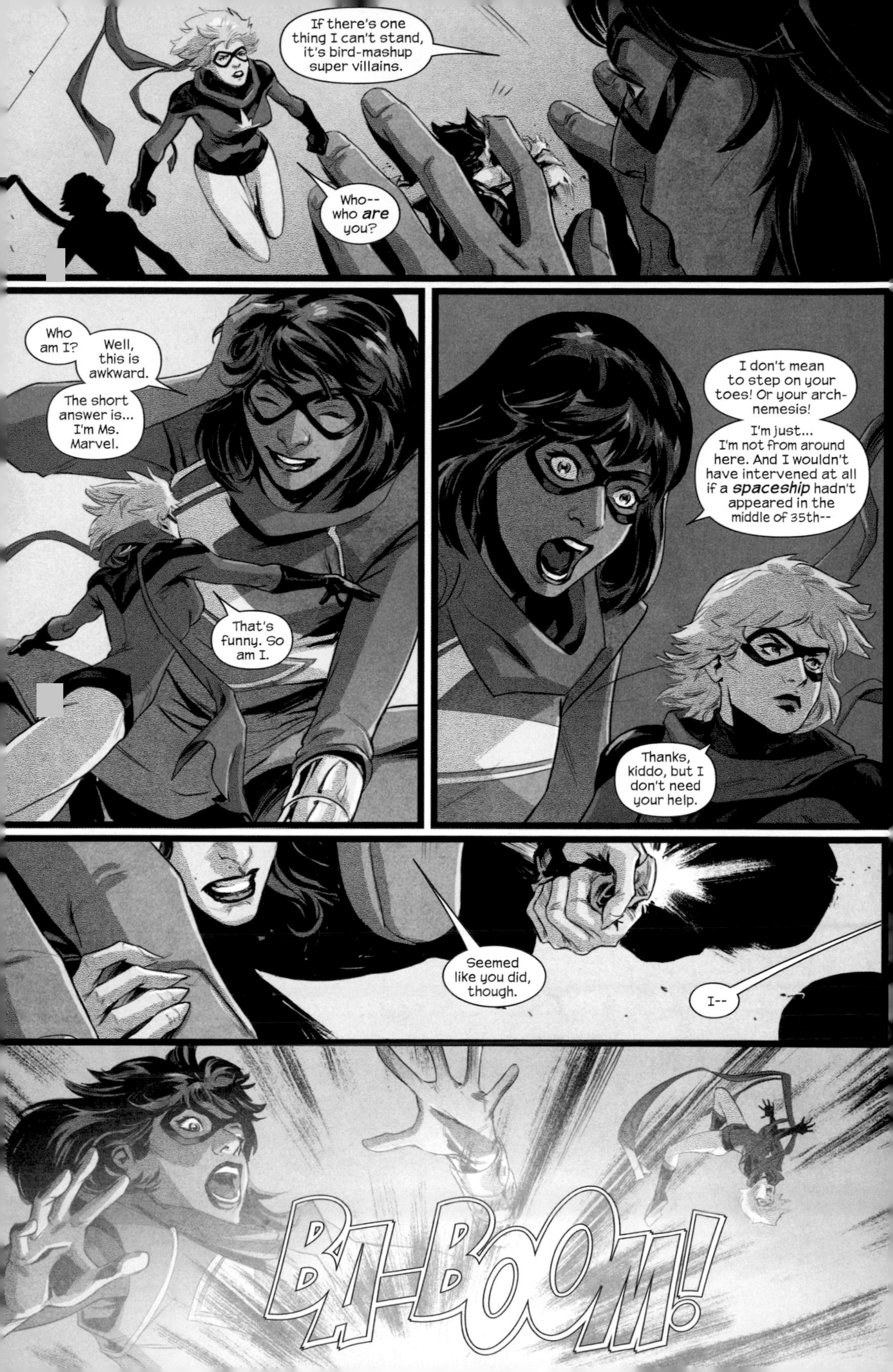
If there's one thing I can't stand, it's bird-mashup super villains.
Who-- who *are* you?
Who am I?
Well, this is awkward.
The short answer is... I'm Ms. Marvel.
That's funny. So am I.
I don't mean to step on your toes! Or your arch-nemesis!
I'm just... I'm not from around here. And I wouldn't have intervened at all if a *spaceship* hadn't appeared in the middle of 35th--
Thanks, kiddo, but I don't need your help.
Seemed like you did, though.
I--
BA-BOOM!

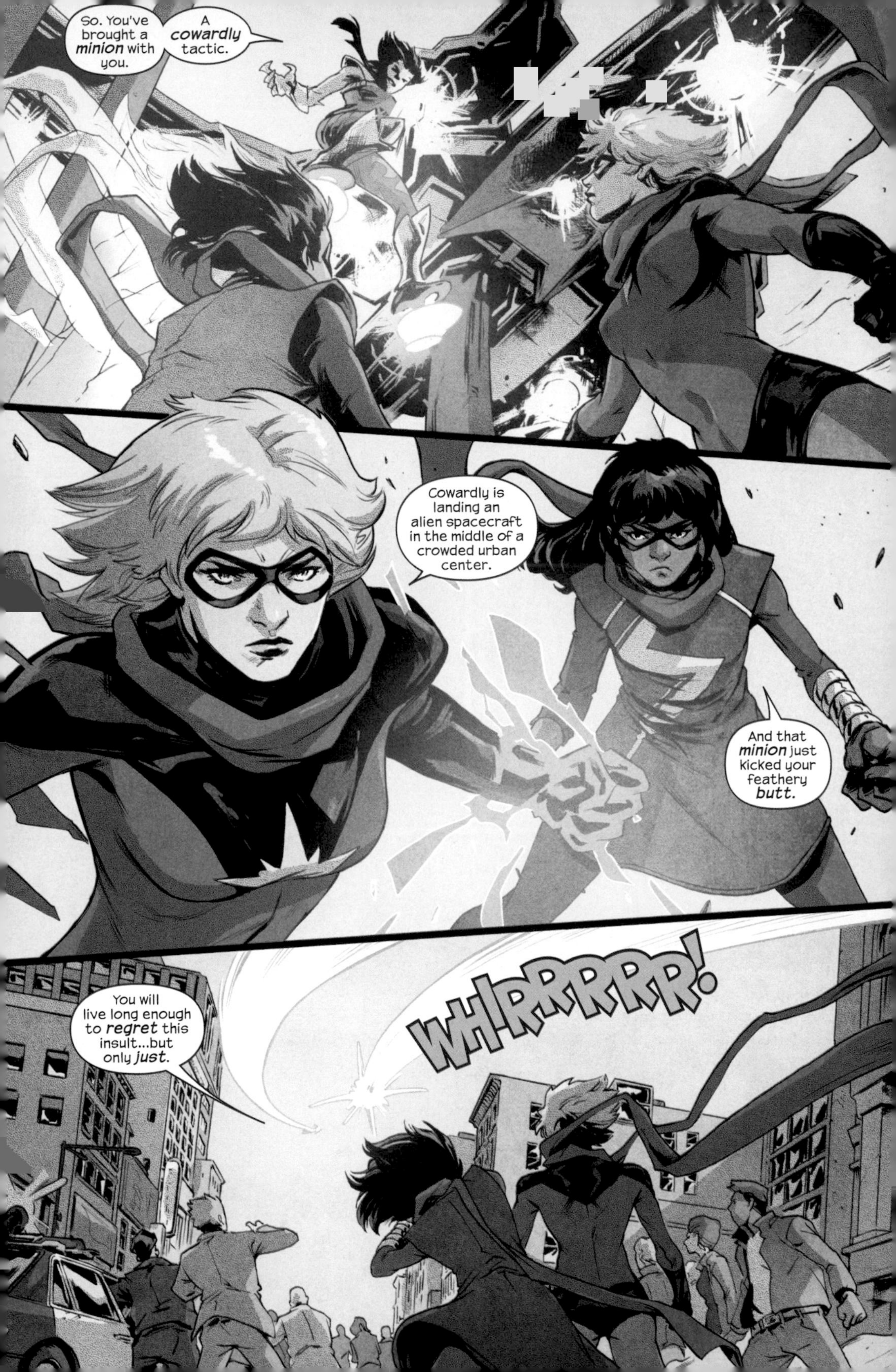
So. You've brought a *minion* with you.
A *cowardly* tactic.
Cowardly is landing an alien spacecraft in the middle of a crowded urban center.
And that *minion* just kicked your feathery *butt.*
You will live long enough to *regret* this insult...but only *just*.
WHIRRRRR!

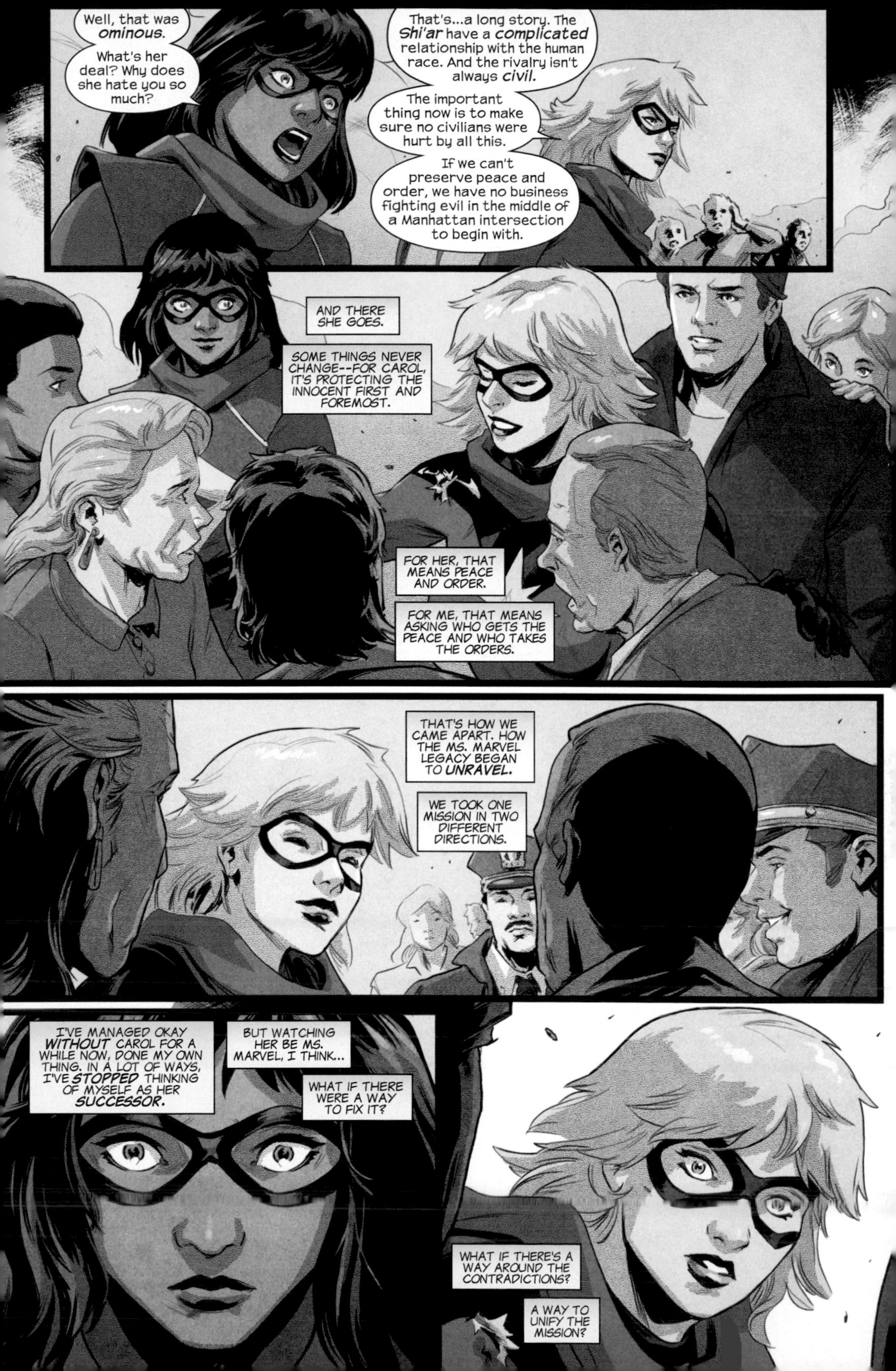

Well, that was *ominous*.
What's her deal? Why does she hate you so much?
That's...a long story. The *Shi'ar* have a *complicated* relationship with the human race. And the rivalry isn't always *civil*.
The important thing now is to make sure no civilians were hurt by all this.
If we can't preserve peace and order, we have no business fighting evil in the middle of a Manhattan intersection to begin with.
AND THERE SHE GOES.
SOME THINGS NEVER CHANGE--FOR CAROL, IT'S PROTECTING THE INNOCENT FIRST AND FOREMOST.
FOR HER, THAT MEANS PEACE AND ORDER.
FOR ME, THAT MEANS ASKING WHO GETS THE PEACE AND WHO TAKES THE ORDERS.
THAT'S HOW WE CAME APART. HOW THE MS. MARVEL LEGACY BEGAN TO *UNRAVEL*.
WE TOOK ONE MISSION IN TWO DIFFERENT DIRECTIONS.
I'VE MANAGED OKAY *WITHOUT* CAROL FOR A WHILE NOW, DONE MY OWN THING. IN A LOT OF WAYS, I'VE *STOPPED* THINKING OF MYSELF AS HER *SUCCESSOR*.
BUT WATCHING HER BE MS. MARVEL, I THINK...
WHAT IF THERE WERE A WAY TO FIX IT?
WHAT IF THERE'S A WAY AROUND THE CONTRADICTIONS?
A WAY TO UNIFY THE MISSION?

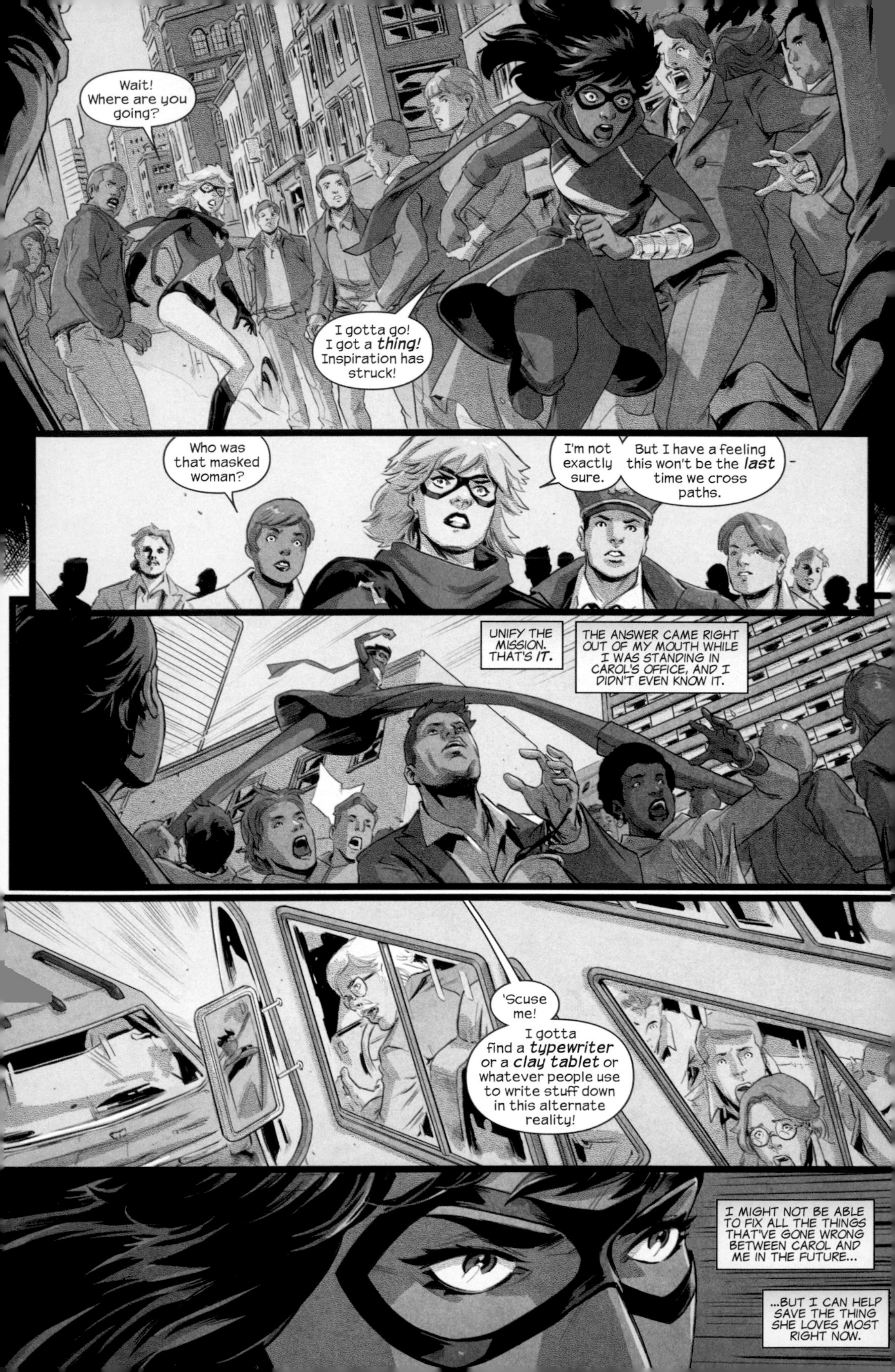

Wait! Where are you going?
I gotta go! I got a *thing!* Inspiration has struck!
Who was that masked woman?
I'm not exactly sure.
But I have a feeling this won't be the *last* time we cross paths.
UNIFY THE MISSION. THAT'S *IT*.
THE ANSWER CAME RIGHT OUT OF MY MOUTH WHILE I WAS STANDING IN CAROL'S OFFICE, AND I DIDN'T EVEN KNOW IT.
'Scuse me!
I gotta find a *typewriter* or a *clay tablet* or whatever people use to write stuff down in this alternate reality!
I MIGHT NOT BE ABLE TO FIX ALL THE THINGS THAT'VE GONE WRONG BETWEEN CAROL AND ME IN THE FUTURE...
...BUT I CAN HELP SAVE THE THING SHE LOVES MOST RIGHT NOW.

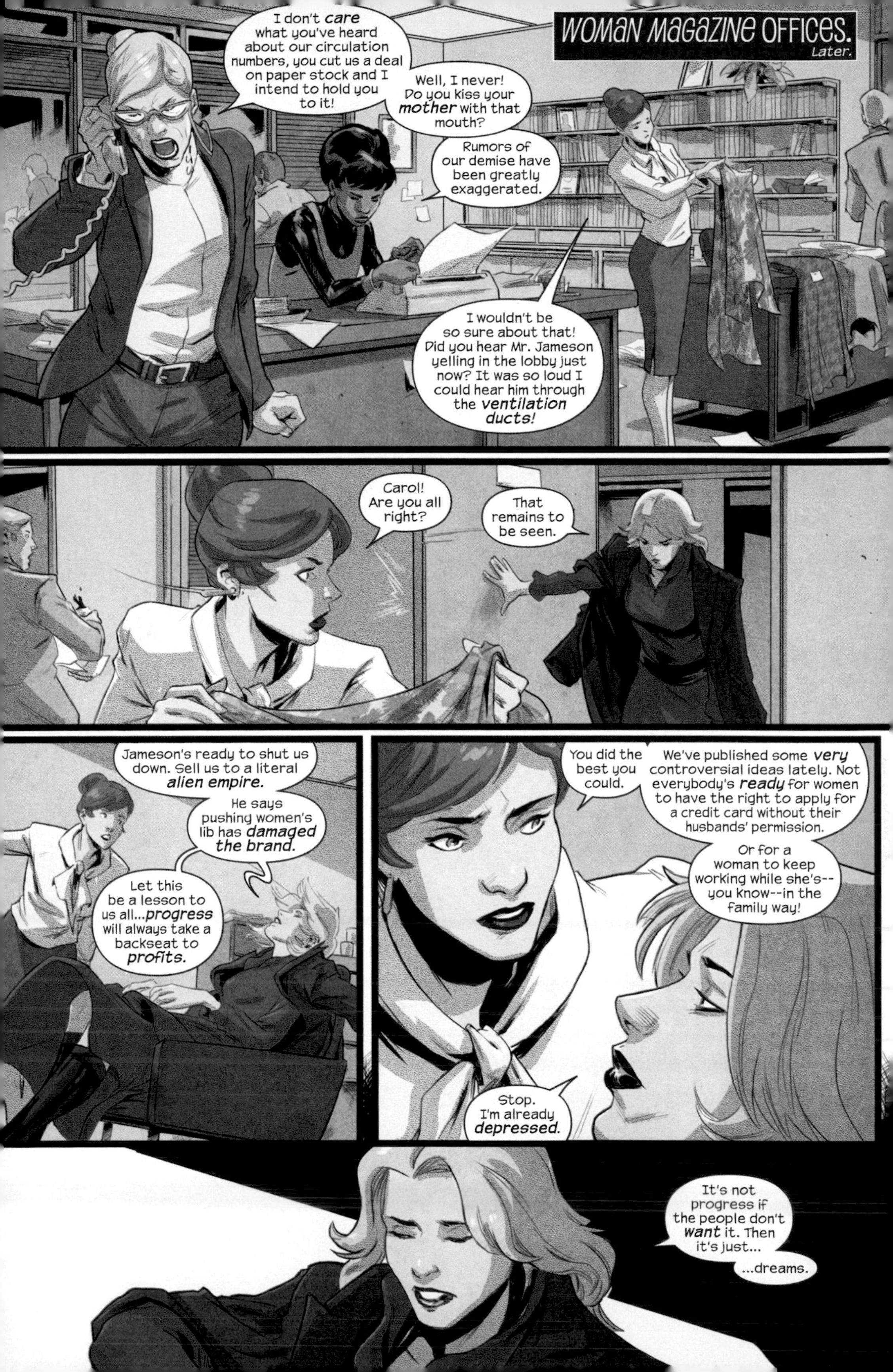
WOMAN MAGAZINE OFFICES.
Later.
I don't care what you've heard about our circulation numbers, you cut us a deal on paper stock and I intend to hold you to it!
Well, I never! Do you kiss your mother with that mouth?
Rumors of our demise have been greatly exaggerated.
I wouldn't be so sure about that! Did you hear Mr. Jameson yelling in the lobby just now? It was so loud I could hear him through the ventilation ducts!
Carol! Are you all right?
That remains to be seen.
Jameson's ready to shut us down. Sell us to a literal alien empire.
He says pushing women's lib has damaged the brand.
Let this be a lesson to us all...progress will always take a backseat to profits.
You did the best you could.
We've published some very controversial ideas lately. Not everybody's ready for women to have the right to apply for a credit card without their husbands' permission.
Or for a woman to keep working while she's--you know--in the family way!
Stop. I'm already depressed.
It's not progress if the people don't want it. Then it's just...
...dreams.

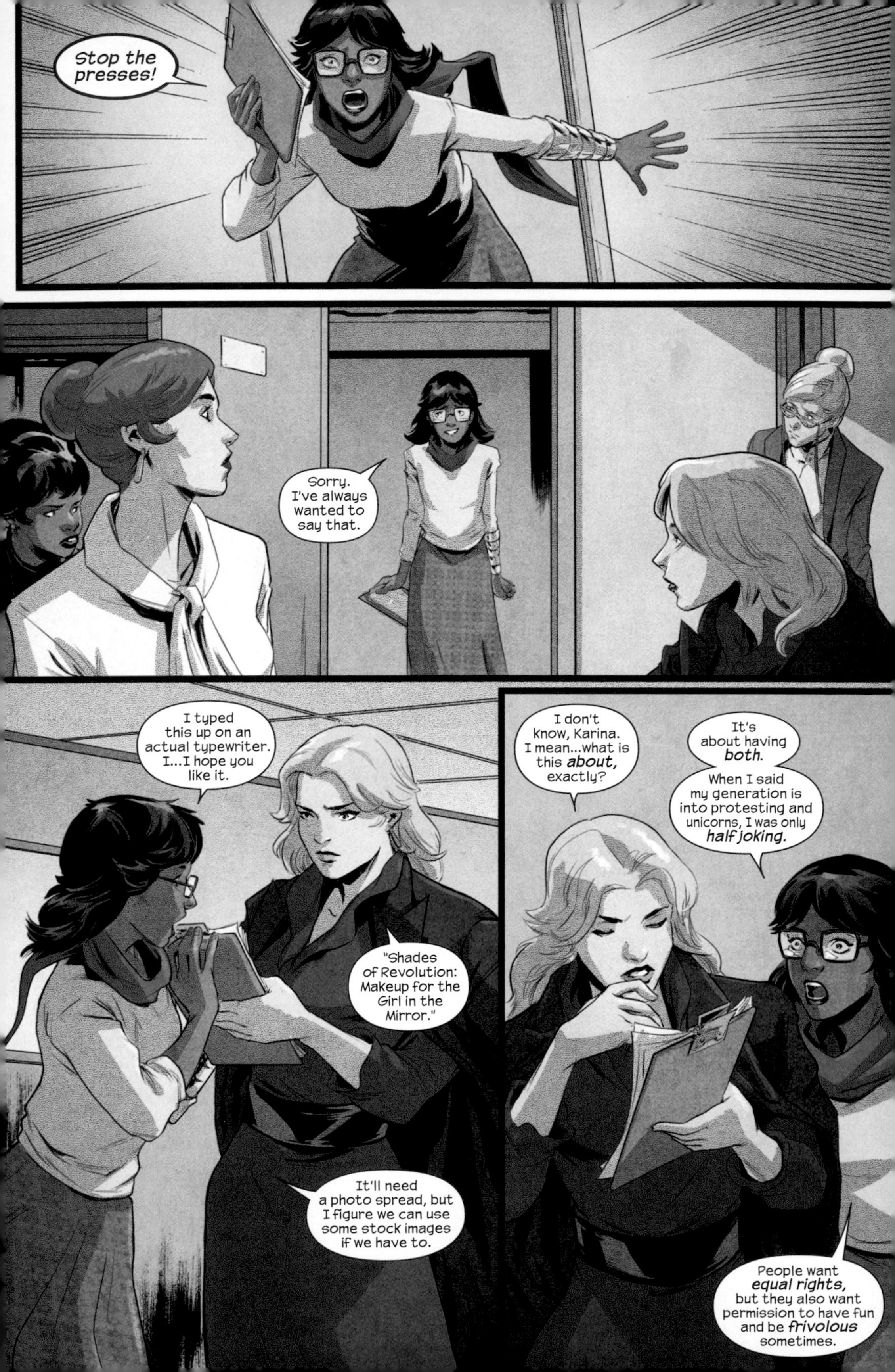
Stop the presses!
Sorry. I've always wanted to say that.
I typed this up on an actual typewriter. I...I hope you like it.
"Shades of Revolution: Makeup for the Girl in the Mirror."
It'll need a photo spread, but I figure we can use some stock images if we have to.
I don't know, Karina. I mean...what is this about, exactly?
It's about having both.
When I said my generation is into protesting and unicorns, I was only half joking.
People want equal rights, but they also want permission to have fun and be frivolous sometimes.

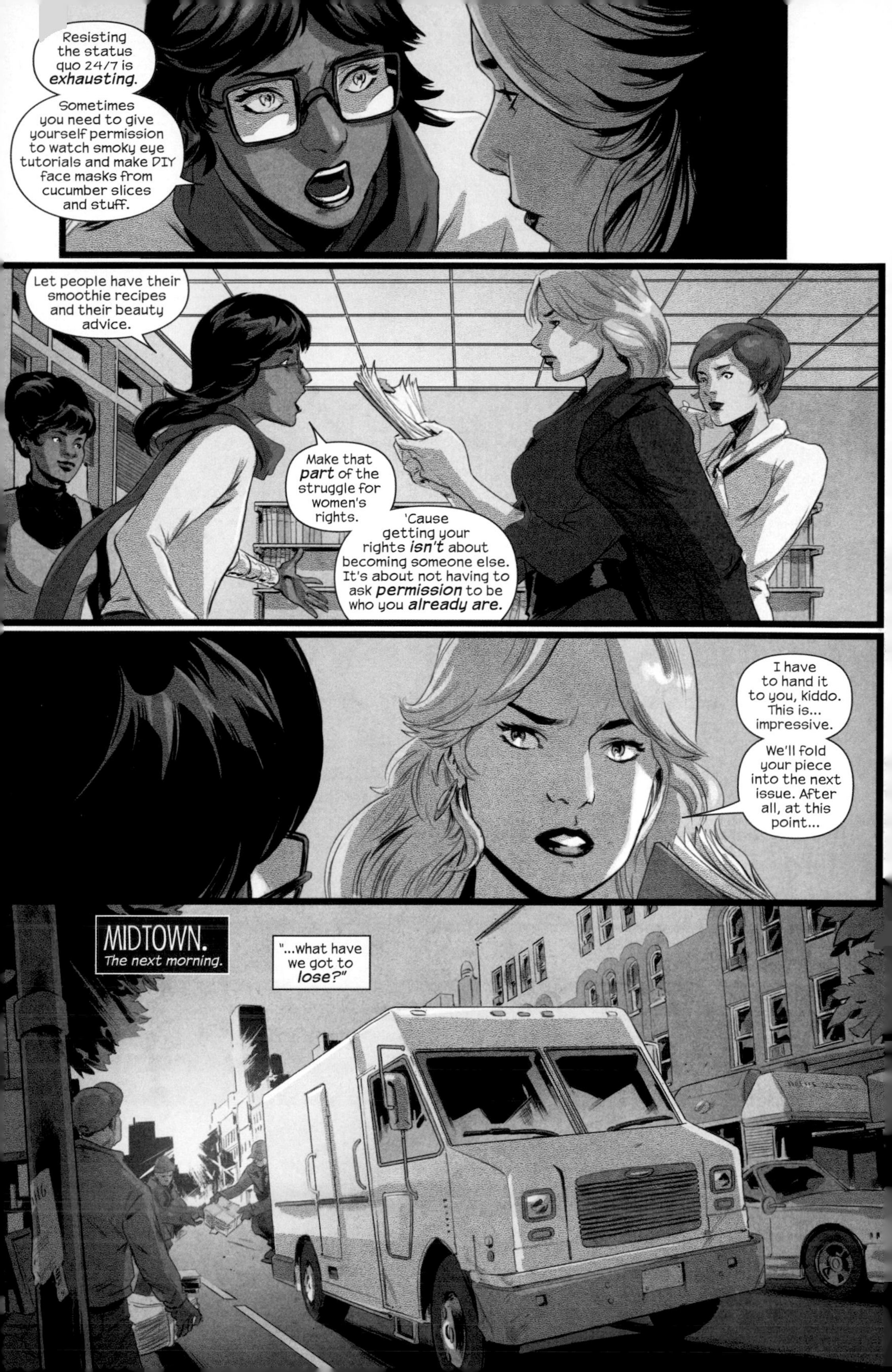
Resisting the status quo 24/7 is *exhausting*.
Sometimes you need to give yourself permission to watch smoky eye tutorials and make DIY face masks from cucumber slices and stuff.
Let people have their smoothie recipes and their beauty advice.
Make that *part* of the struggle for women's rights.
'Cause getting your rights *isn't* about becoming someone else. It's about not having to ask *permission* to be who you *already are*.
I have to hand it to you, kiddo. This is... impressive.
We'll fold your piece into the next issue. After all, at this point...
MIDTOWN. The next morning.
"...what have we got to *lose?*"

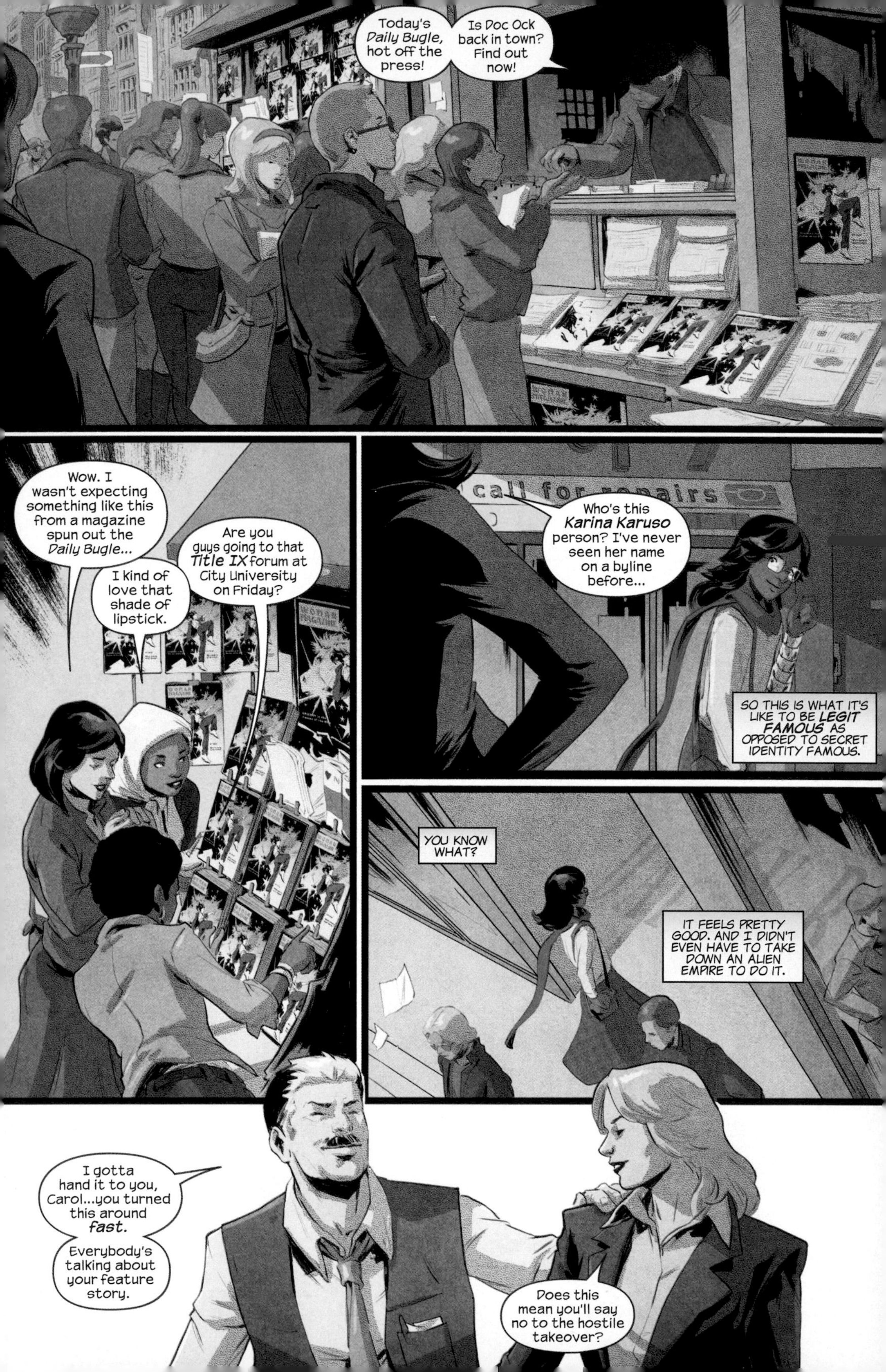
Today's Daily Bugle, hot off the press!
Is Doc Ock back in town? Find out now!
Wow. I wasn't expecting something like this from a magazine spun out the Daily Bugle...
I kind of love that shade of lipstick.
Are you guys going to that Title IX forum at City University on Friday?
call for repairs
Who's this Karina Karuso person? I've never seen her name on a byline before...
SO THIS IS WHAT IT'S LIKE TO BE LEGIT FAMOUS AS OPPOSED TO SECRET IDENTITY FAMOUS.
YOU KNOW WHAT?
IT FEELS PRETTY GOOD. AND I DIDN'T EVEN HAVE TO TAKE DOWN AN ALIEN EMPIRE TO DO IT.
I gotta hand it to you, Carol...you turned this around fast.
Everybody's talking about your feature story.
Does this mean you'll say no to the hostile takeover?

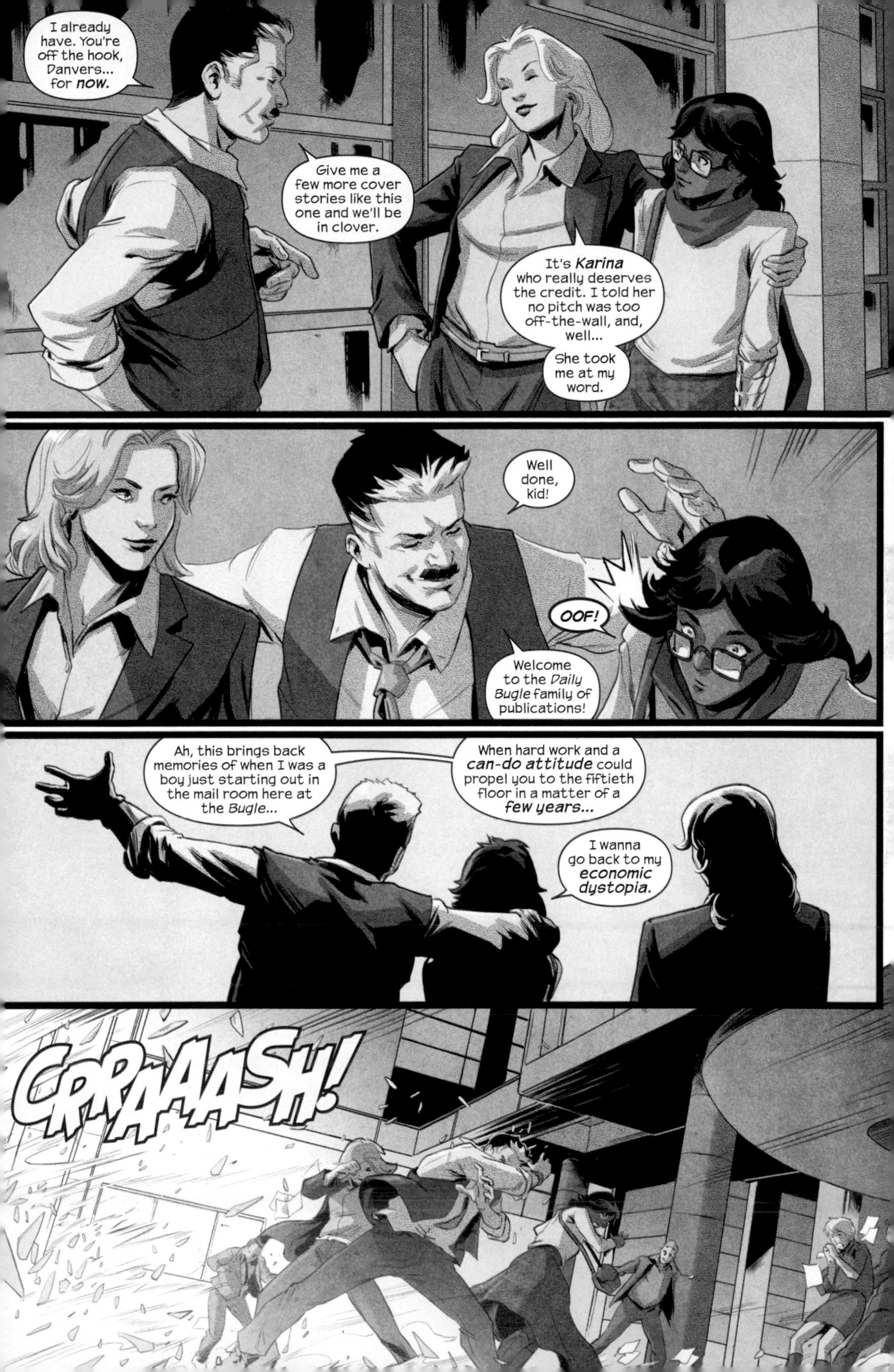
I already have. You're off the hook, Danvers... for *now.*
Give me a few more cover stories like this one and we'll be in clover.
It's *Karina* who really deserves the credit. I told her no pitch was too off-the-wall, and, well...
She took me at my word.
Well done, kid!
OOF!
Welcome to the *Daily Bugle* family of publications!
Ah, this brings back memories of when I was a boy just starting out in the mail room here at the *Bugle*...
When hard work and a *can-do attitude* could propel you to the fiftieth floor in a matter of a *few years...*
I wanna go back to my *economic dystopia.*
CRRAAASH!

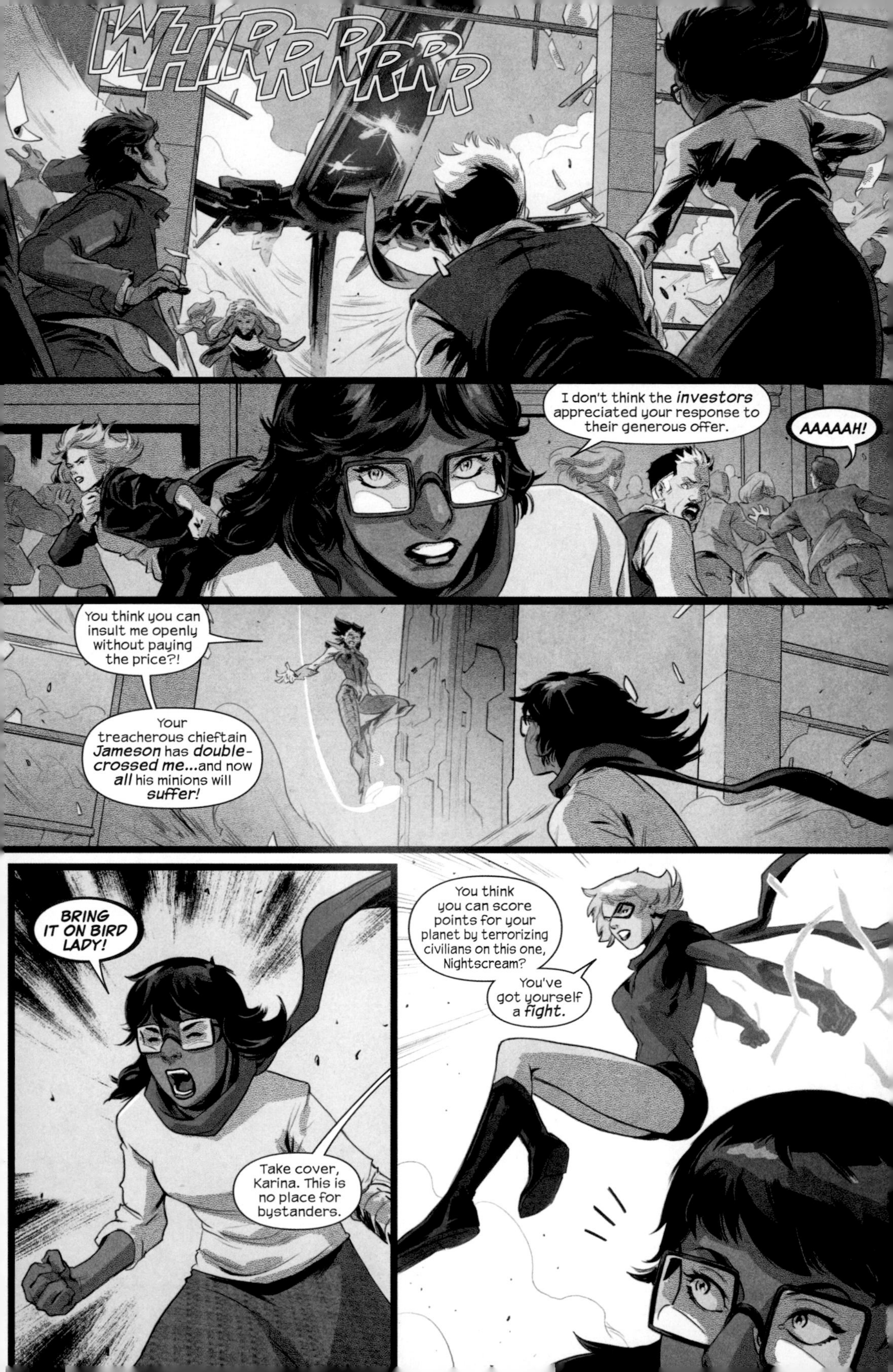
WHIRRRRRR
I don't think the *investors* appreciated your response to their generous offer.
AAAAAH!
You think you can insult me openly without paying the price?!
Your treacherous chieftain *Jameson* has *double-crossed me...*and now *all* his minions will *suffer!*
BRING IT ON BIRD LADY!
Take cover, Karina. This is no place for bystanders.
You think you can score points for your planet by terrorizing civilians on this one, Nightscream?
You've got yourself a *fight.*

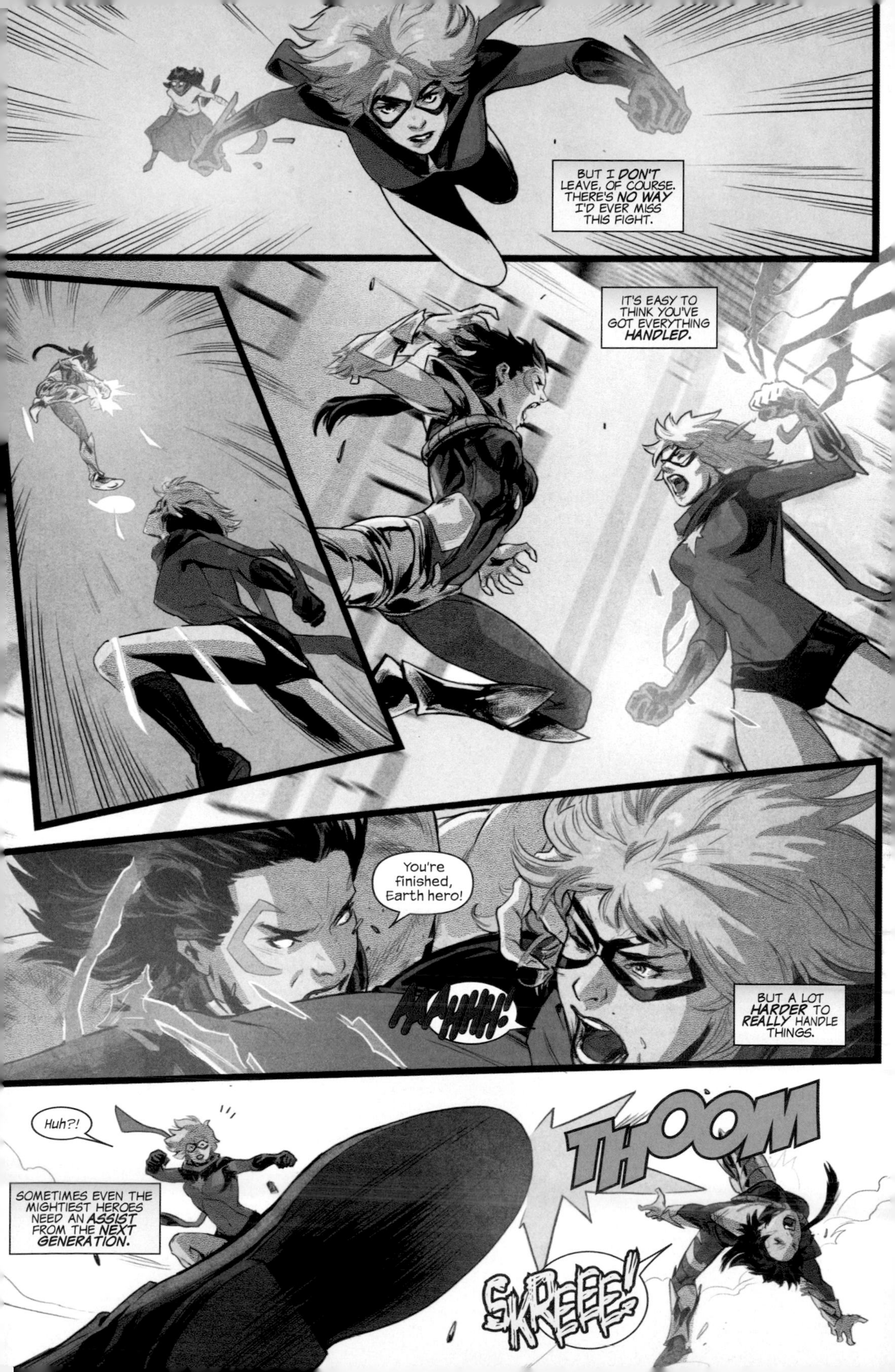

BUT I DON'T LEAVE, OF COURSE. THERE'S NO WAY I'D EVER MISS THIS FIGHT.
IT'S EASY TO THINK YOU'VE GOT EVERYTHING HANDLED.
You're finished, Earth hero!
AAAHHH!
BUT A LOT HARDER TO REALLY HANDLE THINGS.
Huh?!
SOMETIMES EVEN THE MIGHTIEST HEROES NEED AN ASSIST FROM THE NEXT GENERATION.
THOOM
SKREEE!

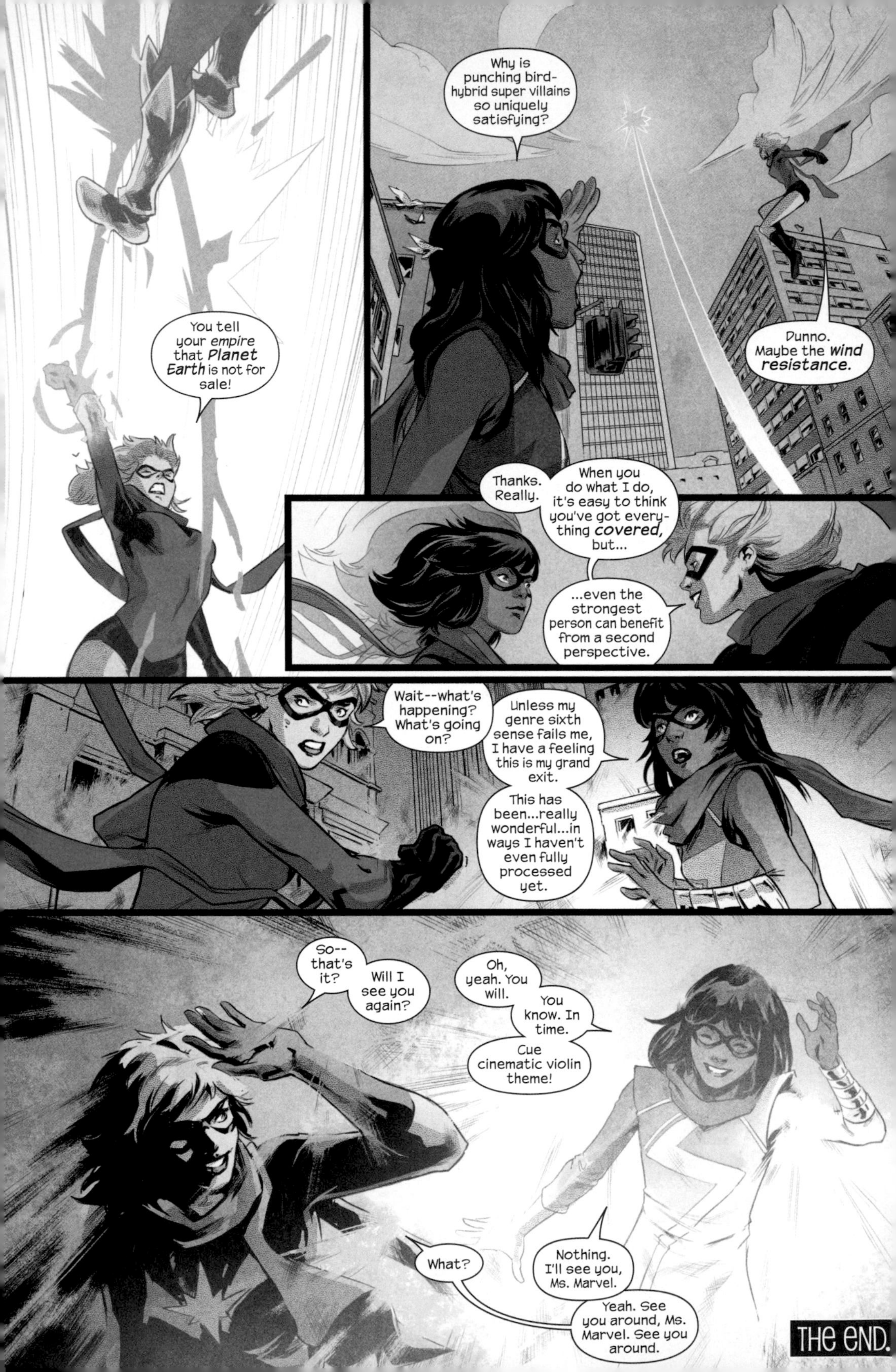
You tell your empire that Planet Earth is not for sale!
Why is punching bird-hybrid super villains so uniquely satisfying?
Dunno. Maybe the wind resistance.
Thanks. Really.
When you do what I do, it's easy to think you've got every-thing covered, but...
...even the strongest person can benefit from a second perspective.
Wait--what's happening? What's going on?
Unless my genre sixth sense fails me, I have a feeling this is my grand exit.
This has been...really wonderful...in ways I haven't even fully processed yet.
So--that's it?
Will I see you again?
Oh, yeah. You will.
You know. In time.
Cue cinematic violin theme!
What?
Nothing. I'll see you, Ms. Marvel.
Yeah. See you around, Ms. Marvel. See you around.
THE END.

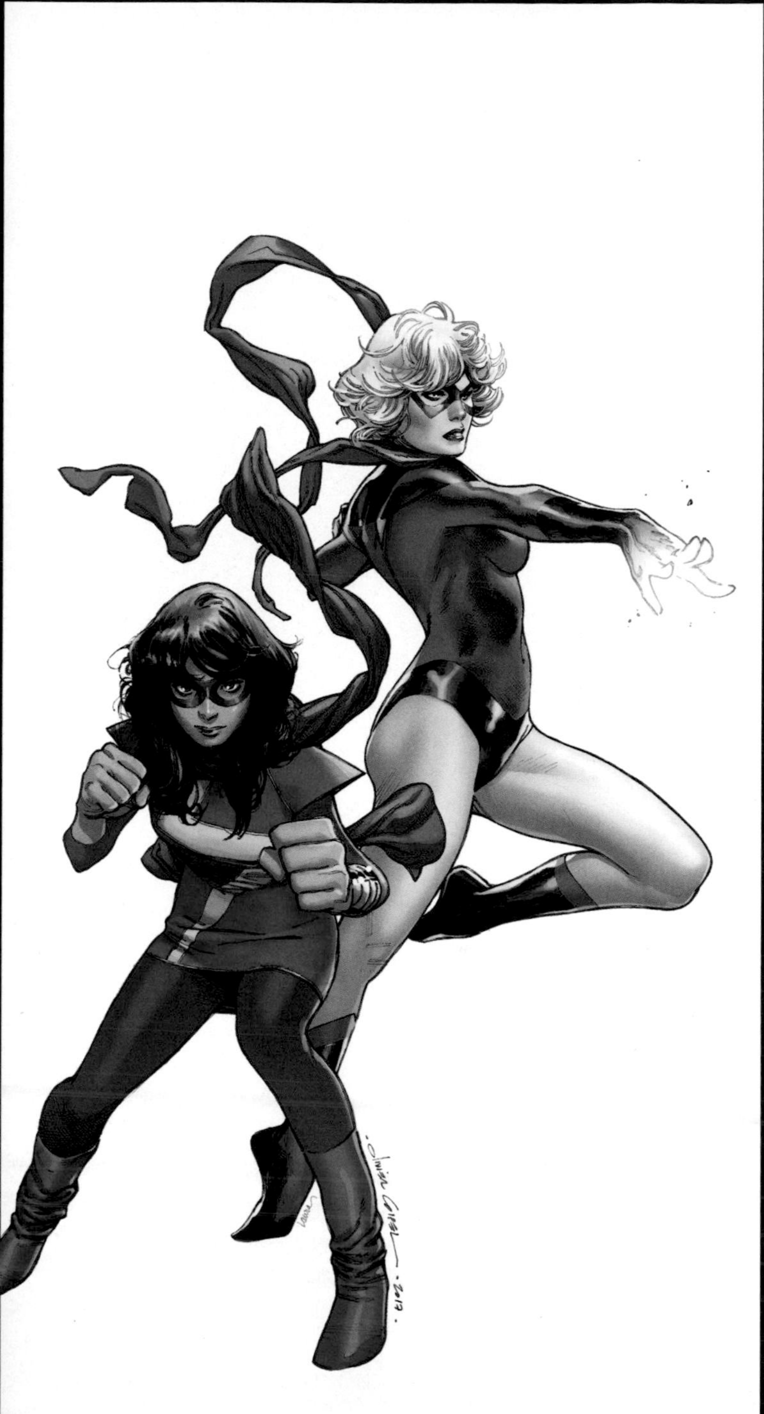

GENERATIONS: MS. MARVEL & MS. MARVEL

VARIANT BY OLIVIER COIPEL & LAURA MARTIN

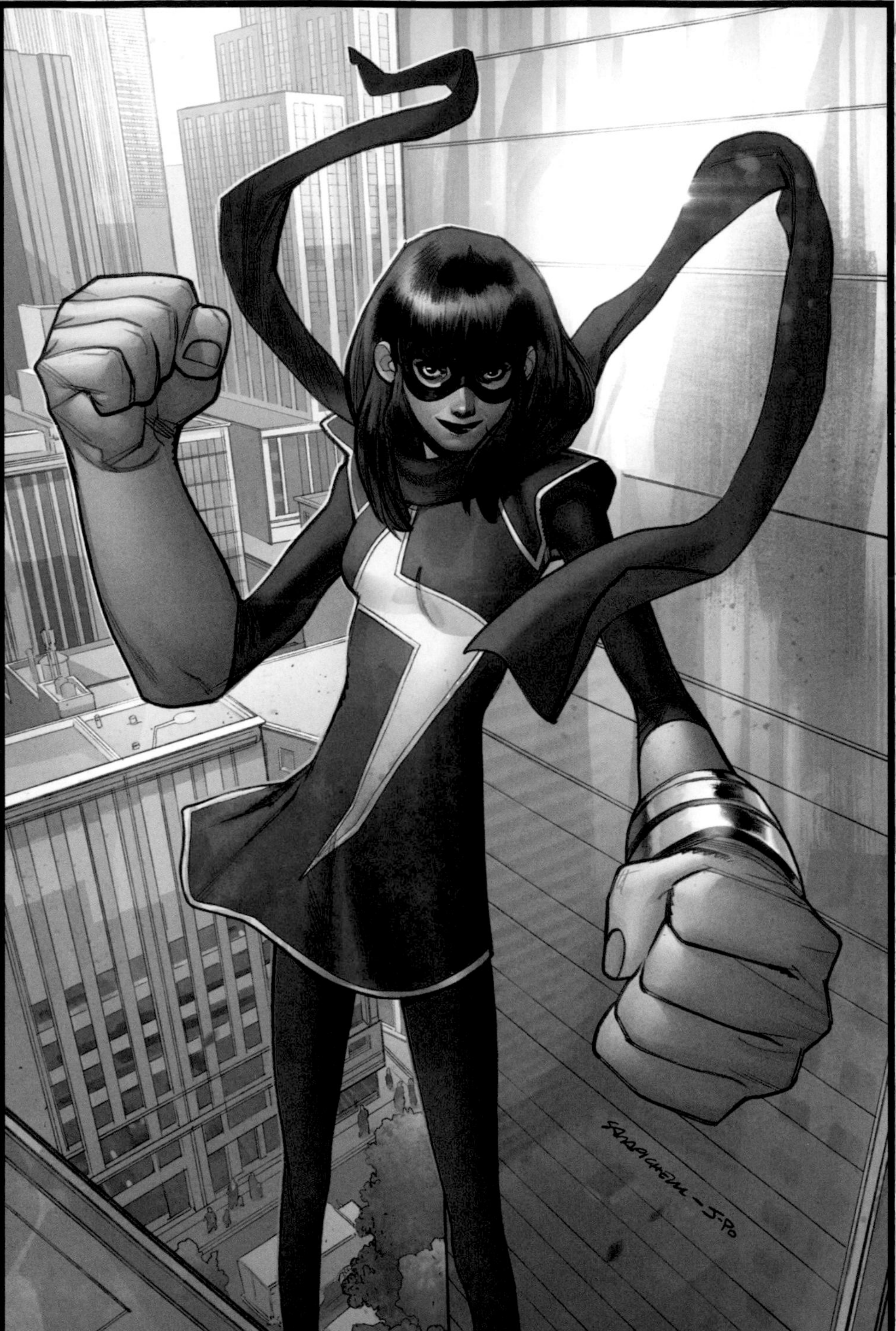

MS. MARVEL #38

TAKE A DEEP DIVE INTO KAMALA'S JERSEY CITY WITH BRUNO, NAKIA, ZOE AND MORE IN THIS SPECIAL JAM-PACKED CELEBRATION OF MS. MARVEL AND HER AMAZING FRIENDS!

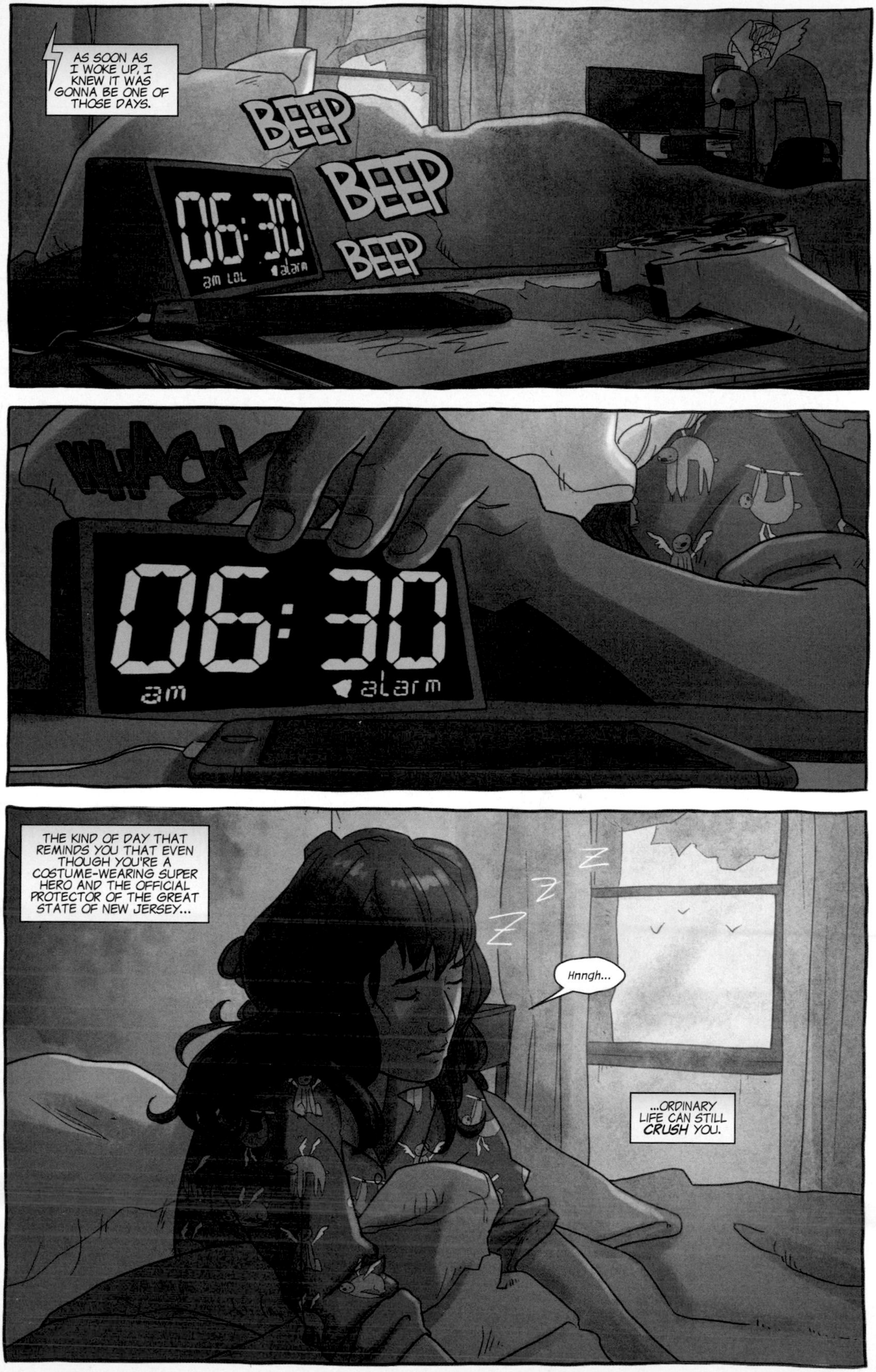
AS SOON AS I WOKE UP, I KNEW IT WAS GONNA BE ONE OF THOSE DAYS.
BEEP
BEEP
BEEP
06:30
am LOL alarm
WHACK!
06:30
am alarm
THE KIND OF DAY THAT REMINDS YOU THAT EVEN THOUGH YOU'RE A COSTUME-WEARING SUPER HERO AND THE OFFICIAL PROTECTOR OF THE GREAT STATE OF NEW JERSEY...
Z
Z
Z
Hnngh...
...ORDINARY LIFE CAN STILL CRUSH YOU.

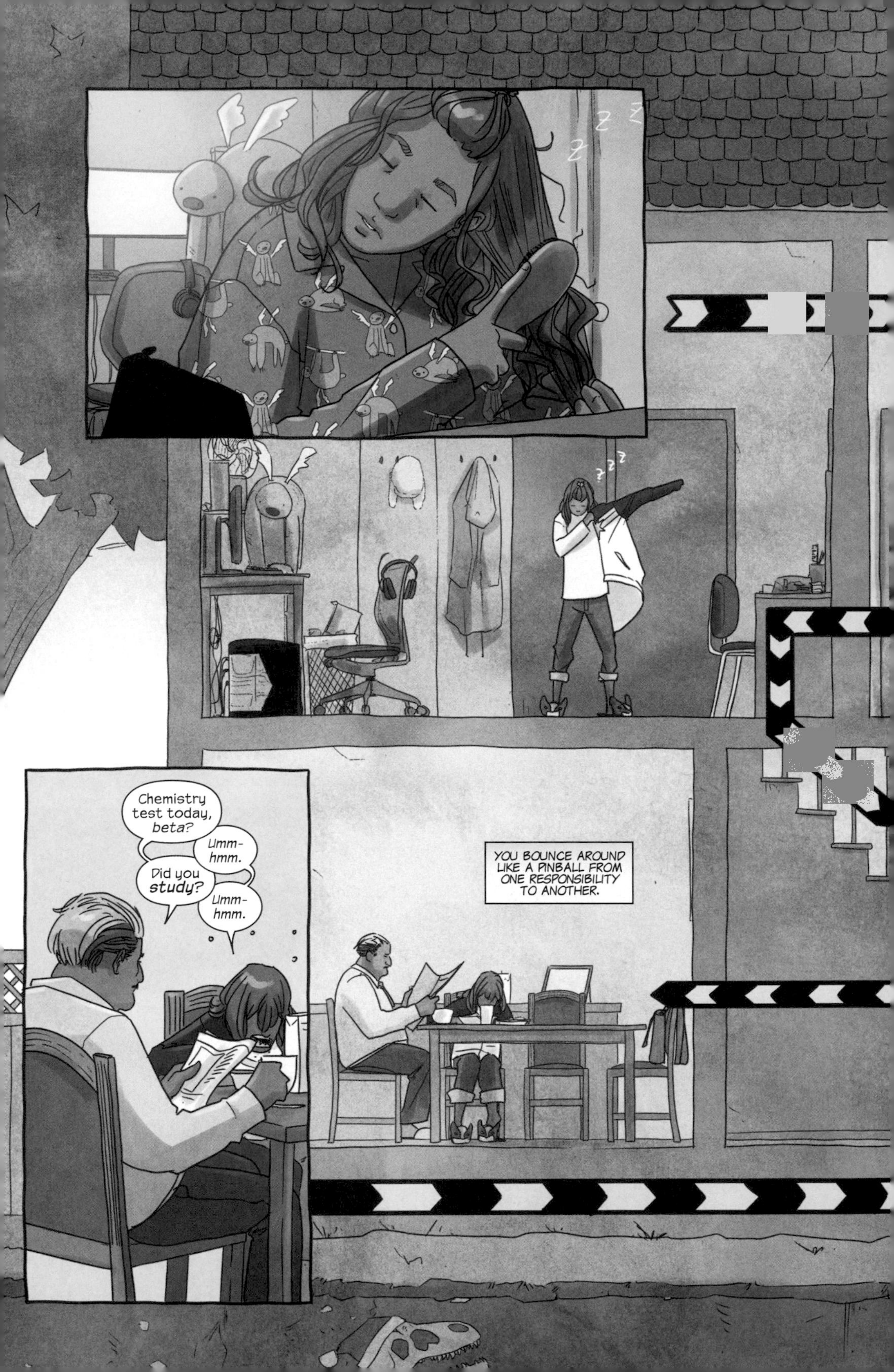
Chemistry test today, beta?
Umm-hmm.
Did you study?
Umm-hmm.
YOU BOUNCE AROUND LIKE A PINBALL FROM ONE RESPONSIBILITY TO ANOTHER.

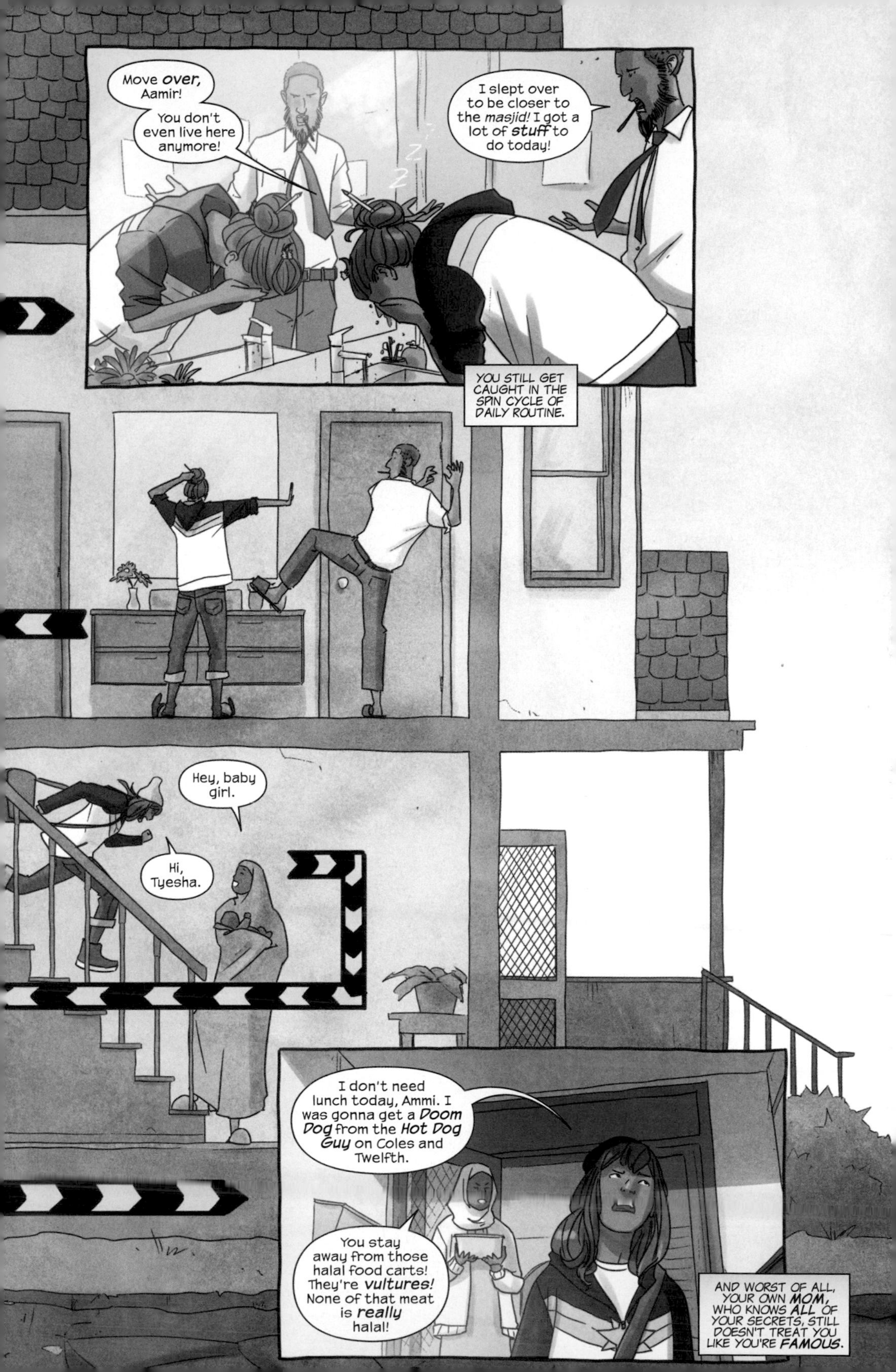

Move over, Aamir!
You don't even live here anymore!
I slept over to be closer to the masjid! I got a lot of stuff to do today!
YOU STILL GET CAUGHT IN THE SPIN CYCLE OF DAILY ROUTINE.
Hey, baby girl.
Hi, Tyesha.
I don't need lunch today, Ammi. I was gonna get a Doom Dog from the Hot Dog Guy on Coles and Twelfth.
You stay away from those halal food carts! They're vultures! None of that meat is really halal!
AND WORST OF ALL, YOUR OWN MOM, WHO KNOWS ALL OF YOUR SECRETS, STILL DOESN'T TREAT YOU LIKE YOU'RE FAMOUS.

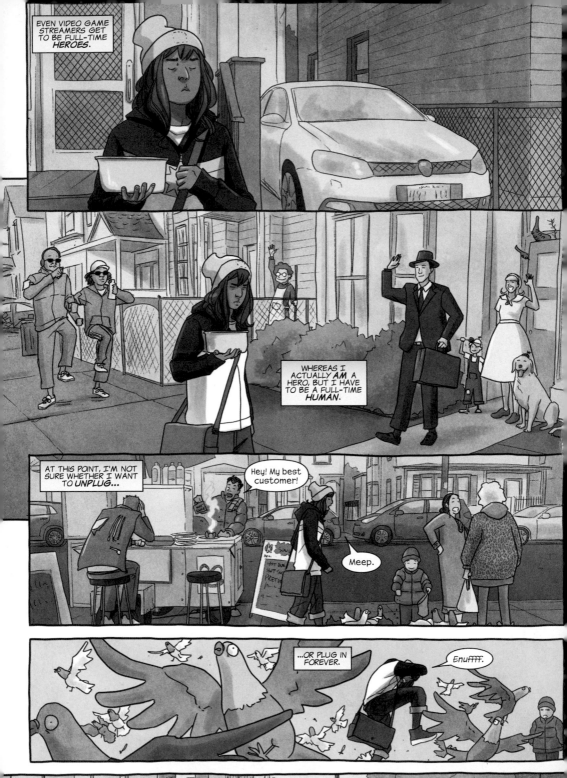

EVEN VIDEO GAME STREAMERS GET TO BE FULL-TIME *HEROES.*

WHEREAS I ACTUALLY *AM* A HERO, BUT I HAVE TO BE A FULL-TIME *HUMAN.*

AT THIS POINT, I'M NOT SURE WHETHER I WANT TO *UNPLUG...*

Hey! My best customer!

Meep.

...OR PLUG IN FOREVER.

Enuffff.

IT DOESN'T HELP THAT THIS IS ALSO ONE OF THE DAYS JERSEY CITY DECIDES TO BE SUNNY AND CHEERFUL AND BEAUTIFUL, LIKE IT'S CONSPIRING AGAINST MY BAD MOOD.

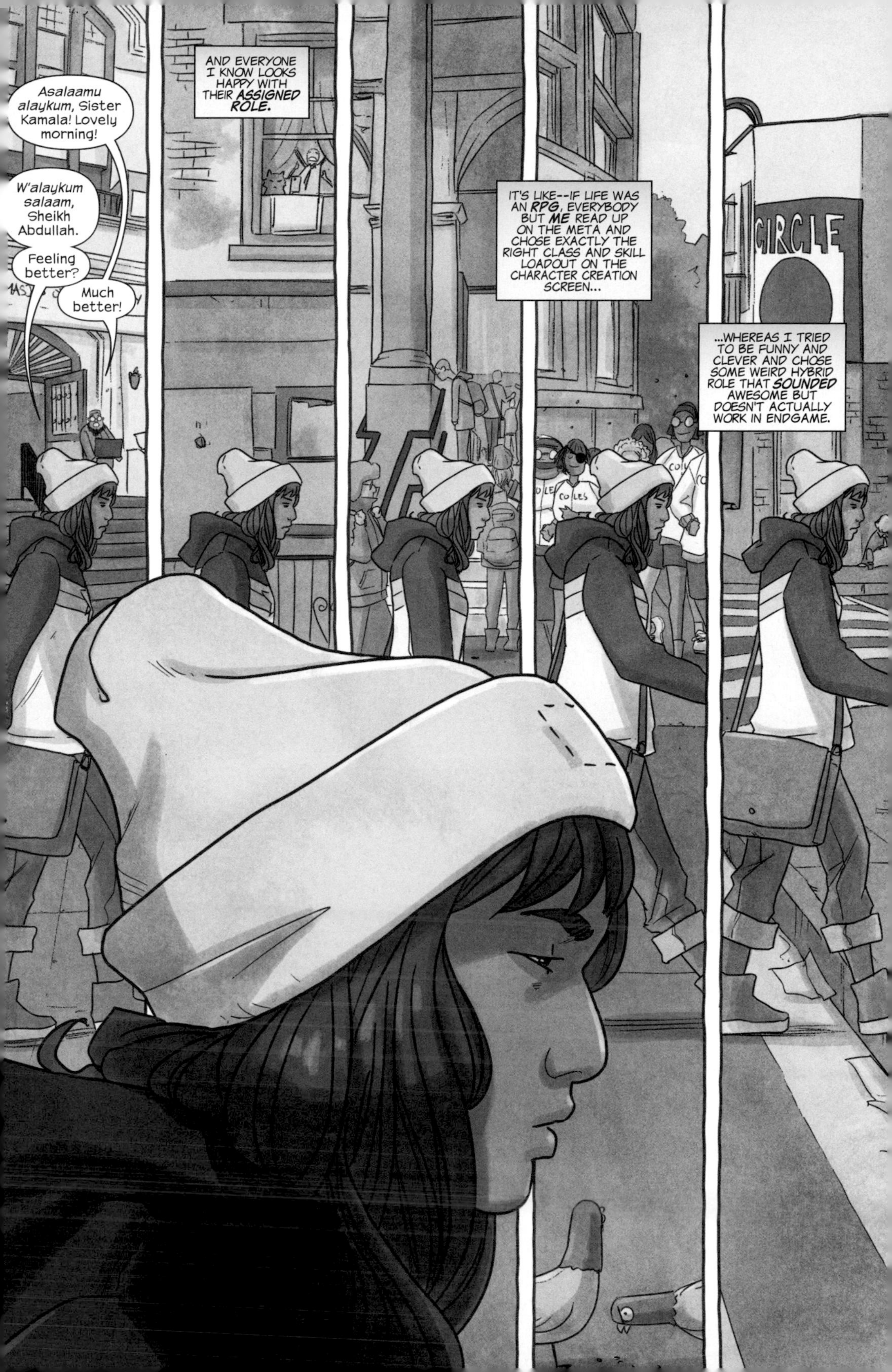

Asalaamu alaykum, Sister Kamala! Lovely morning!
W'alaykum salaam, Sheikh Abdullah.
Feeling better?
Much better!
AND EVERYONE I KNOW LOOKS HAPPY WITH THEIR ASSIGNED ROLE.
IT'S LIKE--IF LIFE WAS AN RPG, EVERYBODY BUT ME READ UP ON THE META AND CHOSE EXACTLY THE RIGHT CLASS AND SKILL LOADOUT ON THE CHARACTER CREATION SCREEN...
...WHEREAS I TRIED TO BE FUNNY AND CLEVER AND CHOSE SOME WEIRD HYBRID ROLE THAT SOUNDED AWESOME BUT DOESN'T ACTUALLY WORK IN ENDGAME.
CIRCLE

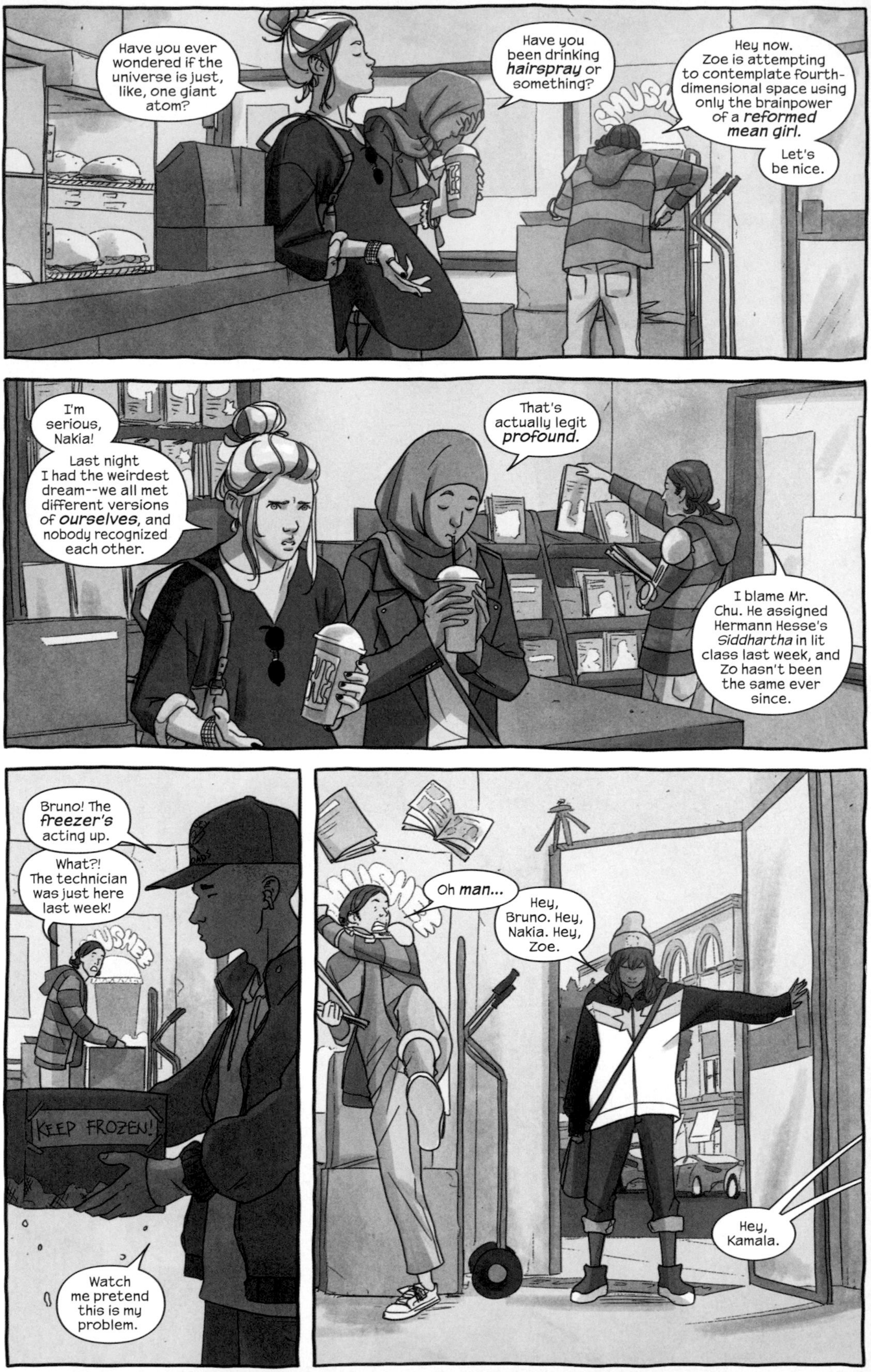
Have you ever wondered if the universe is just, like, one giant atom?
Have you been drinking *hairspray* or something?
Hey now. Zoe is attempting to contemplate fourth-dimensional space using only the brainpower of a *reformed mean girl.*
Let's be nice.
I'm serious, Nakia!
Last night I had the weirdest dream--we all met different versions of *ourselves*, and nobody recognized each other.
That's actually legit *profound.*
I blame Mr. Chu. He assigned Hermann Hesse's *Siddhartha* in lit class last week, and Zo hasn't been the same ever since.
Bruno! The *freezer's* acting up.
What?! The technician was just here last week!
KEEP FROZEN!
Watch me pretend this is my problem.
Oh *man*...
Hey, Bruno. Hey, Nakia. Hey, Zoe.
Hey, Kamala.

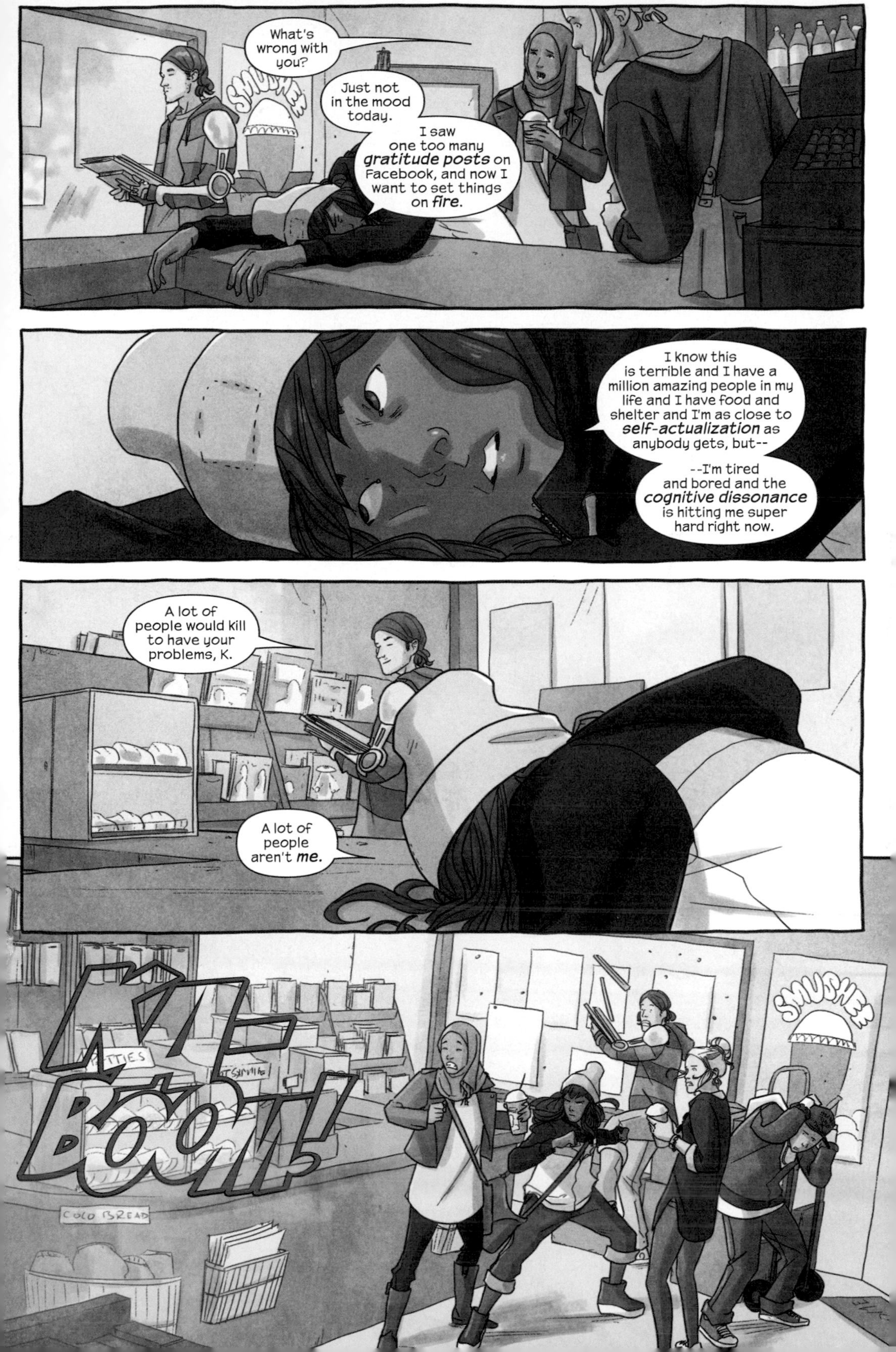

What's wrong with you?
Just not in the mood today.
I saw one too many *gratitude posts* on Facebook, and now I want to set things on *fire*.
I know this is terrible and I have a million amazing people in my life and I have food and shelter and I'm as close to *self-actualization* as anybody gets, but--
--I'm tired and bored and the *cognitive dissonance* is hitting me super hard right now.
A lot of people would kill to have your problems, K.
A lot of people aren't *me*.
SMUSHEE
KA-BOOM!
COLD BREAD

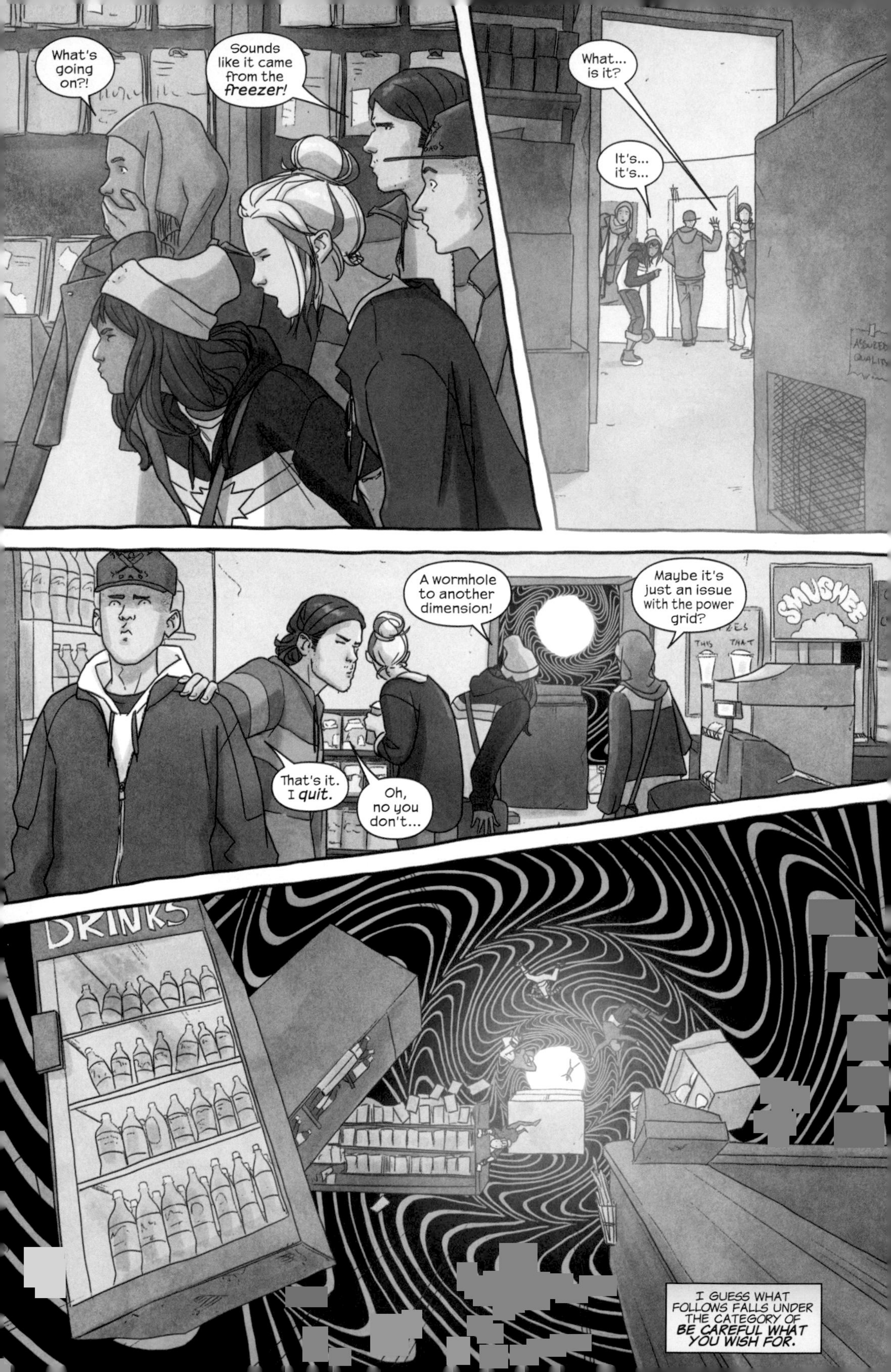
What's going on?!
Sounds like it came from the *freezer!*
What... is it?
It's... it's...
A wormhole to another dimension!
Maybe it's just an issue with the power grid?
SMUSHEE
That's it. I *quit.*
Oh, no you don't...
DRINKS
I GUESS WHAT FOLLOWS FALLS UNDER THE CATEGORY OF **BE CAREFUL WHAT YOU WISH FOR.**

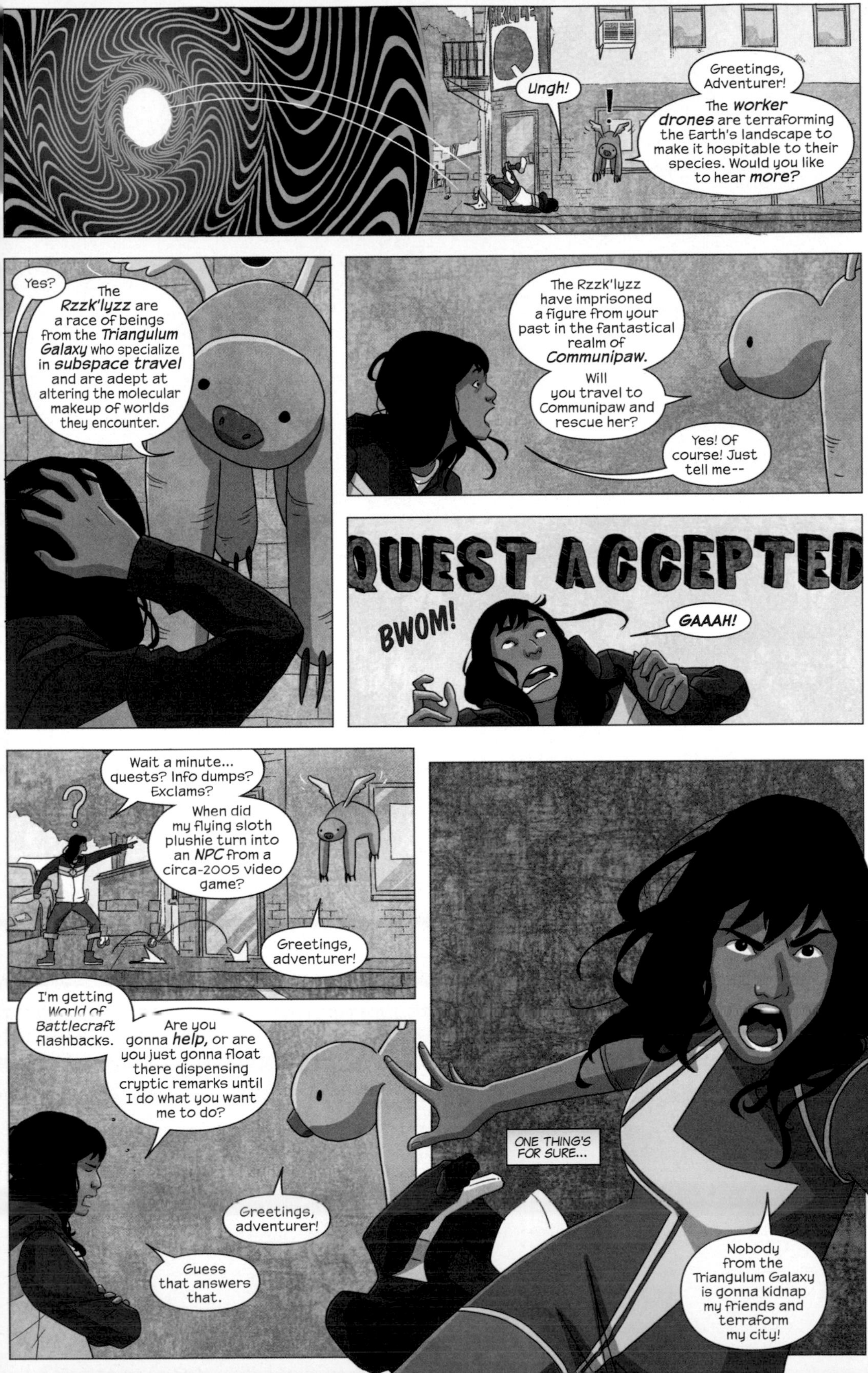
Ungh!
Greetings, Adventurer! The worker drones are terraforming the Earth's landscape to make it hospitable to their species. Would you like to hear more?
Yes?
The Rzzk'lyzz are a race of beings from the Triangulum Galaxy who specialize in subspace travel and are adept at altering the molecular makeup of worlds they encounter.
The Rzzk'lyzz have imprisoned a figure from your past in the fantastical realm of Communipaw.
Will you travel to Communipaw and rescue her?
Yes! Of course! Just tell me--
QUEST ACCEPTED
BWOM!
GAAAH!
Wait a minute... quests? Info dumps? Exclams?
When did my flying sloth plushie turn into an NPC from a circa-2005 video game?
Greetings, adventurer!
I'm getting World of Battlecraft flashbacks.
Are you gonna help, or are you just gonna float there dispensing cryptic remarks until I do what you want me to do?
Greetings, adventurer!
Guess that answers that.
ONE THING'S FOR SURE...
Nobody from the Triangulum Galaxy is gonna kidnap my friends and terraform my city!

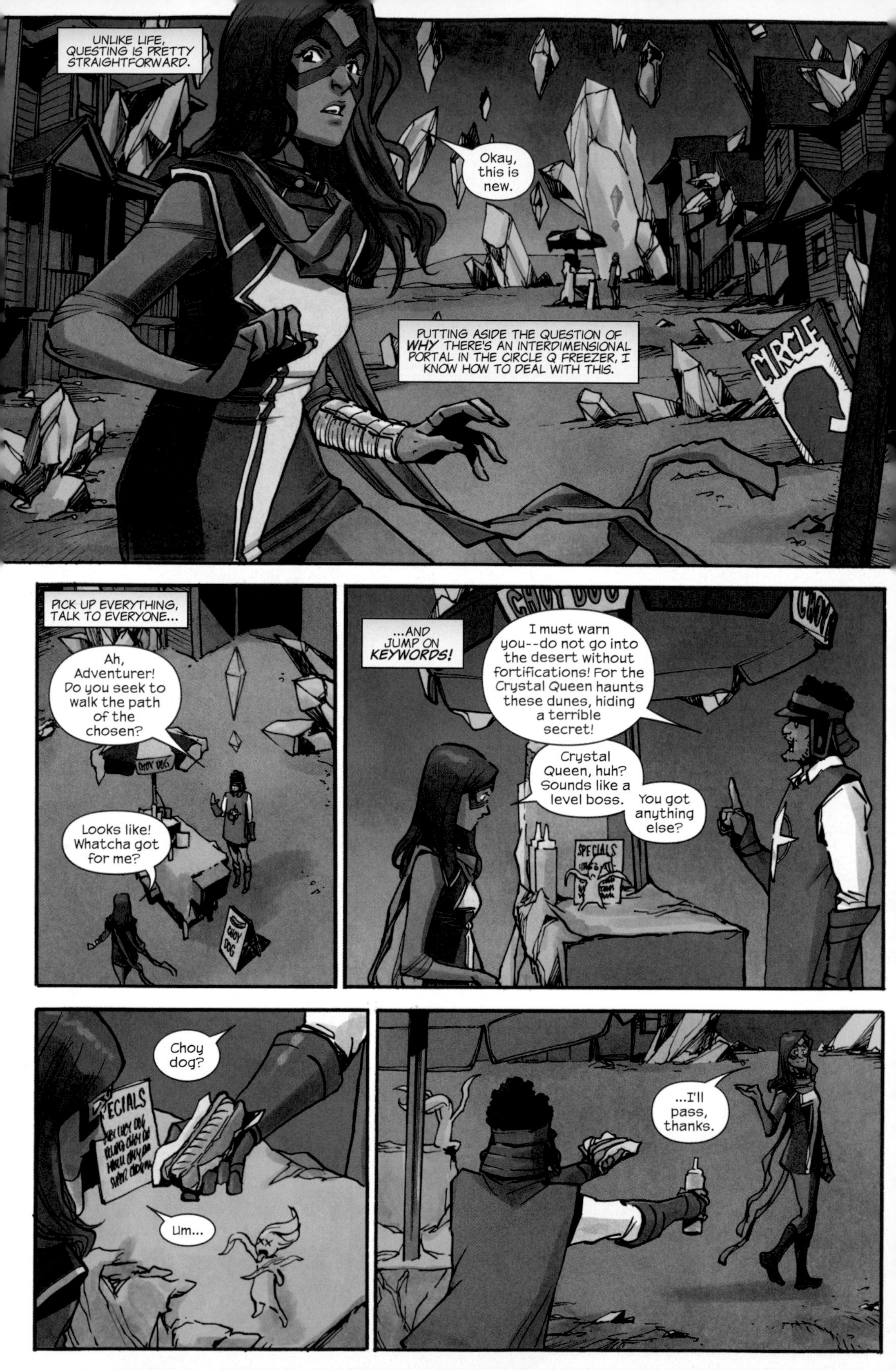
UNLIKE LIFE, QUESTING IS PRETTY STRAIGHTFORWARD.
Okay, this is new.
PUTTING ASIDE THE QUESTION OF *WHY* THERE'S AN INTERDIMENSIONAL PORTAL IN THE CIRCLE Q FREEZER, I KNOW HOW TO DEAL WITH THIS.
CIRCLE
PICK UP EVERYTHING, TALK TO EVERYONE...
Ah, Adventurer! Do you seek to walk the path of the chosen?
Looks like! Whatcha got for me?
CHOY DOG
...AND JUMP ON *KEYWORDS!*
I must warn you--do not go into the desert without fortifications! For the Crystal Queen haunts these dunes, hiding a terrible secret!
Crystal Queen, huh? Sounds like a level boss.
You got anything else?
SPECIALS
Choy dog?
Um...
...I'll pass, thanks.

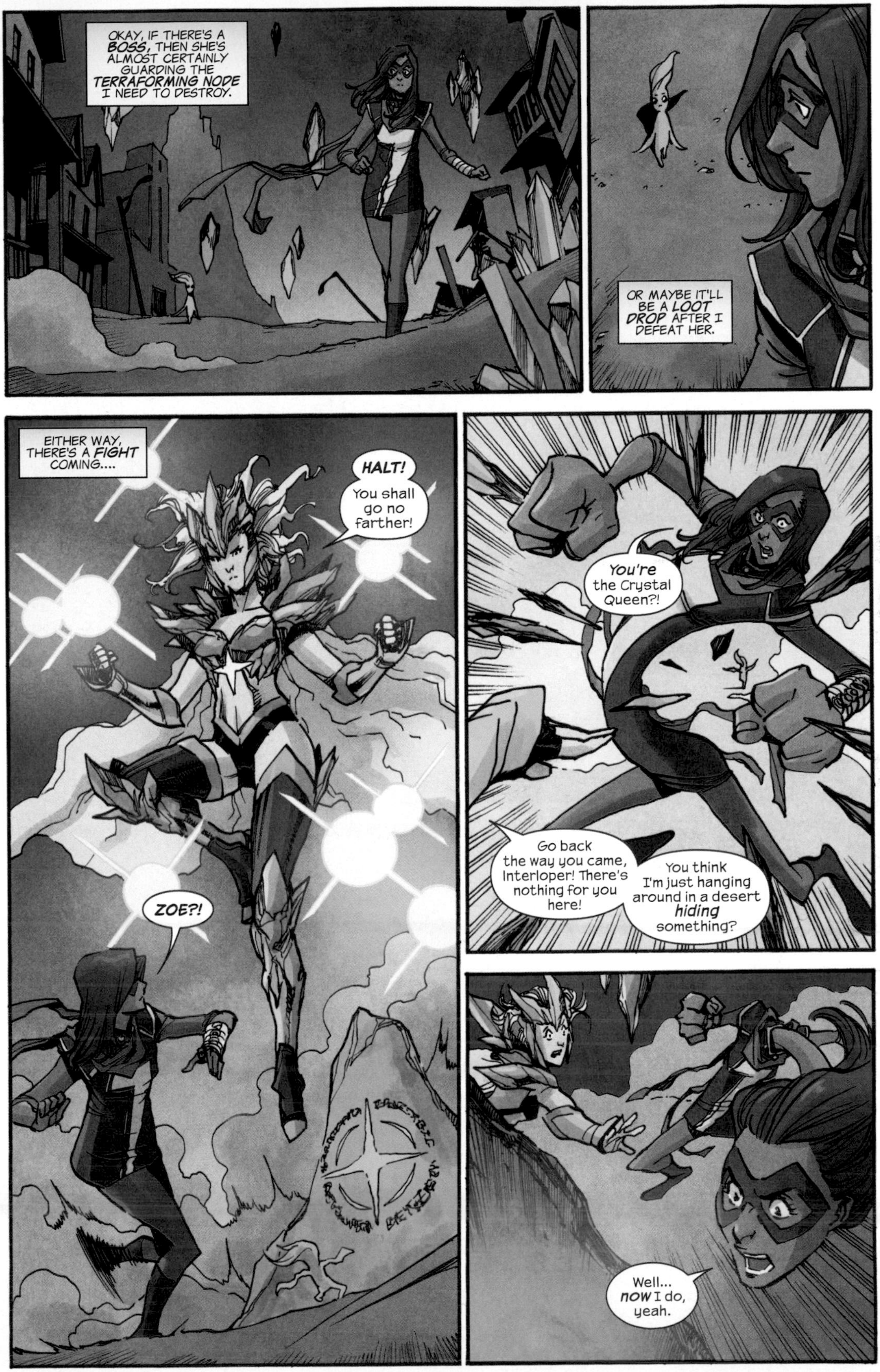
OKAY, IF THERE'S A BOSS, THEN SHE'S ALMOST CERTAINLY GUARDING THE TERRAFORMING NODE I NEED TO DESTROY.
OR MAYBE IT'LL BE A LOOT DROP AFTER I DEFEAT HER.
EITHER WAY, THERE'S A FIGHT COMING....
HALT! You shall go no farther!
ZOE?!
You're the Crystal Queen?!
Go back the way you came, Interloper! There's nothing for you here!
You think I'm just hanging around in a desert hiding something?
Well... now I do, yeah.

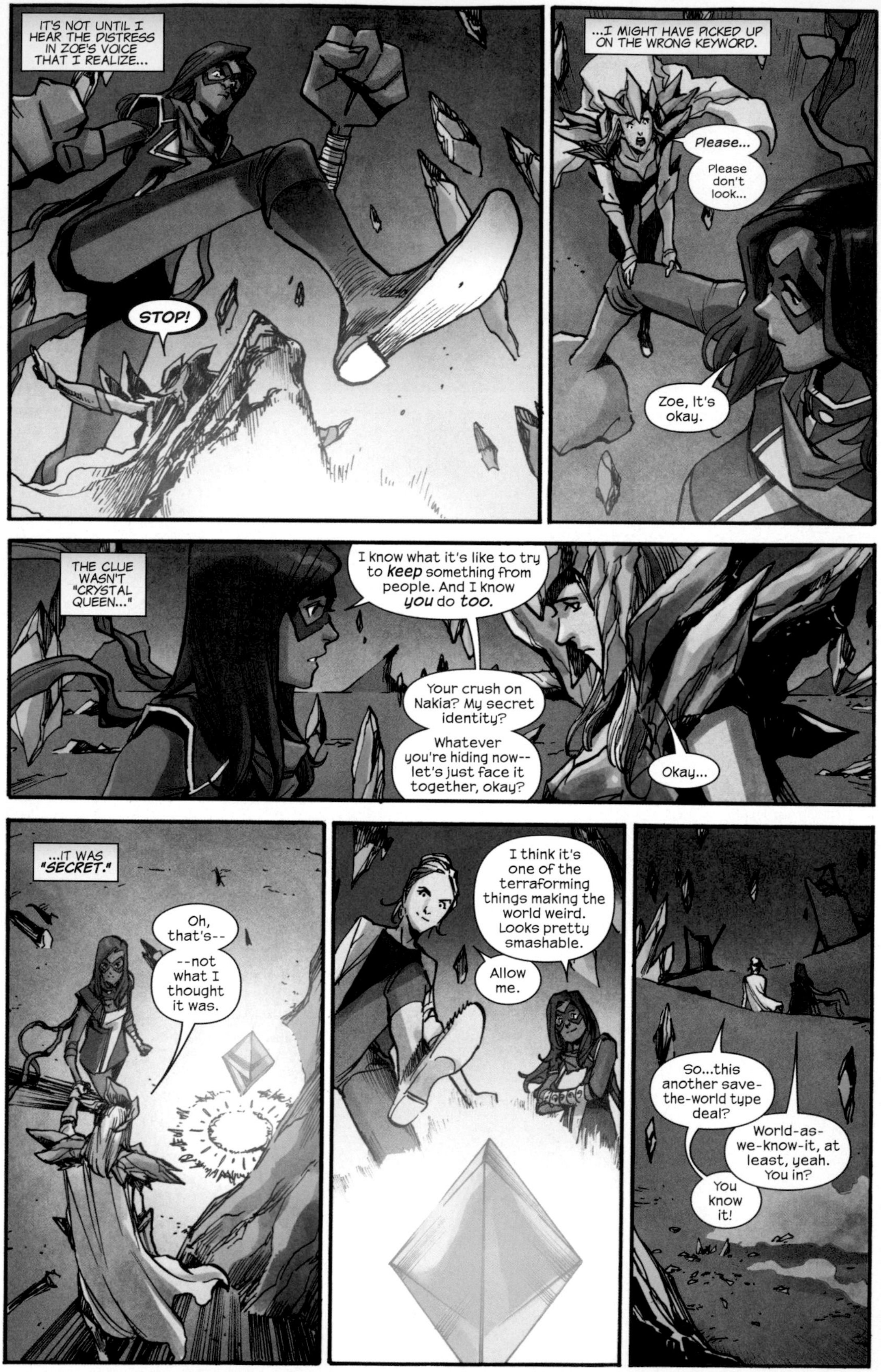
IT'S NOT UNTIL I HEAR THE DISTRESS IN ZOE'S VOICE THAT I REALIZE...
STOP!
...I MIGHT HAVE PICKED UP ON THE WRONG KEYWORD.
Please...
Please don't look...
Zoe, It's okay.
THE CLUE WASN'T "CRYSTAL QUEEN..."
I know what it's like to try to keep something from people. And I know you do too.
Your crush on Nakia? My secret identity?
Whatever you're hiding now--let's just face it together, okay?
Okay...
...IT WAS "SECRET."
Oh, that's--
--not what I thought it was.
I think it's one of the terraforming things making the world weird. Looks pretty smashable.
Allow me.
So...this another save-the-world type deal?
World-as-we-know-it, at least, yeah. You in?
You know it!

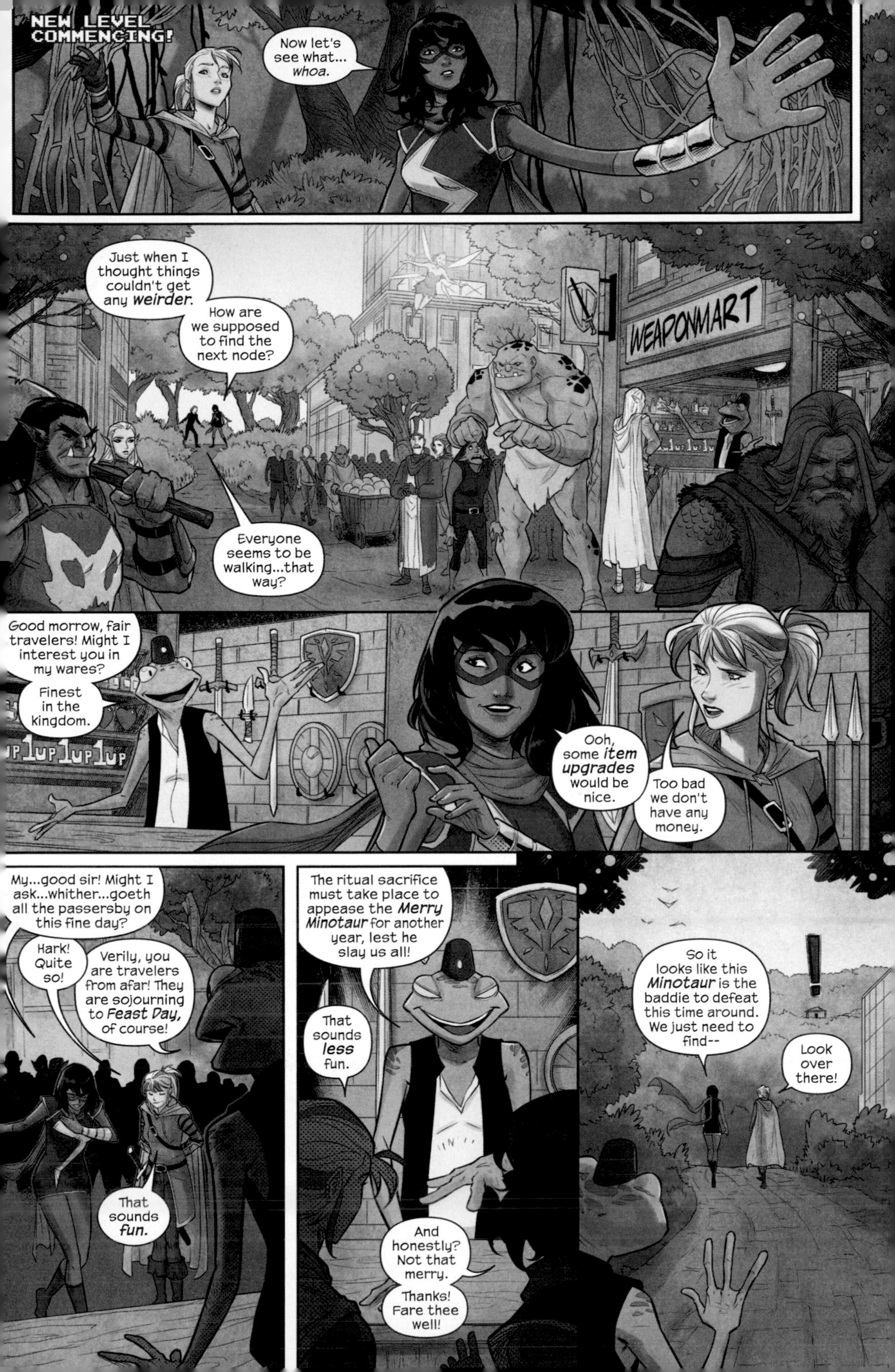
NEW LEVEL COMMENCING!
Now let's see what... whoa.
Just when I thought things couldn't get any weirder.
How are we supposed to find the next node?
Everyone seems to be walking...that way?
WEAPONMART
Good morrow, fair travelers! Might I interest you in my wares?
Finest in the kingdom.
Ooh, some item upgrades would be nice.
Too bad we don't have any money.
My...good sir! Might I ask...whither...goeth all the passersby on this fine day?
Hark! Quite so!
Verily, you are travelers from afar! They are sojourning to Feast Day, of course!
That sounds fun.
The ritual sacrifice must take place to appease the Merry Minotaur for another year, lest he slay us all!
That sounds less fun.
And honestly? Not that merry.
Thanks! Fare thee well!
So it looks like this Minotaur is the baddie to defeat this time around. We just need to find--
Look over there!

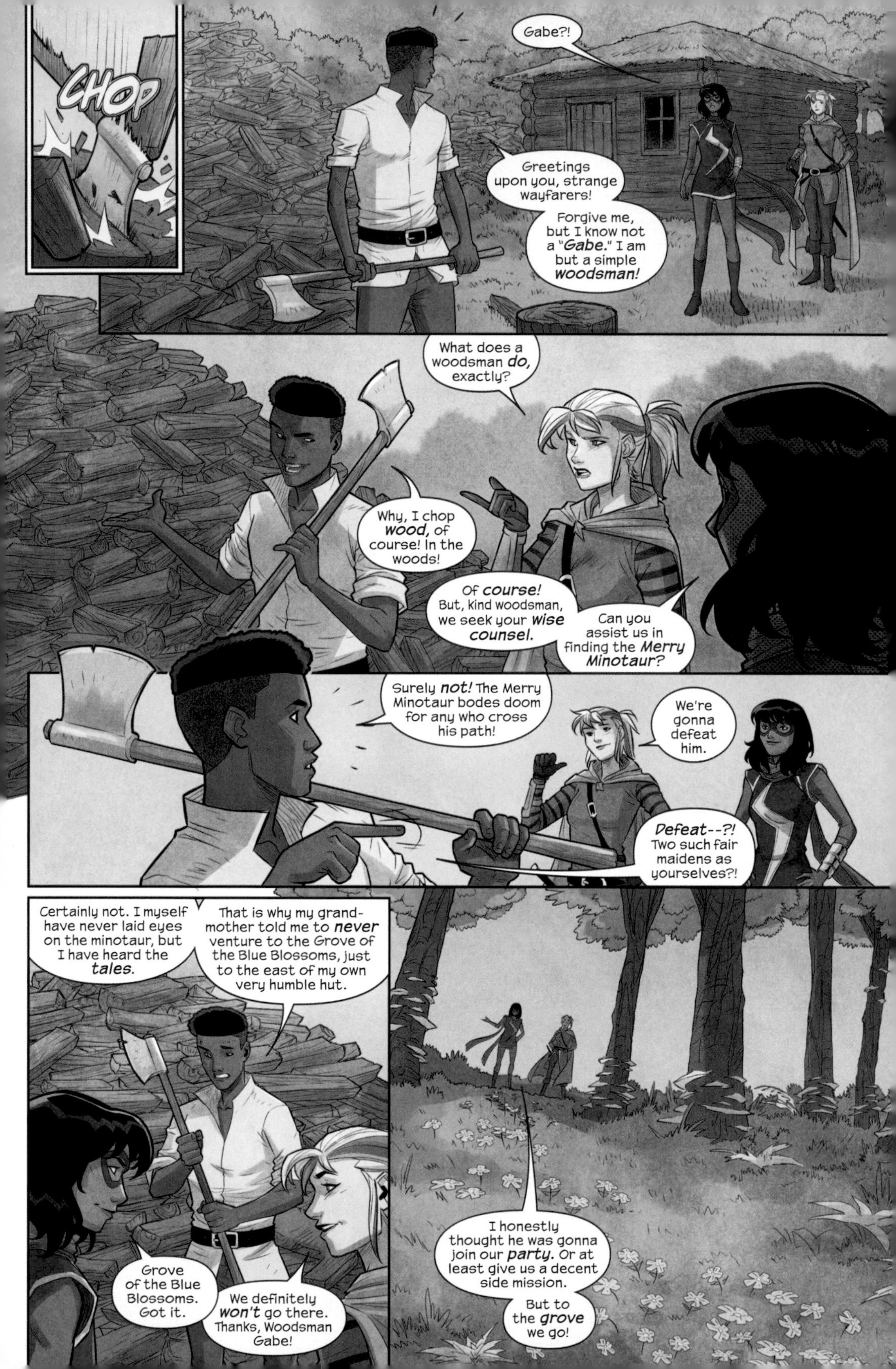

CHOP
Gabe?!
Greetings upon you, strange wayfarers!
Forgive me, but I know not a "Gabe." I am but a simple woodsman!
What does a woodsman do, exactly?
Why, I chop wood, of course! In the woods!
Of course! But, kind woodsman, we seek your wise counsel.
Can you assist us in finding the Merry Minotaur?
Surely not! The Merry Minotaur bodes doom for any who cross his path!
We're gonna defeat him.
Defeat--?! Two such fair maidens as yourselves?!
Certainly not. I myself have never laid eyes on the minotaur, but I have heard the tales.
That is why my grand-mother told me to never venture to the Grove of the Blue Blossoms, just to the east of my own very humble hut.
Grove of the Blue Blossoms. Got it.
We definitely won't go there. Thanks, Woodsman Gabe!
I honestly thought he was gonna join our party. Or at least give us a decent side mission.
But to the grove we go!

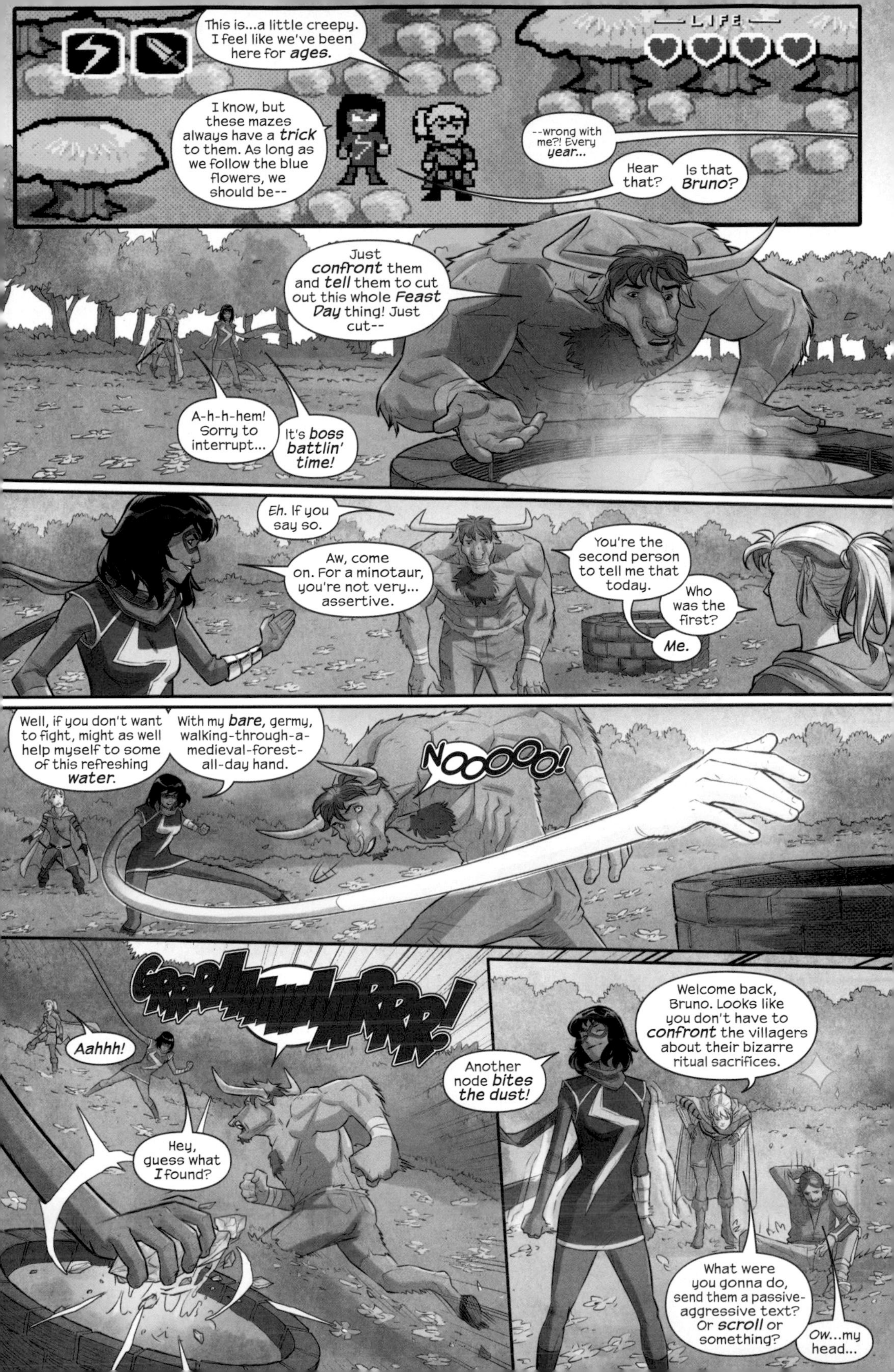
LIFE
This is...a little creepy. I feel like we've been here for *ages*.
I know, but these mazes always have a *trick* to them. As long as we follow the blue flowers, we should be--
--wrong with me?! Every *year*...
Hear that?
Is that *Bruno?*
Just *confront* them and *tell* them to cut out this whole *Feast Day* thing! Just cut--
A-h-h-hem! Sorry to interrupt...
It's *boss battlin' time!*
Eh. If you say so.
Aw, come on. For a minotaur, you're not very... assertive.
You're the second person to tell me that today.
Who was the first?
Me.
Well, if you don't want to fight, might as well help myself to some of this refreshing *water*.
With my *bare*, germy, walking-through-a-medieval-forest-all-day hand.
NOOOOO!
Aahhh!
Hey, guess what *I* found?
Another node *bites the dust!*
Welcome back, Bruno. Looks like you don't have to *confront* the villagers about their bizarre ritual sacrifices.
What were you gonna do, send them a passive-aggressive text? Or *scroll* or something?
Ow...my head...

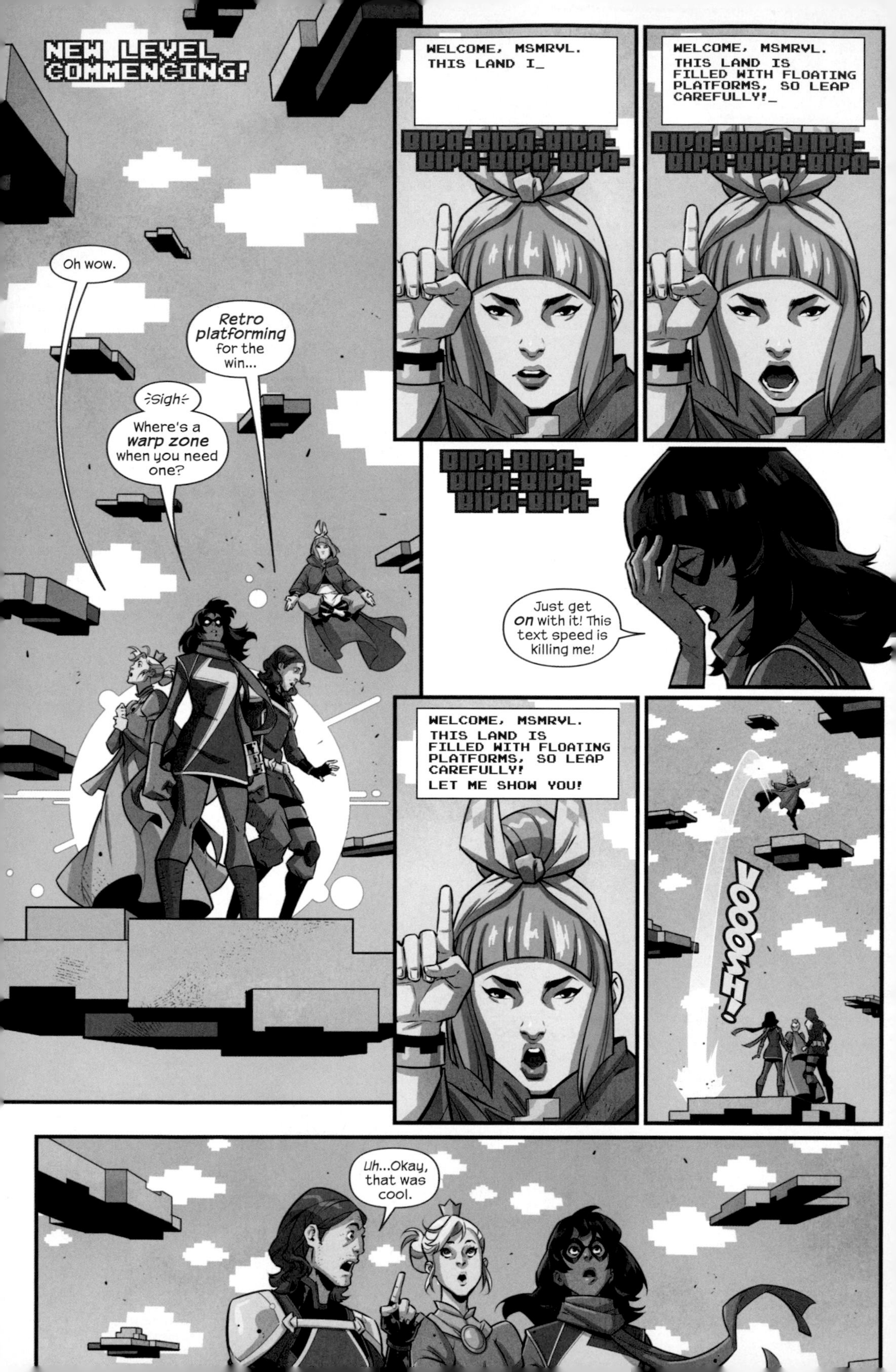
NEW LEVEL COMMENCING!
Oh wow.
Retro platforming for the win...
Sigh
Where's a warp zone when you need one?
WELCOME, MSMRVL. THIS LAND I_
BIPA-BIPA-BIPA-BIPA-BIPA-BIPA-
WELCOME, MSMRVL. THIS LAND IS FILLED WITH FLOATING PLATFORMS, SO LEAP CAREFULLY!_
BIPA-BIPA-BIPA-BIPA-BIPA-BIPA-
BIPA-BIPA-BIPA-BIPA-BIPA-BIPA-
Just get on with it! This text speed is killing me!
WELCOME, MSMRVL. THIS LAND IS FILLED WITH FLOATING PLATFORMS, SO LEAP CAREFULLY! LET ME SHOW YOU!
VOOOOSH!
Uh...Okay, that was cool.

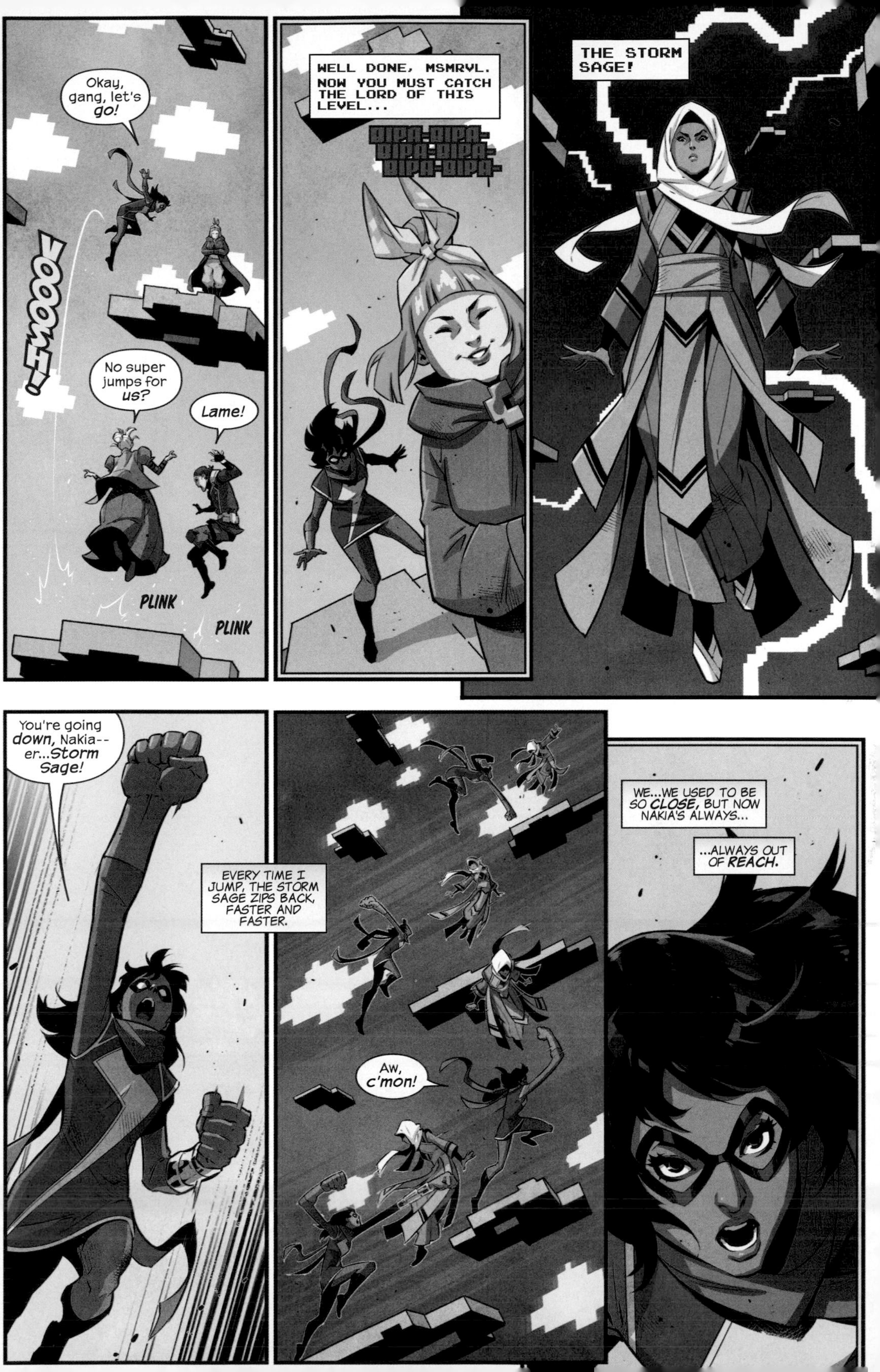

Okay, gang, let's go!
VOOOM!
No super jumps for us?
Lame!
PLINK
PLINK
WELL DONE, MSMRVL. NOW YOU MUST CATCH THE LORD OF THIS LEVEL...
BIPA-BIPA-BIPA-BIPA-BIPA-BIPA-
THE STORM SAGE!
You're going down, Nakia-- er...Storm Sage!
EVERY TIME I JUMP, THE STORM SAGE ZIPS BACK, FASTER AND FASTER.
Aw, c'mon!
WE...WE USED TO BE SO CLOSE, BUT NOW NAKIA'S ALWAYS...
...ALWAYS OUT OF REACH.

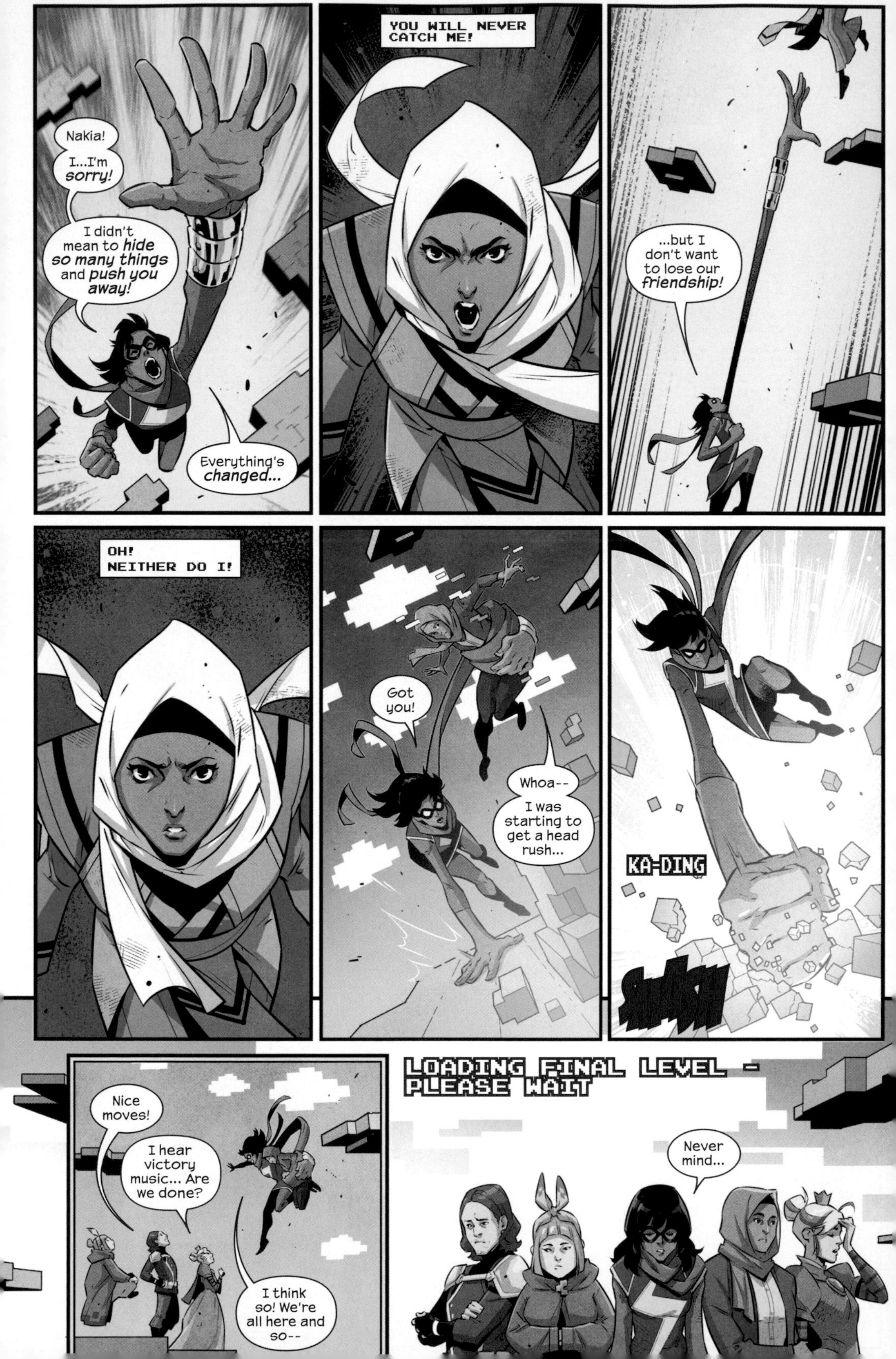
Nakia!
I...I'm sorry!
I didn't mean to hide so many things and push you away!
Everything's changed...
YOU WILL NEVER CATCH ME!
...but I don't want to lose our friendship!
OH! NEITHER DO I!
Got you!
Whoa-- I was starting to get a head rush...
KA-DING
Nice moves!
I hear victory music... Are we done?
I think so! We're all here and so--
LOADING FINAL LEVEL - PLEASE WAIT
Never mind...

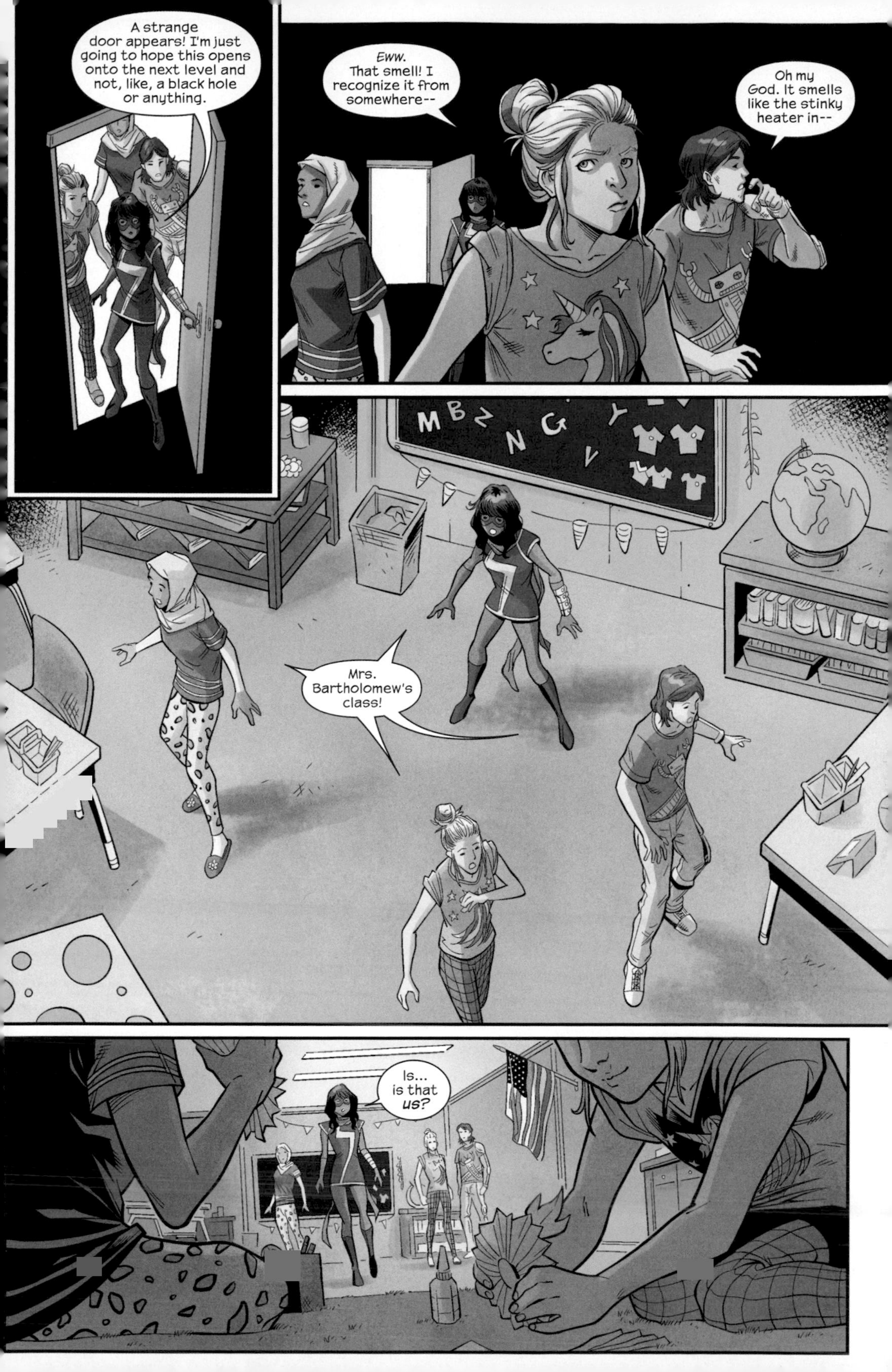
A strange door appears! I'm just going to hope this opens onto the next level and not, like, a black hole or anything.
Eww. That smell! I recognize it from somewhere--
Oh my God. It smells like the stinky heater in--
M B Z N G Y V
Mrs. Bartholomew's class!
Is... is that *us?*

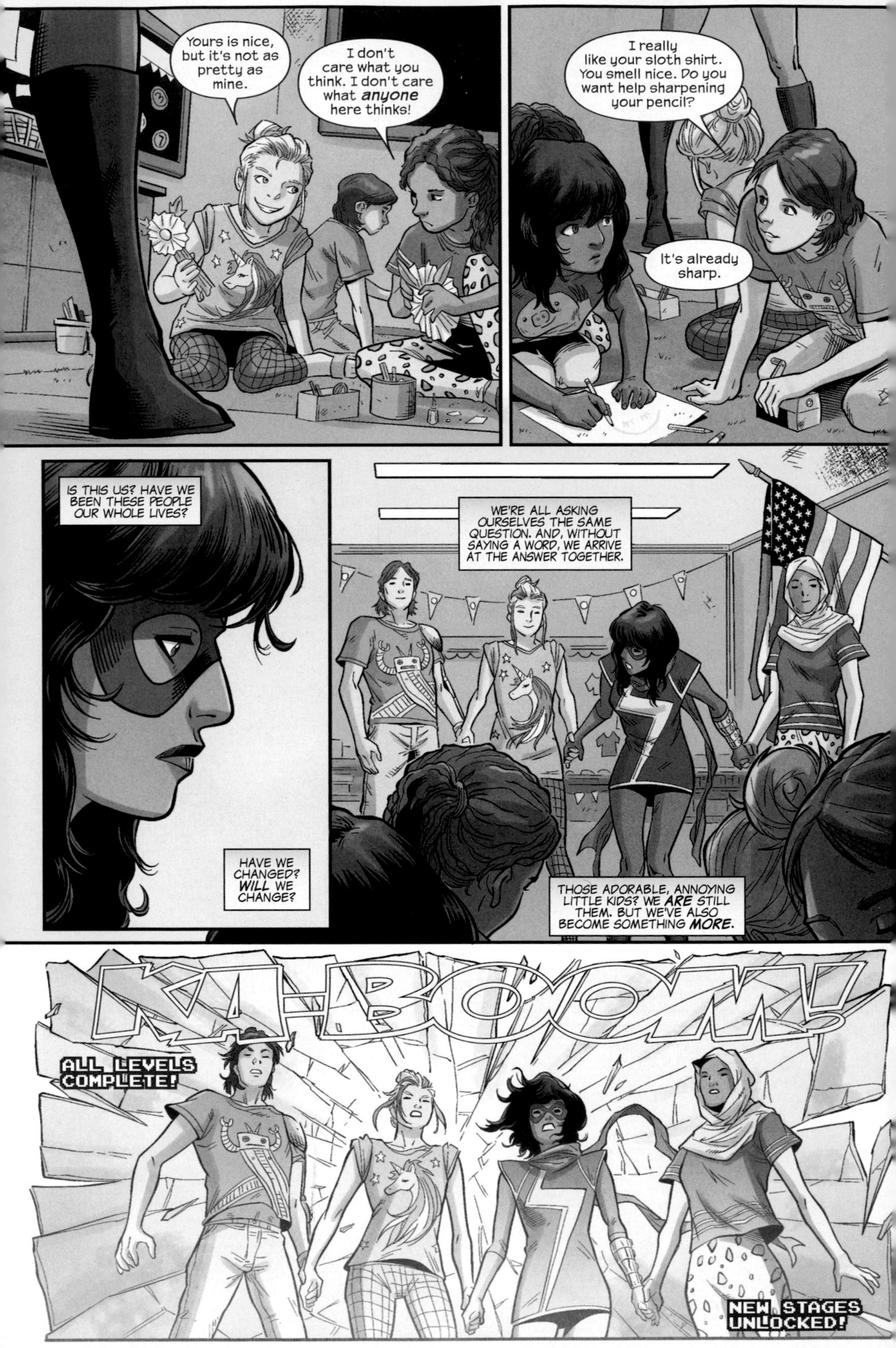

Yours is nice, but it's not as pretty as mine.
I don't care what you think. I don't care what *anyone* here thinks!
I really like your sloth shirt. You smell nice. Do you want help sharpening your pencil?
It's already sharp.
IS THIS US? HAVE WE BEEN THESE PEOPLE OUR WHOLE LIVES?
HAVE WE CHANGED? *WILL* WE CHANGE?
WE'RE ALL ASKING OURSELVES THE SAME QUESTION. AND, WITHOUT SAYING A WORD, WE ARRIVE AT THE ANSWER TOGETHER.
THOSE ADORABLE, ANNOYING LITTLE KIDS? WE *ARE* STILL THEM. BUT WE'VE ALSO BECOME SOMETHING *MORE*.
KA-BOOM!
ALL LEVELS COMPLETE!
NEW STAGES UNLOCKED!

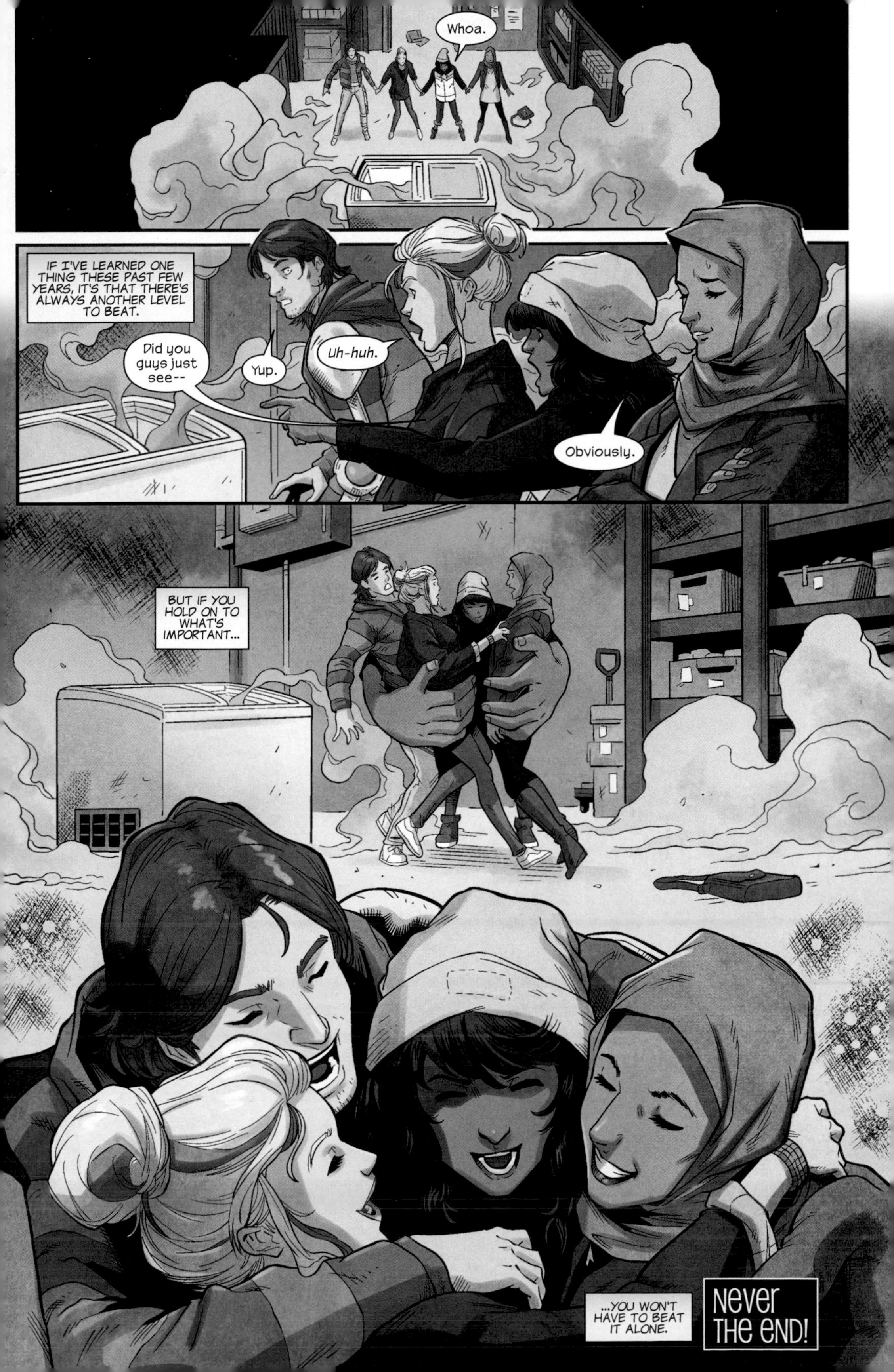
Whoa.
IF I'VE LEARNED ONE THING THESE PAST FEW YEARS, IT'S THAT THERE'S ALWAYS ANOTHER LEVEL TO BEAT.
Did you guys just see--
Yup.
Uh-huh.
Obviously.
BUT IF YOU HOLD ON TO WHAT'S IMPORTANT...
...YOU WON'T HAVE TO BEAT IT ALONE.
Never THE END!

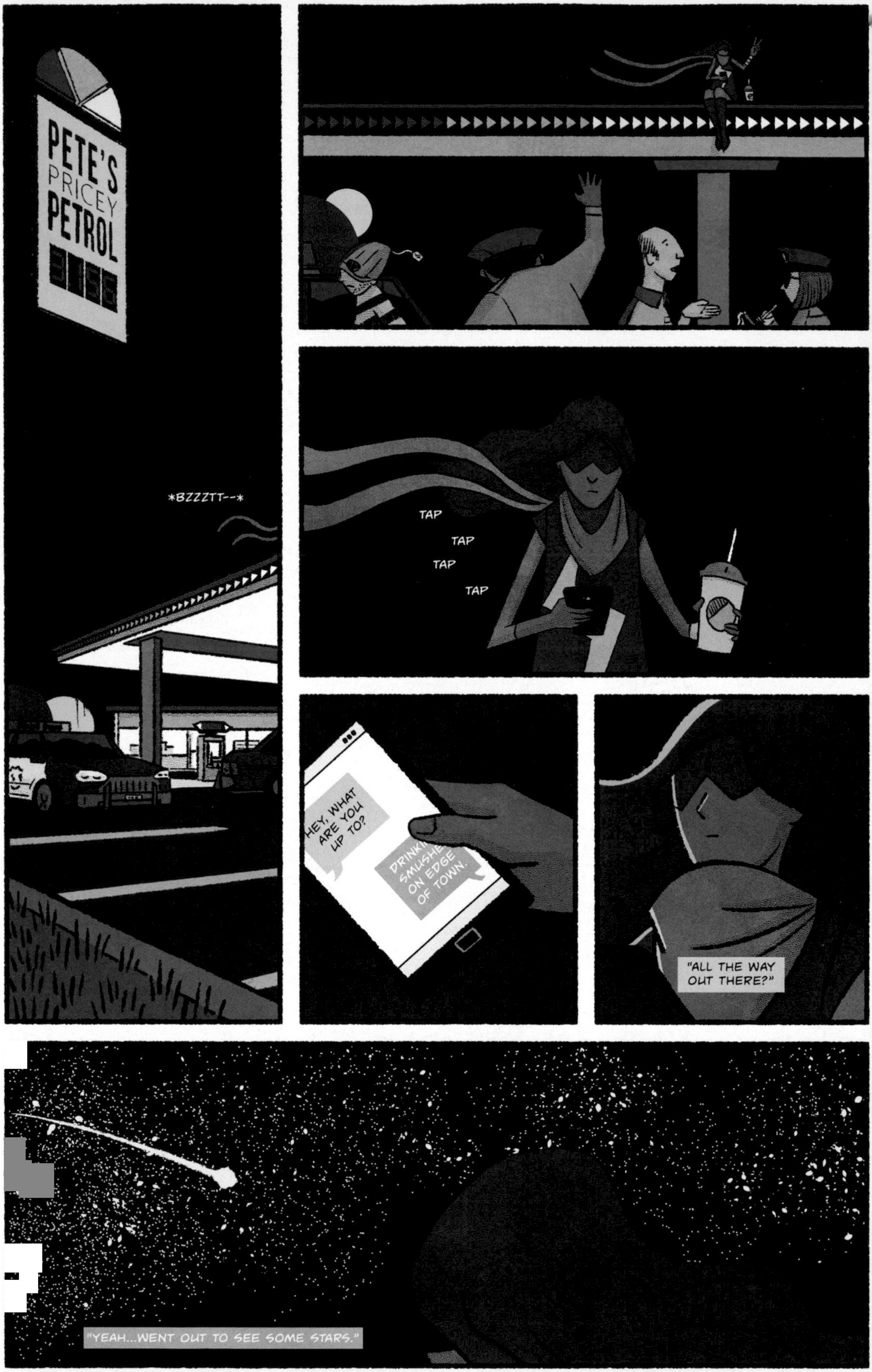
PETE'S
PRICEY
PETROL
BZZZTT--
TAP
TAP
TAP
TAP
HEY, WHAT ARE YOU UP TO?
ON EDGE OF TOWN.
"ALL THE WAY OUT THERE?"
"YEAH...WENT OUT TO SEE SOME STARS."

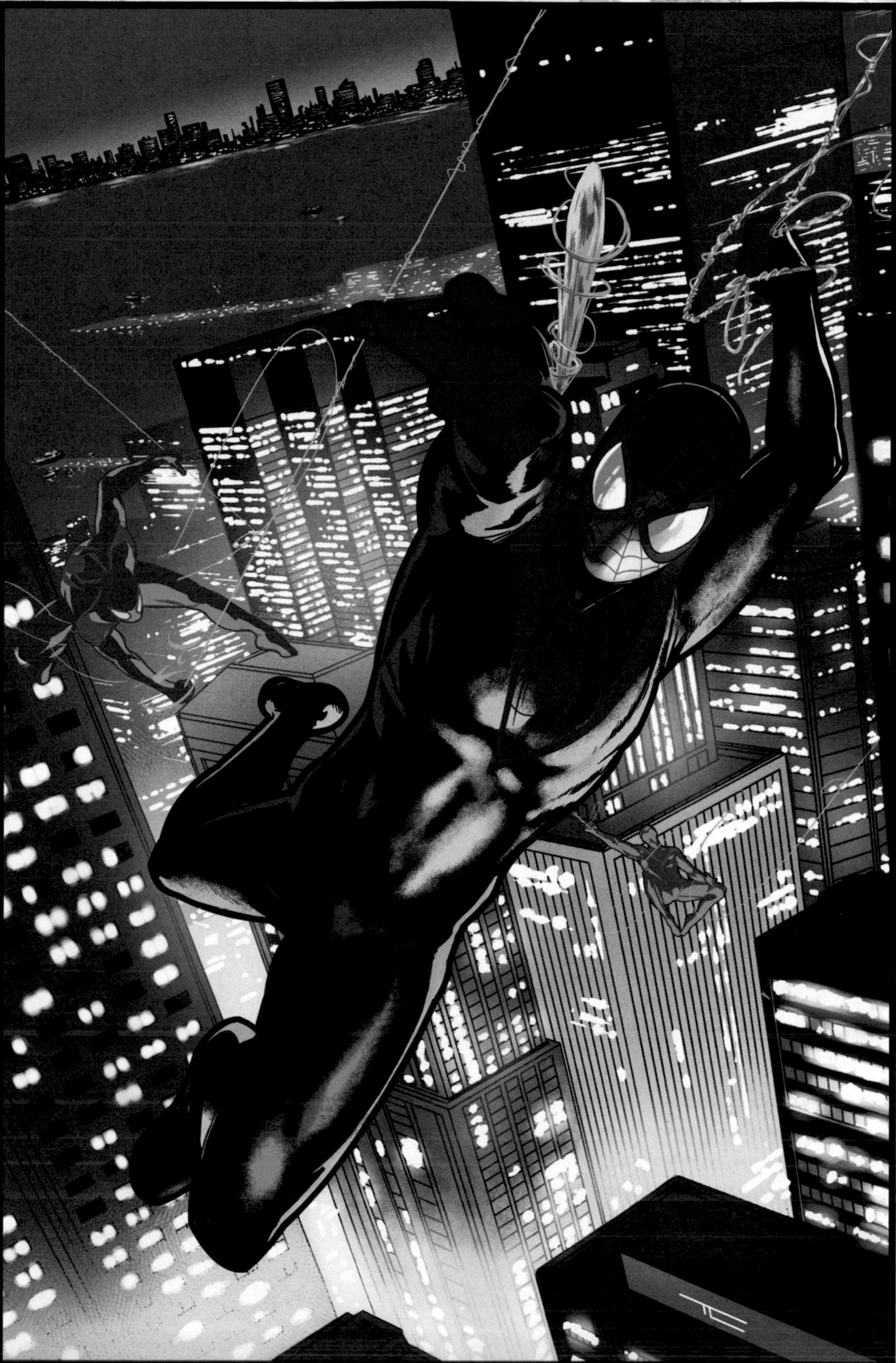

MILES MORALES: SPIDER-MAN #24

KAMALA AND FELLOW TEEN SUPER HERO MILES MORALES ARE LEFT SHAKEN AFTER SYMBIOTE GOD KNULL'S INVASION OF EARTH IN *KING IN BLACK*.

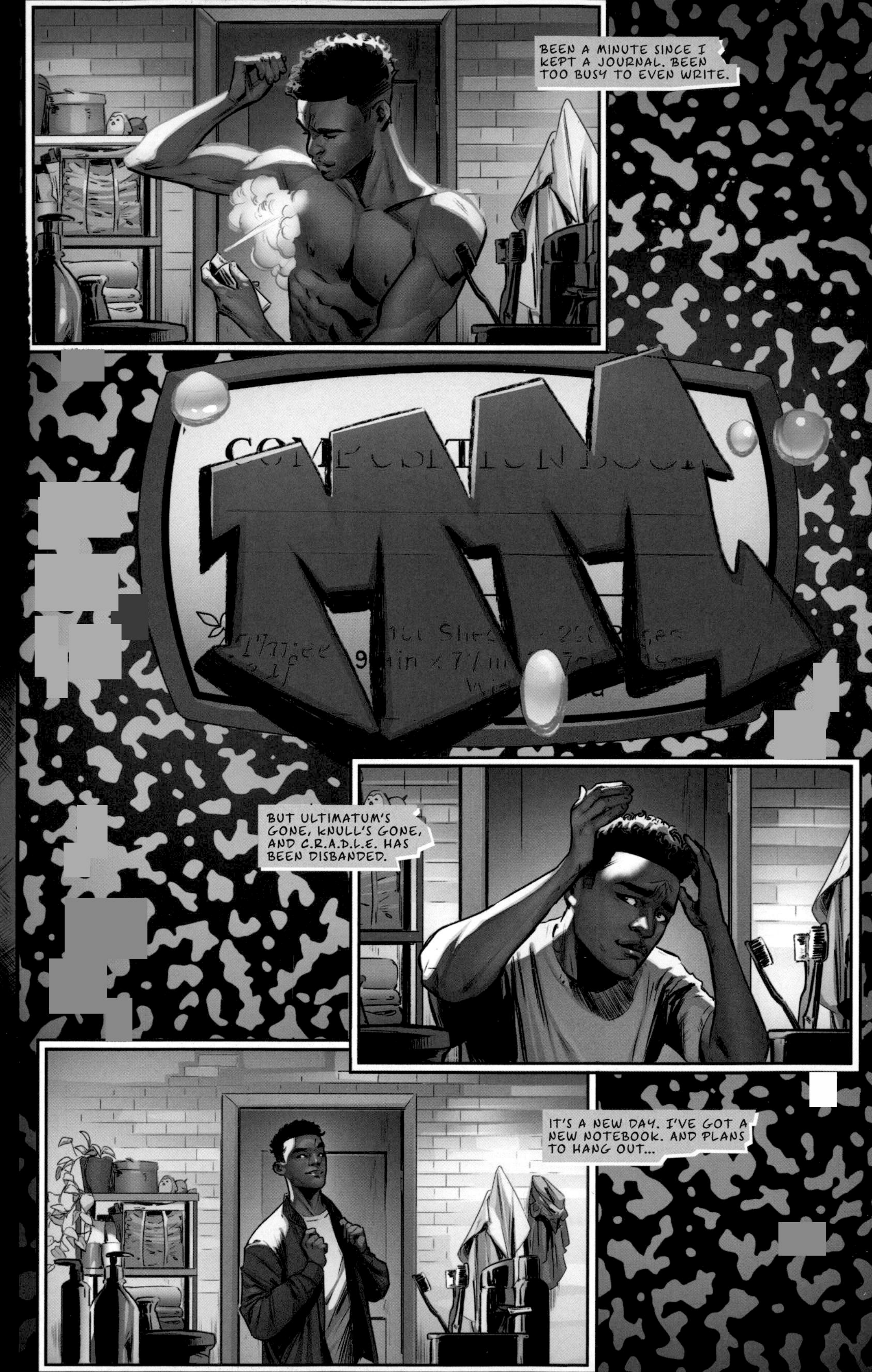
BEEN A MINUTE SINCE I KEPT A JOURNAL. BEEN TOO BUSY TO EVEN WRITE.
BUT ULTIMATUM'S GONE, KNULL'S GONE, AND C.R.A.D.L.E. HAS BEEN DISBANDED.
IT'S A NEW DAY. I'VE GOT A NEW NOTEBOOK. AND PLANS TO HANG OUT...

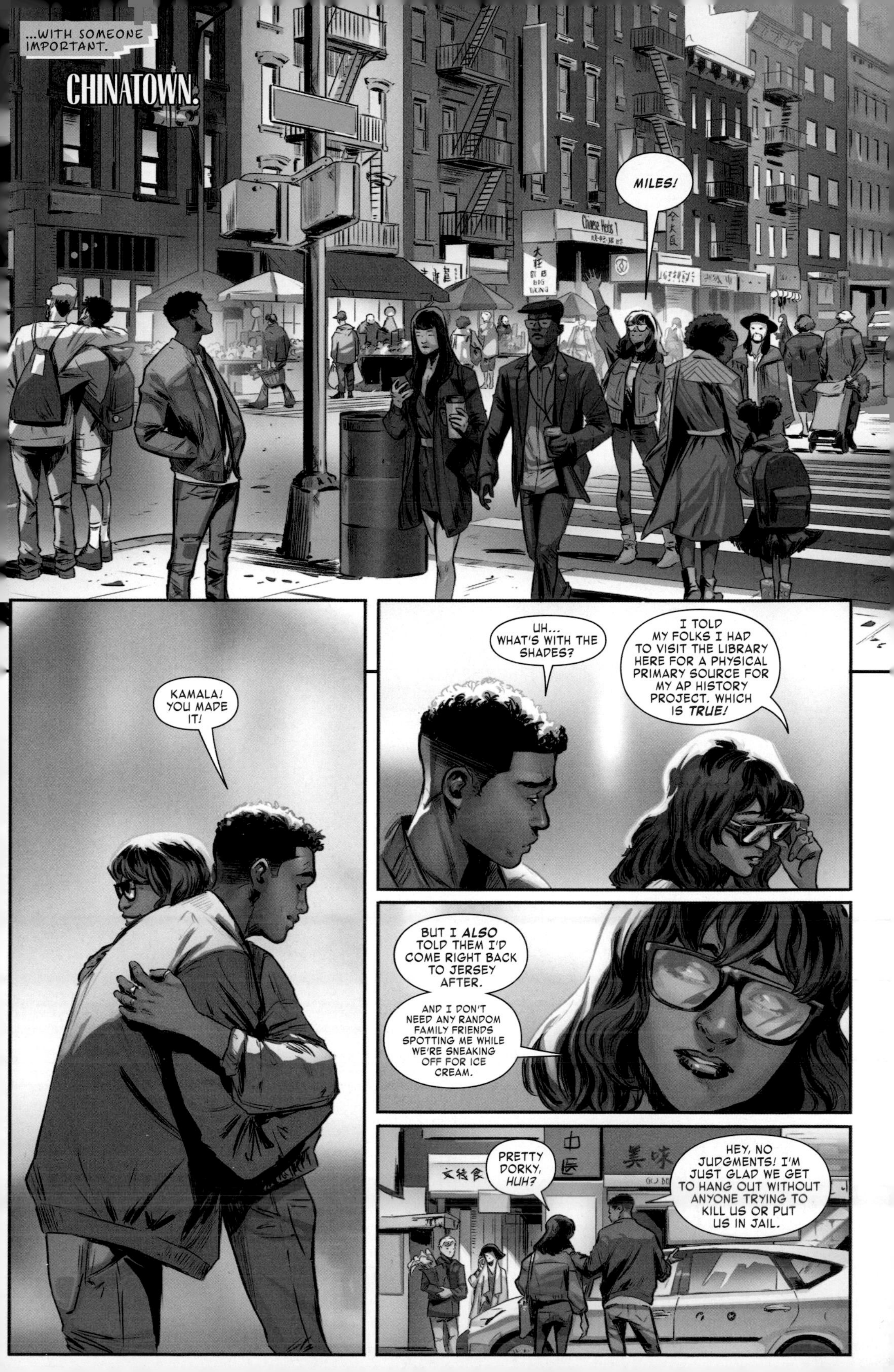
...WITH SOMEONE IMPORTANT.
CHINATOWN.
MILES!
KAMALA! YOU MADE IT!
UH... WHAT'S WITH THE SHADES?
I TOLD MY FOLKS I HAD TO VISIT THE LIBRARY HERE FOR A PHYSICAL PRIMARY SOURCE FOR MY AP HISTORY PROJECT. WHICH IS TRUE!
BUT I ALSO TOLD THEM I'D COME RIGHT BACK TO JERSEY AFTER.
AND I DON'T NEED ANY RANDOM FAMILY FRIENDS SPOTTING ME WHILE WE'RE SNEAKING OFF FOR ICE CREAM.
PRETTY DORKY, HUH?
HEY, NO JUDGMENTS! I'M JUST GLAD WE GET TO HANG OUT WITHOUT ANYONE TRYING TO KILL US OR PUT US IN JAIL.

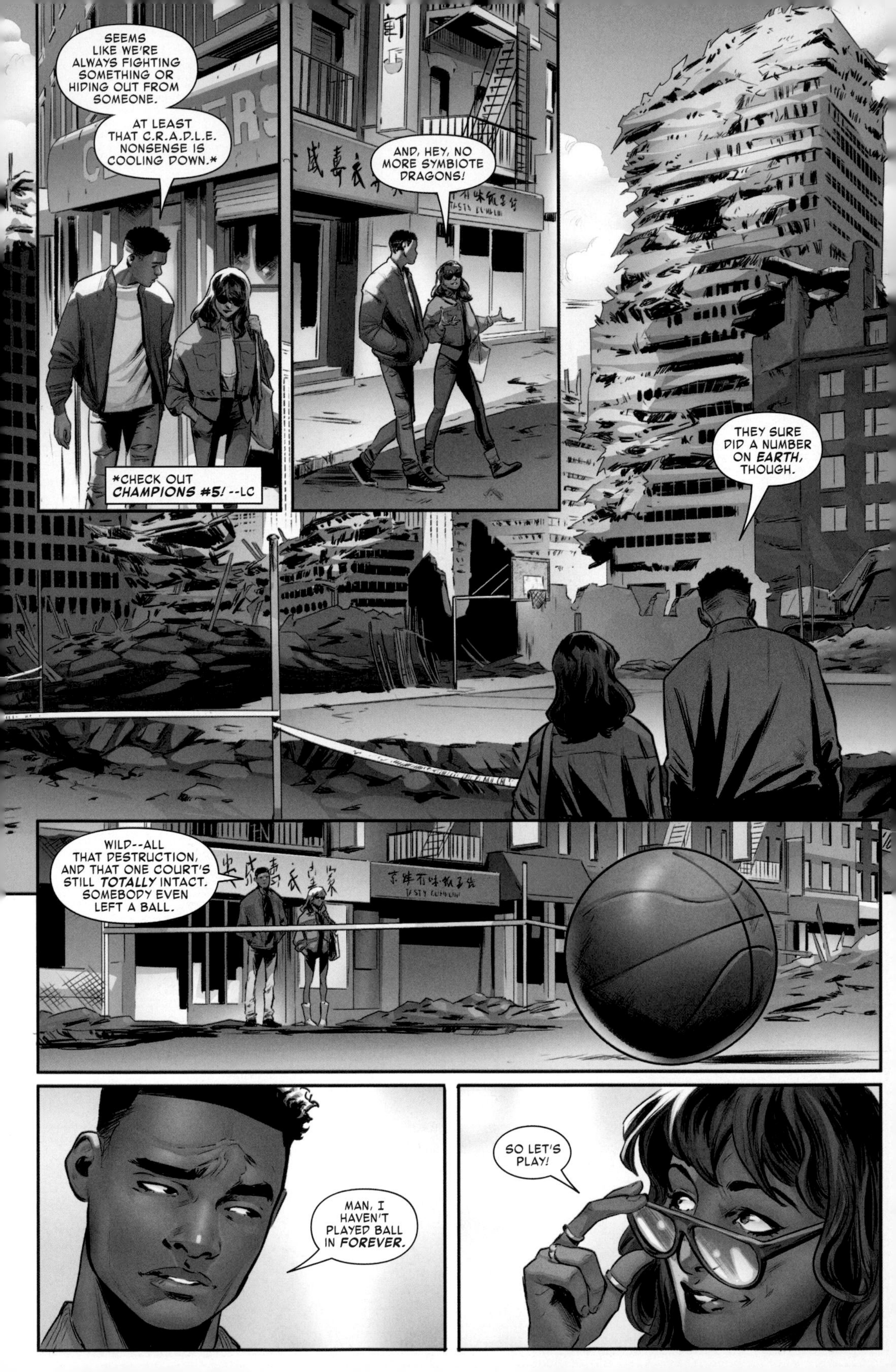
SEEMS LIKE WE'RE ALWAYS FIGHTING SOMETHING OR HIDING OUT FROM SOMEONE.
AT LEAST THAT C.R.A.D.L.E. NONSENSE IS COOLING DOWN.*
*CHECK OUT CHAMPIONS #5! --LC
AND, HEY, NO MORE SYMBIOTE DRAGONS!
THEY SURE DID A NUMBER ON EARTH, THOUGH.
WILD--ALL THAT DESTRUCTION, AND THAT ONE COURT'S STILL TOTALLY INTACT. SOMEBODY EVEN LEFT A BALL.
MAN, I HAVEN'T PLAYED BALL IN FOREVER.
SO LET'S PLAY!

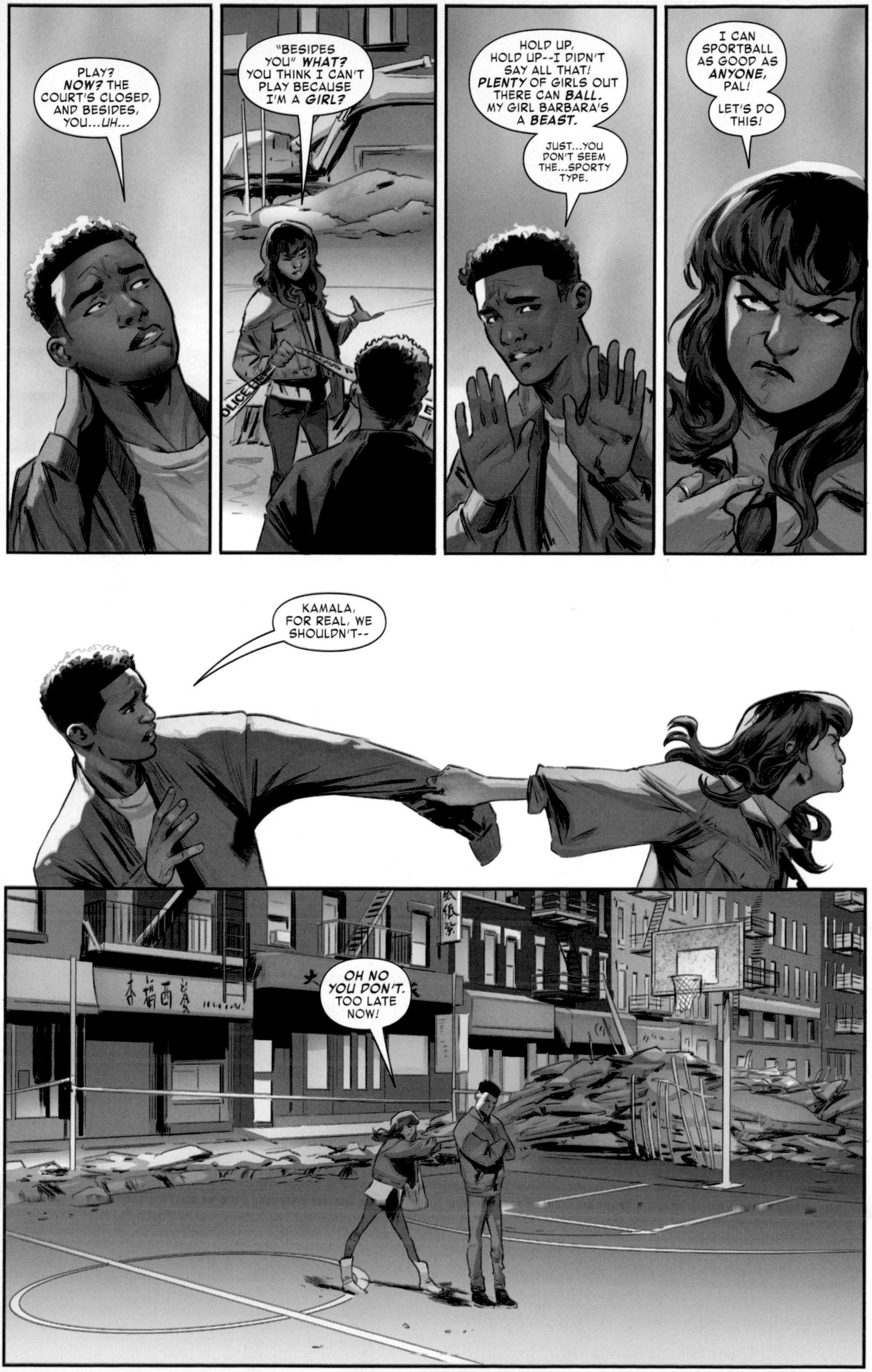
PLAY? NOW? THE COURT'S CLOSED, AND BESIDES, YOU...UH...
"BESIDES YOU" WHAT? YOU THINK I CAN'T PLAY BECAUSE I'M A GIRL?
HOLD UP, HOLD UP--I DIDN'T SAY ALL THAT! PLENTY OF GIRLS OUT THERE CAN BALL. MY GIRL BARBARA'S A BEAST.
JUST...YOU DON'T SEEM THE...SPORTY TYPE.
I CAN SPORTBALL AS GOOD AS ANYONE, PAL!
LET'S DO THIS!
KAMALA, FOR REAL, WE SHOULDN'T--
OH NO YOU DON'T. TOO LATE NOW!

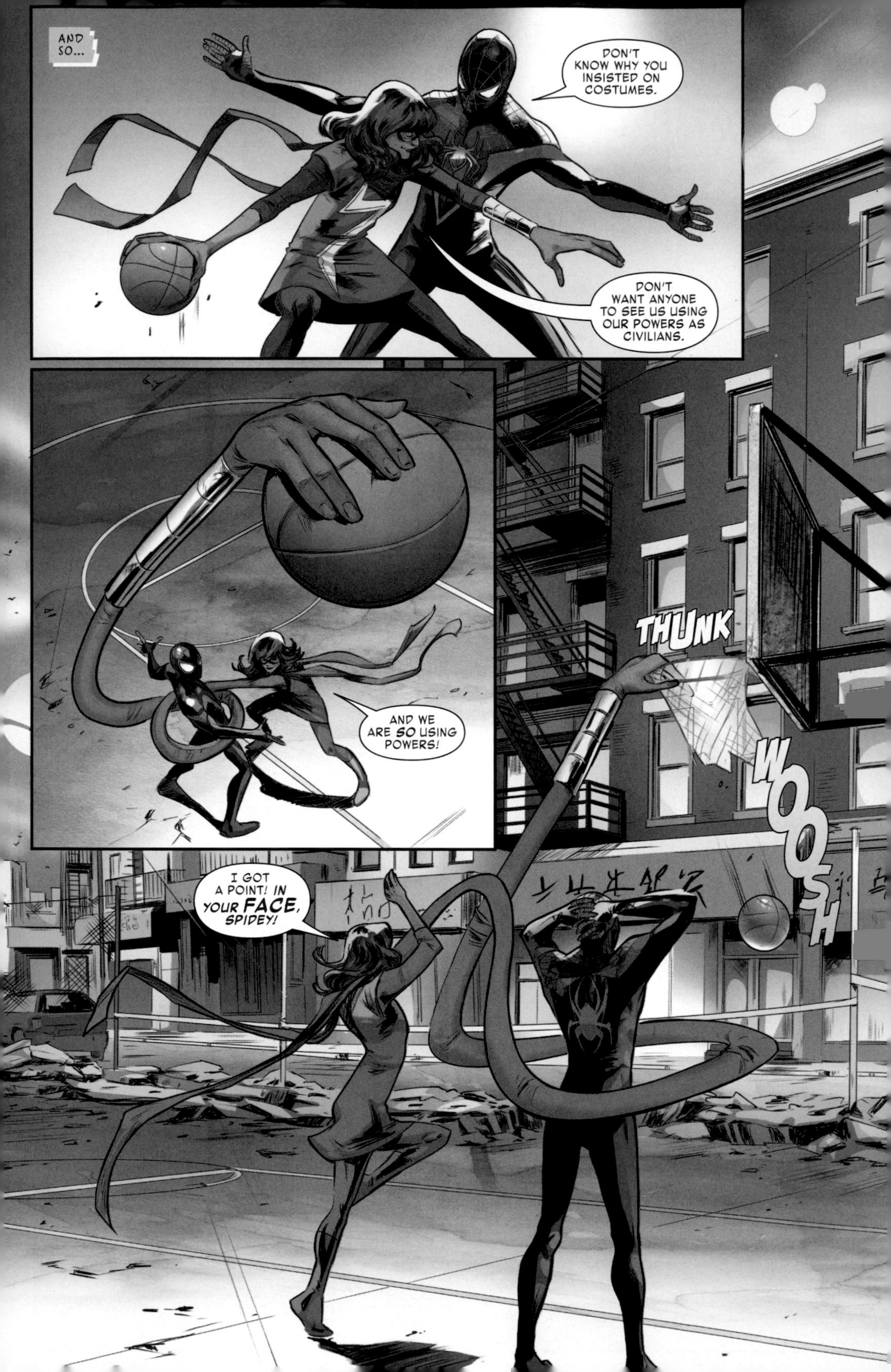
AND SO...
DON'T KNOW WHY YOU INSISTED ON COSTUMES.
DON'T WANT ANYONE TO SEE US USING OUR POWERS AS CIVILIANS.
AND WE ARE SO USING POWERS!
THUNK
WOOSH
I GOT A POINT! IN YOUR FACE, SPIDEY!

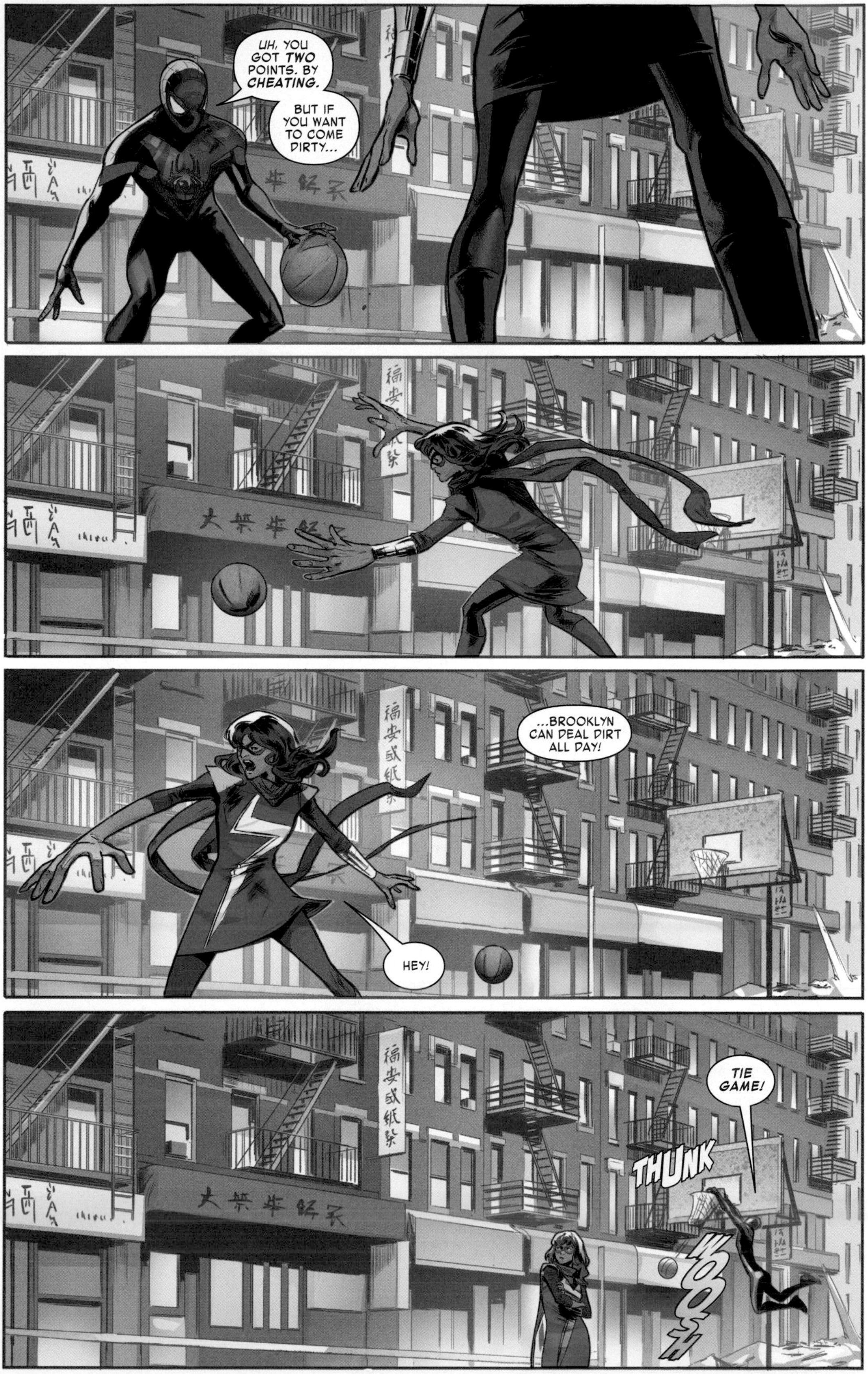
UH, YOU GOT TWO POINTS. BY CHEATING.
BUT IF YOU WANT TO COME DIRTY...
...BROOKLYN CAN DEAL DIRT ALL DAY!
HEY!
TIE GAME!
THUNK
WOOOSH

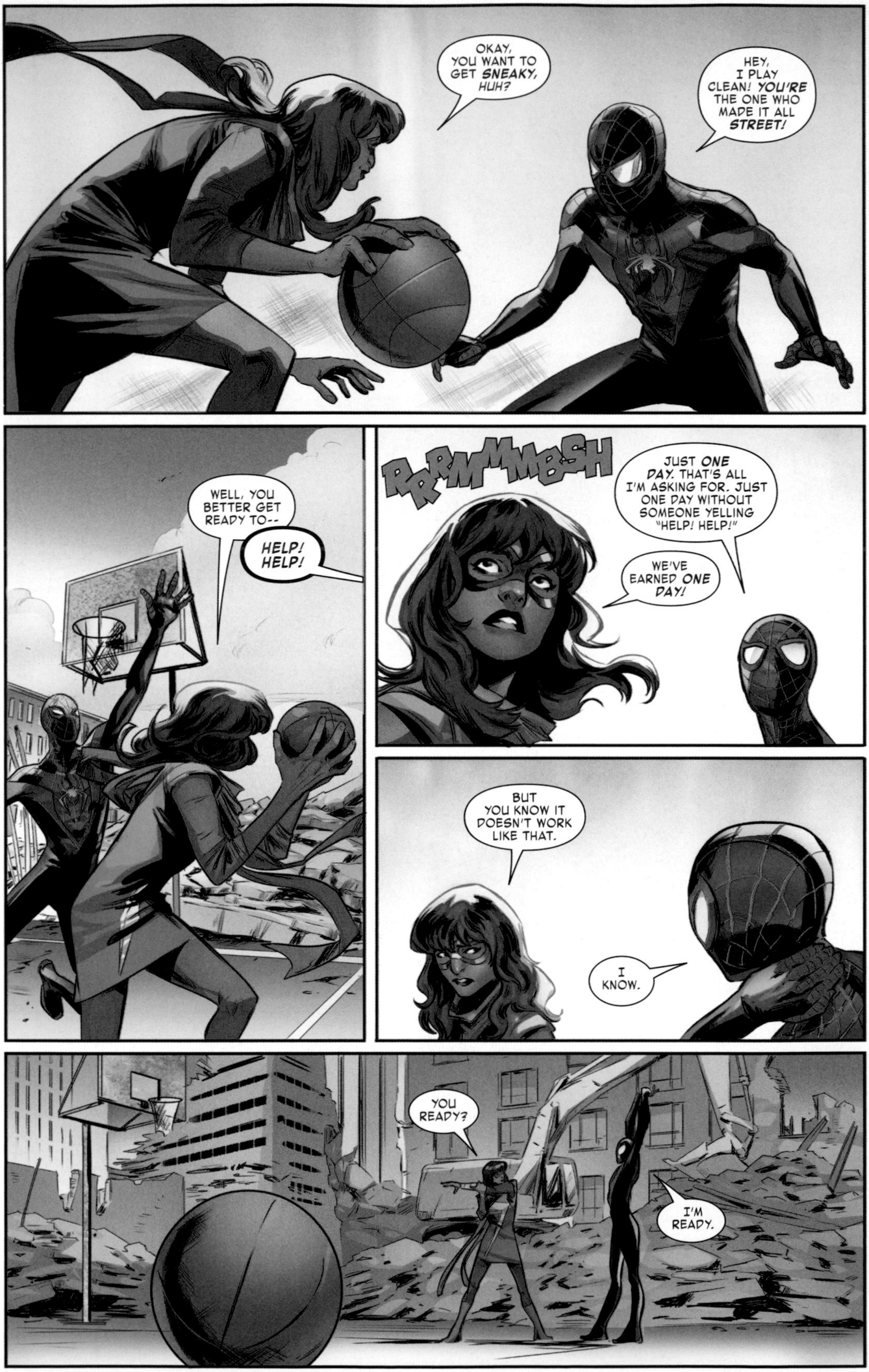
OKAY, YOU WANT TO GET SNEAKY, HUH?
HEY, I PLAY CLEAN! YOU'RE THE ONE WHO MADE IT ALL STREET!
WELL, YOU BETTER GET READY TO--
HELP! HELP!
RRRMMMBSH
JUST ONE DAY. THAT'S ALL I'M ASKING FOR. JUST ONE DAY WITHOUT SOMEONE YELLING "HELP! HELP!"
WE'VE EARNED ONE DAY!
BUT YOU KNOW IT DOESN'T WORK LIKE THAT.
I KNOW.
YOU READY?
I'M READY.

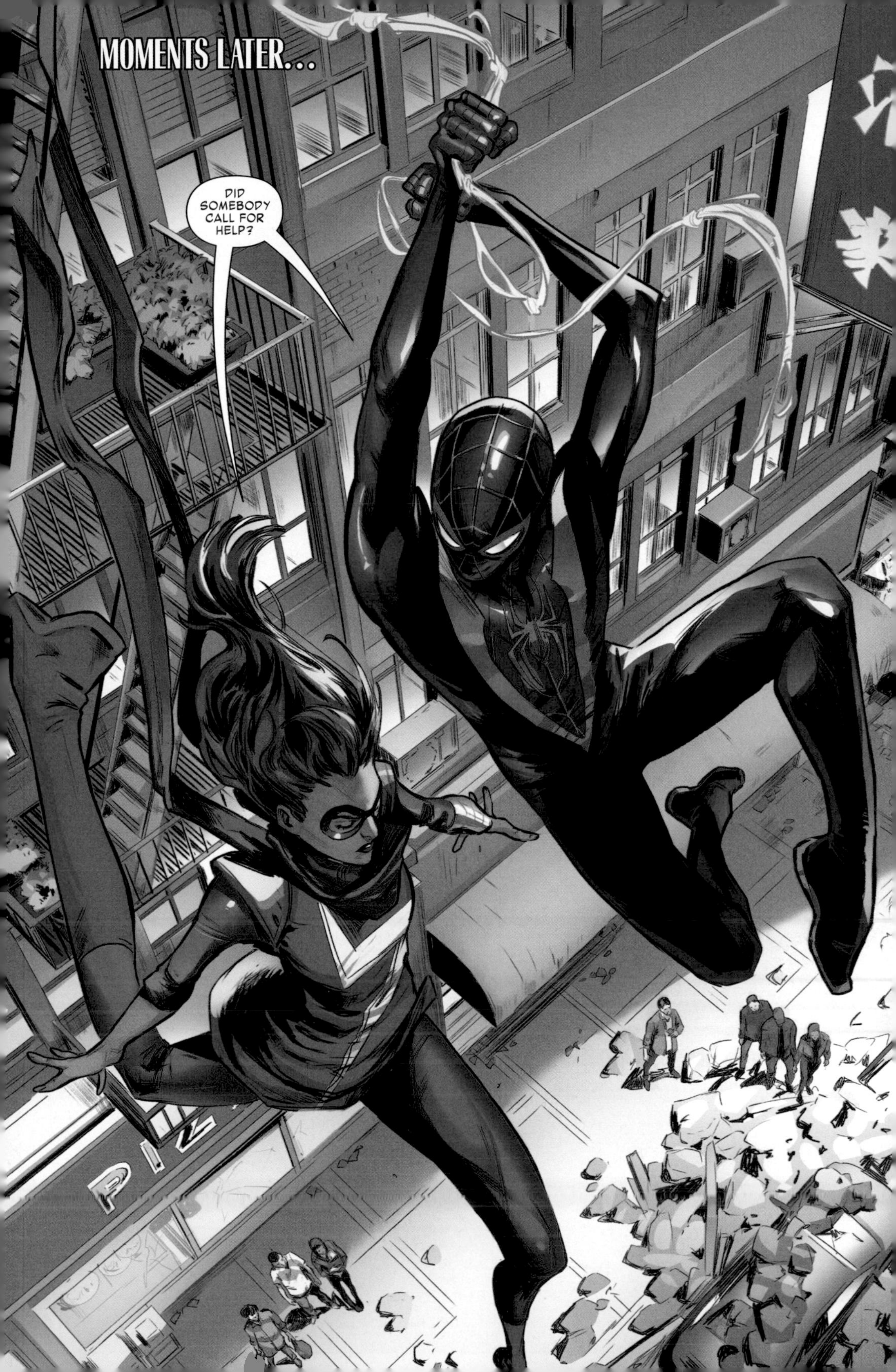
MOMENTS LATER...
DID SOMEBODY CALL FOR HELP?

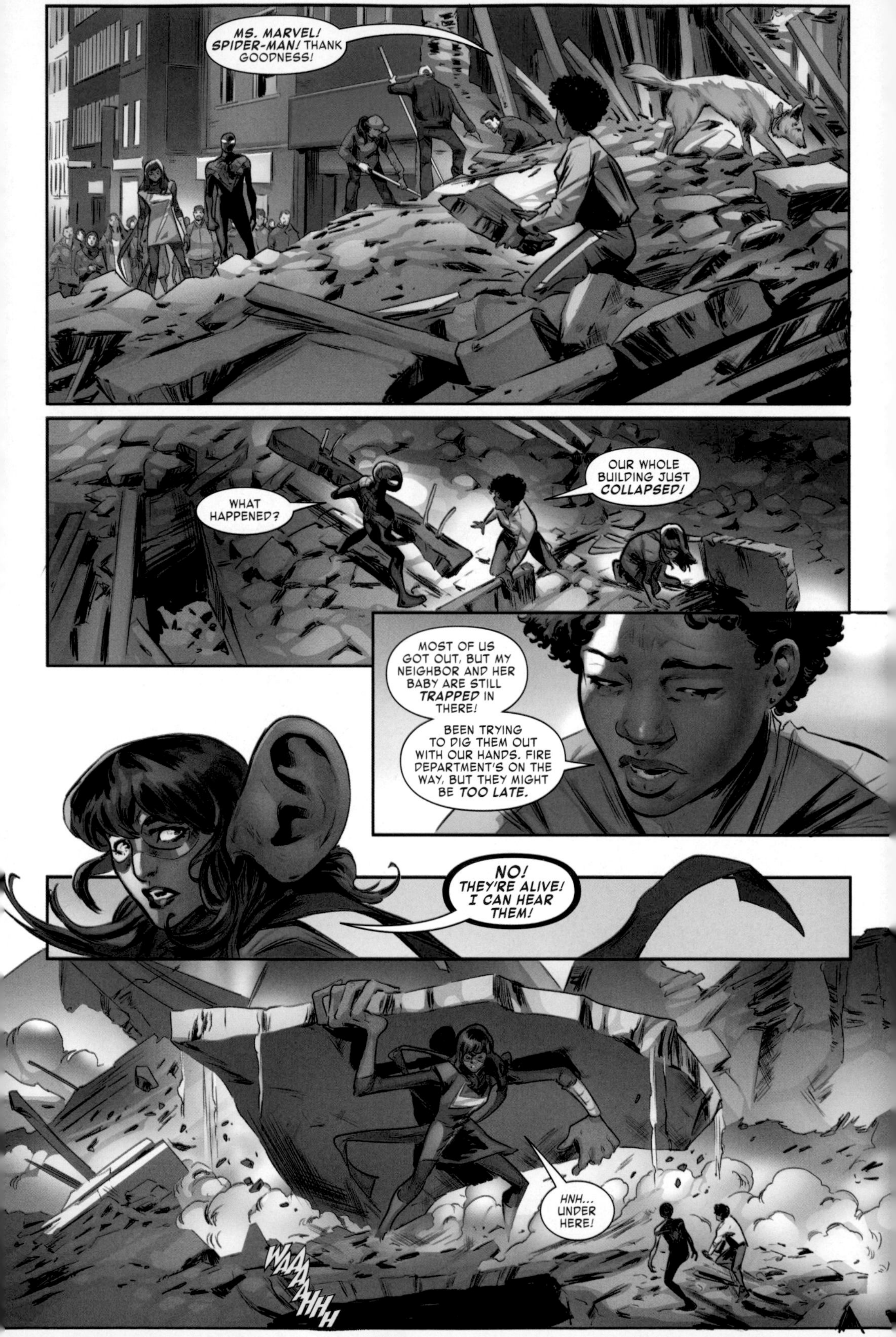

MS. MARVEL! SPIDER-MAN! THANK GOODNESS!
WHAT HAPPENED?
OUR WHOLE BUILDING JUST COLLAPSED!
MOST OF US GOT OUT, BUT MY NEIGHBOR AND HER BABY ARE STILL TRAPPED IN THERE!
BEEN TRYING TO DIG THEM OUT WITH OUR HANDS. FIRE DEPARTMENT'S ON THE WAY, BUT THEY MIGHT BE TOO LATE.
NO! THEY'RE ALIVE! I CAN HEAR THEM!
HNH... UNDER HERE!
WAAAAHHH

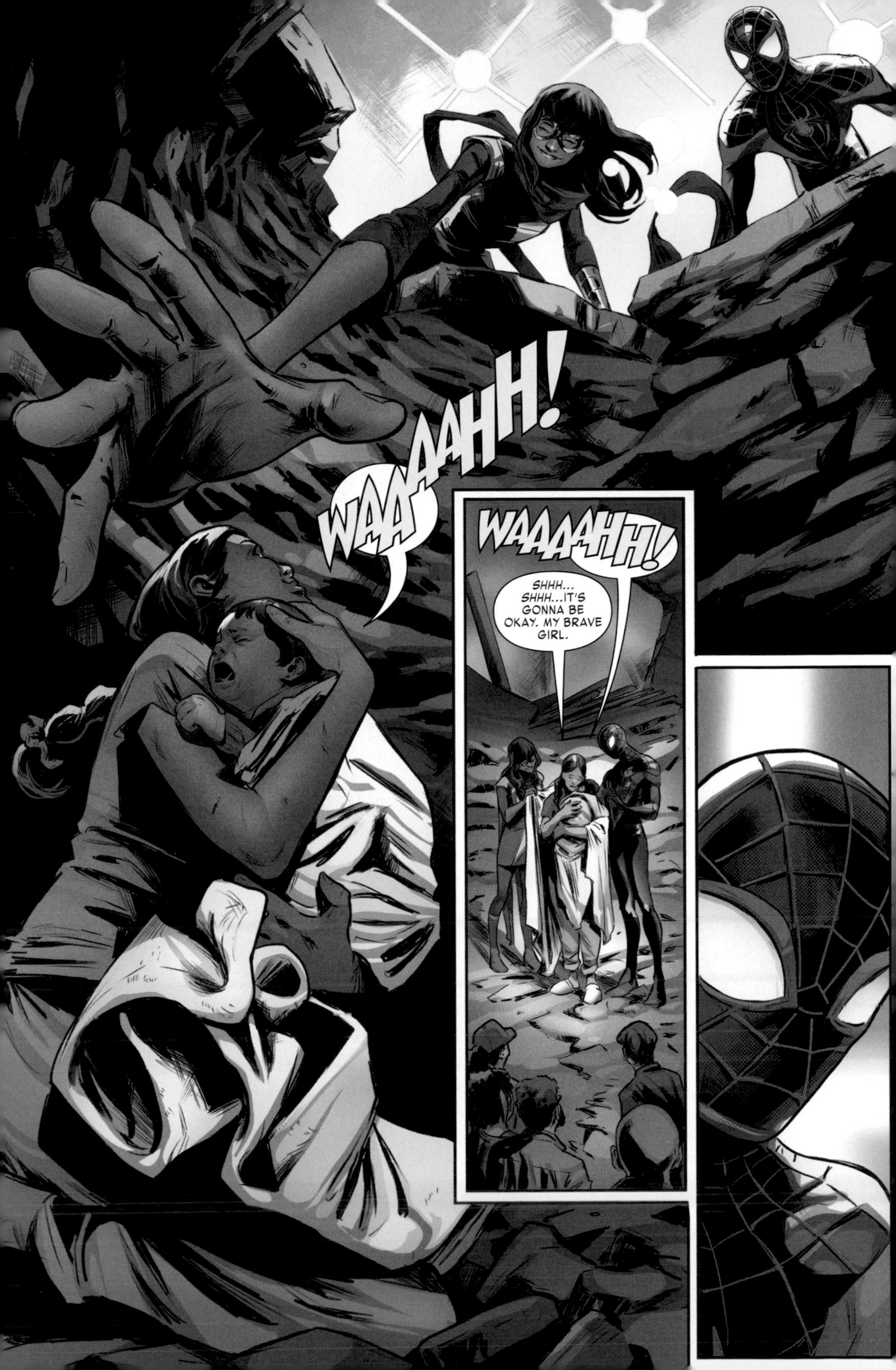
WAAAAHH!
WAAAAHH!
SHHH... SHHH...IT'S GONNA BE OKAY. MY BRAVE GIRL.

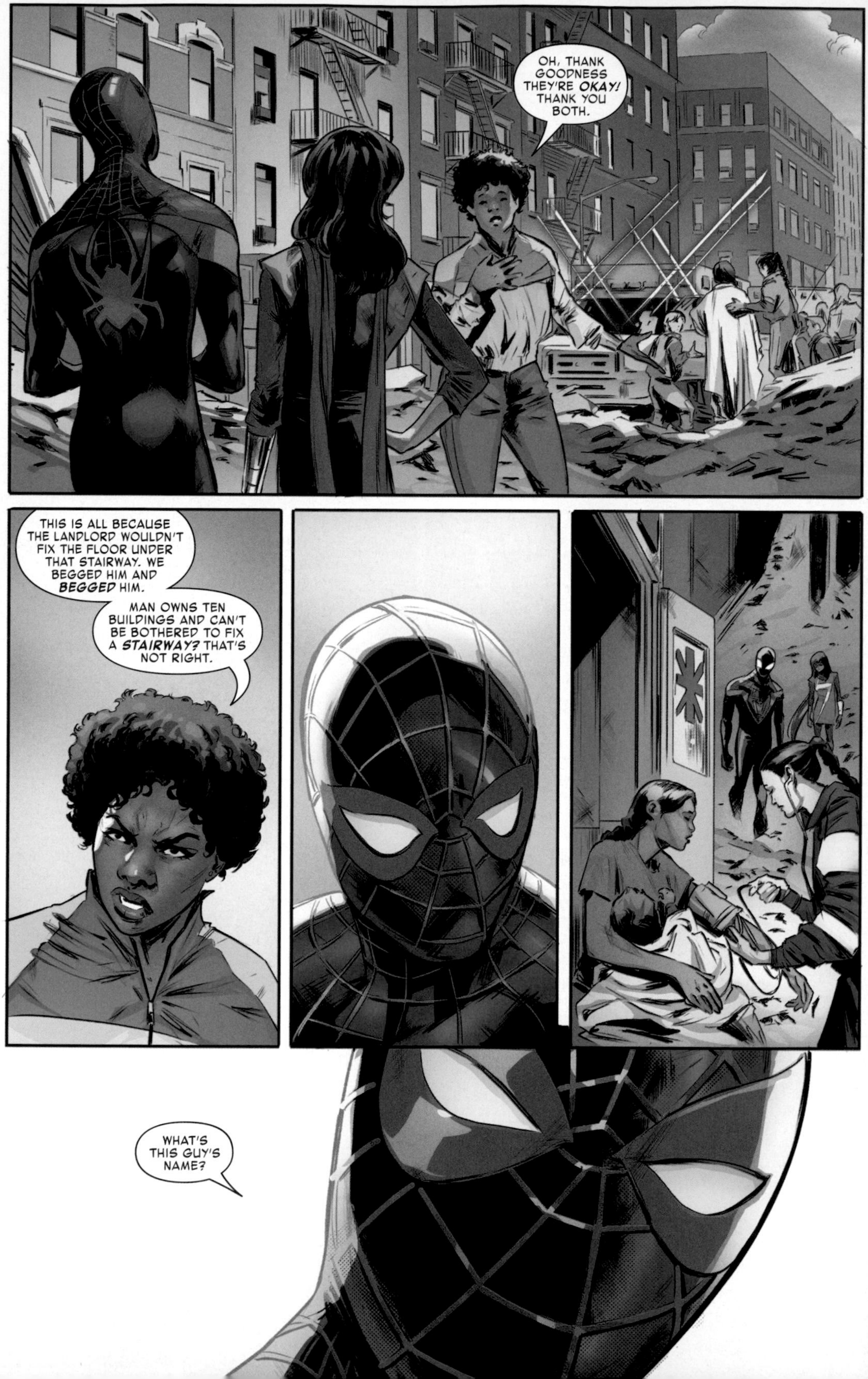
OH, THANK GOODNESS THEY'RE OKAY! THANK YOU BOTH.
THIS IS ALL BECAUSE THE LANDLORD WOULDN'T FIX THE FLOOR UNDER THAT STAIRWAY. WE BEGGED HIM AND BEGGED HIM.
MAN OWNS TEN BUILDINGS AND CAN'T BE BOTHERED TO FIX A STAIRWAY? THAT'S NOT RIGHT.
WHAT'S THIS GUY'S NAME?

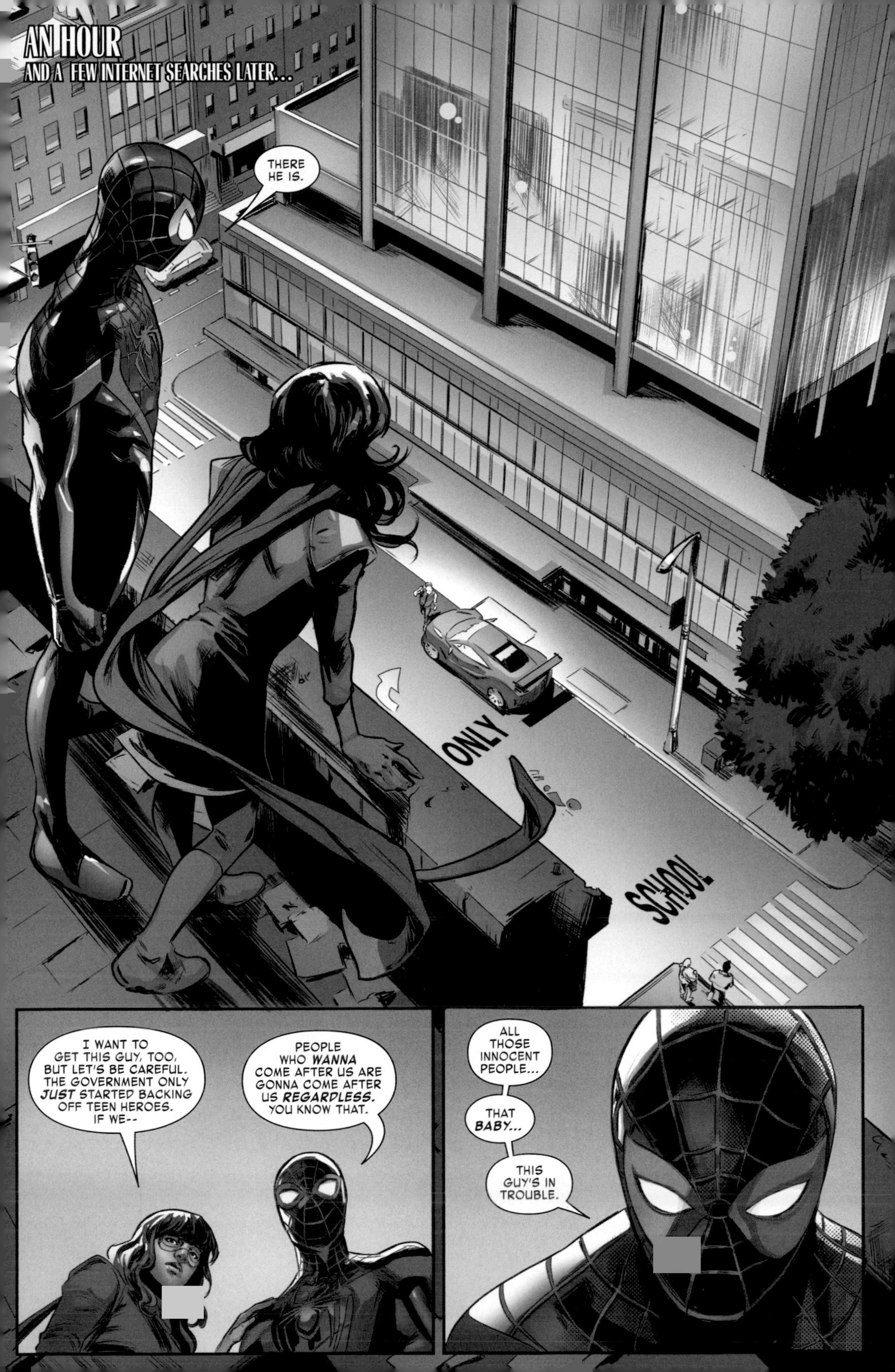
AN HOUR
AND A FEW INTERNET SEARCHES LATER...
THERE HE IS.
ONLY
I WANT TO GET THIS GUY, TOO, BUT LET'S BE CAREFUL. THE GOVERNMENT ONLY *JUST* STARTED BACKING OFF TEEN HEROES. IF WE--
PEOPLE WHO *WANNA* COME AFTER US ARE GONNA COME AFTER US *REGARDLESS.* YOU KNOW THAT.
ALL THOSE INNOCENT PEOPLE...
THAT *BABY...*
THIS GUY'S IN TROUBLE.

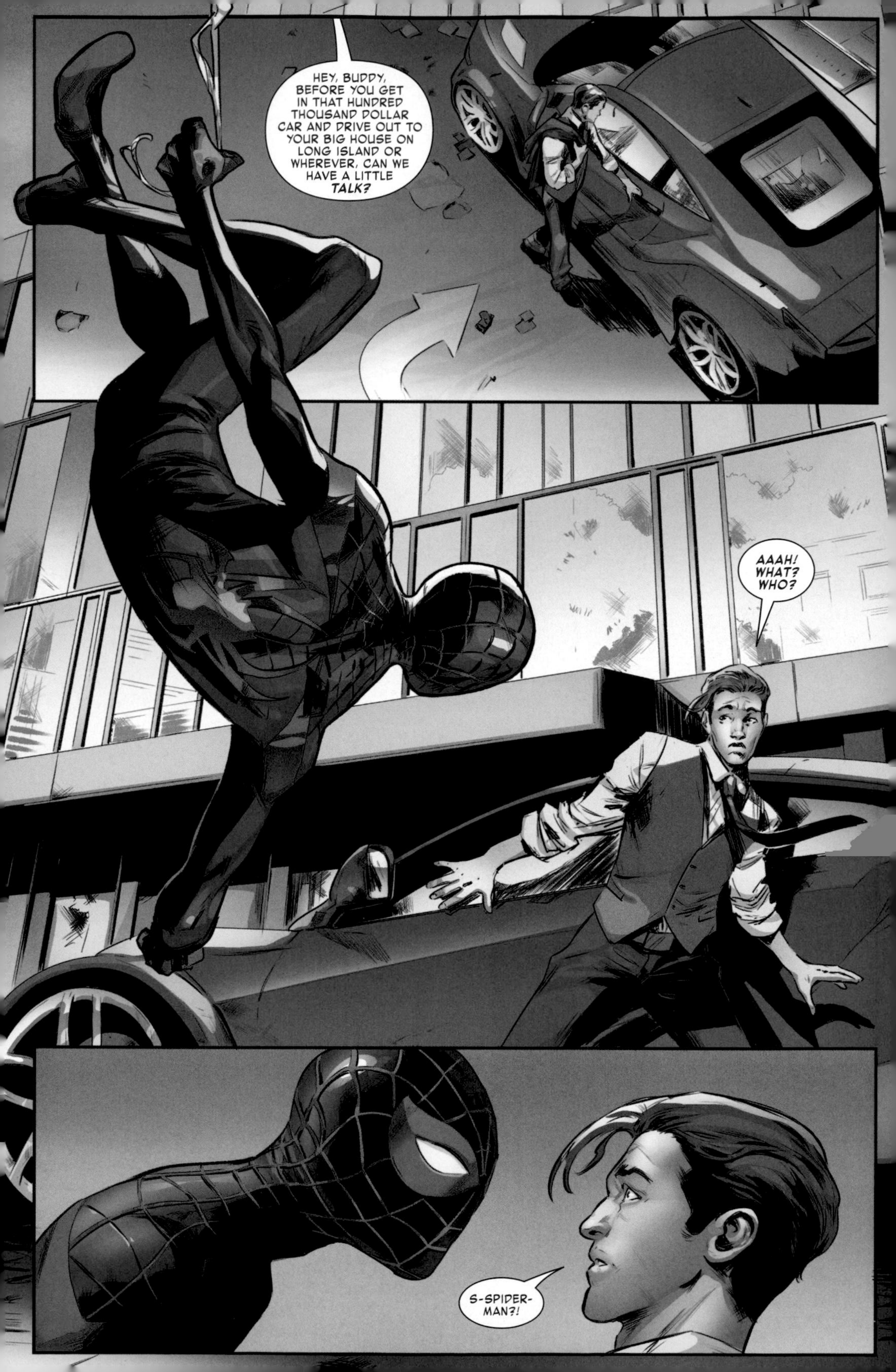
HEY, BUDDY, BEFORE YOU GET IN THAT HUNDRED THOUSAND DOLLAR CAR AND DRIVE OUT TO YOUR BIG HOUSE ON LONG ISLAND OR WHEREVER, CAN WE HAVE A LITTLE *TALK?*
AAAH! WHAT? WHO?
S-SPIDER-MAN?!

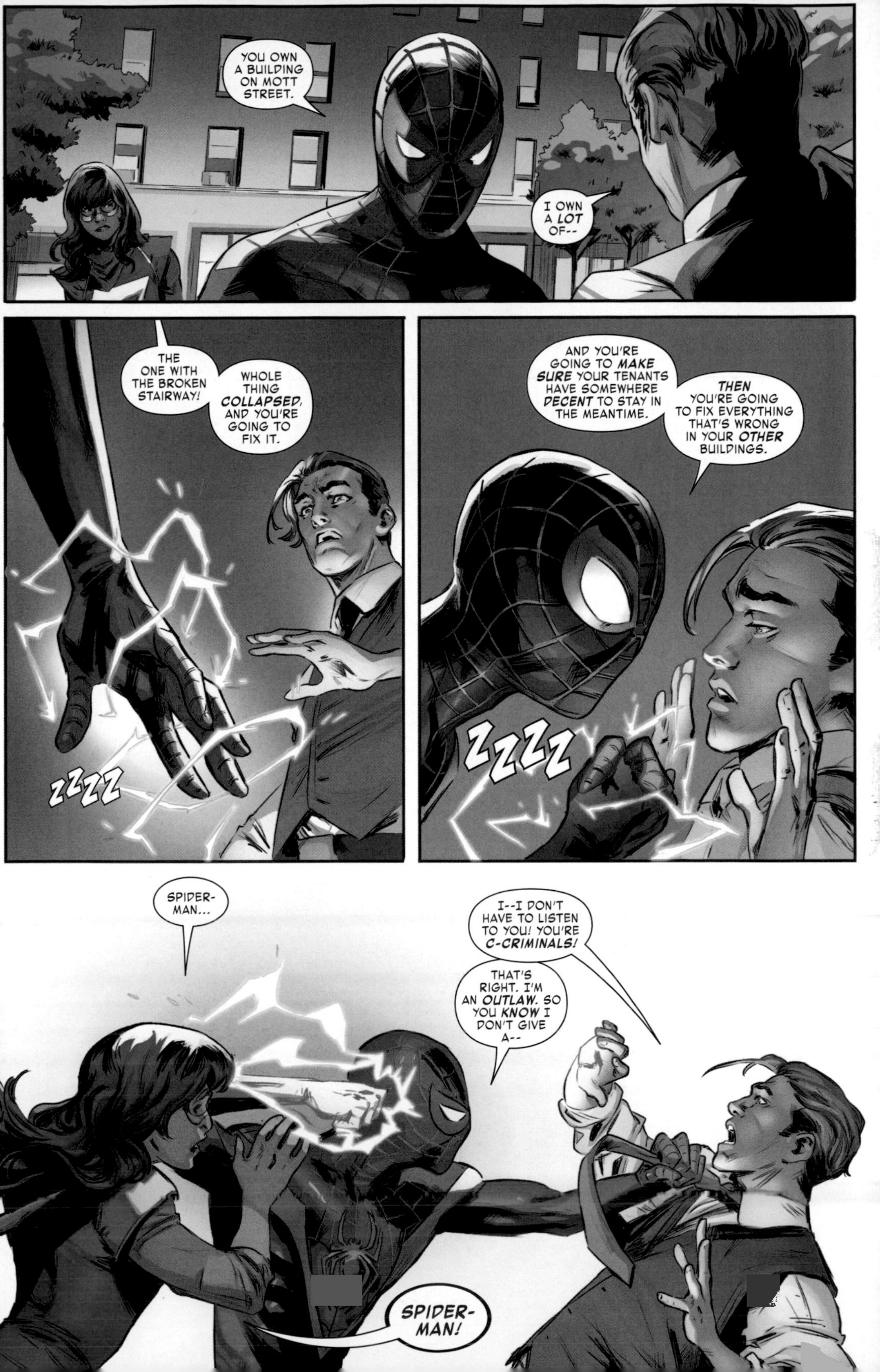

YOU OWN A BUILDING ON MOTT STREET.
I OWN A LOT OF--
THE ONE WITH THE BROKEN STAIRWAY!
WHOLE THING COLLAPSED, AND YOU'RE GOING TO FIX IT.
ZZZZ
AND YOU'RE GOING TO MAKE SURE YOUR TENANTS HAVE SOMEWHERE DECENT TO STAY IN THE MEANTIME.
THEN YOU'RE GOING TO FIX EVERYTHING THAT'S WRONG IN YOUR OTHER BUILDINGS.
ZZZZ
SPIDER-MAN...
I--I DON'T HAVE TO LISTEN TO YOU! YOU'RE C-CRIMINALS!
THAT'S RIGHT. I'M AN OUTLAW. SO YOU KNOW I DON'T GIVE A--
SPIDER-MAN!

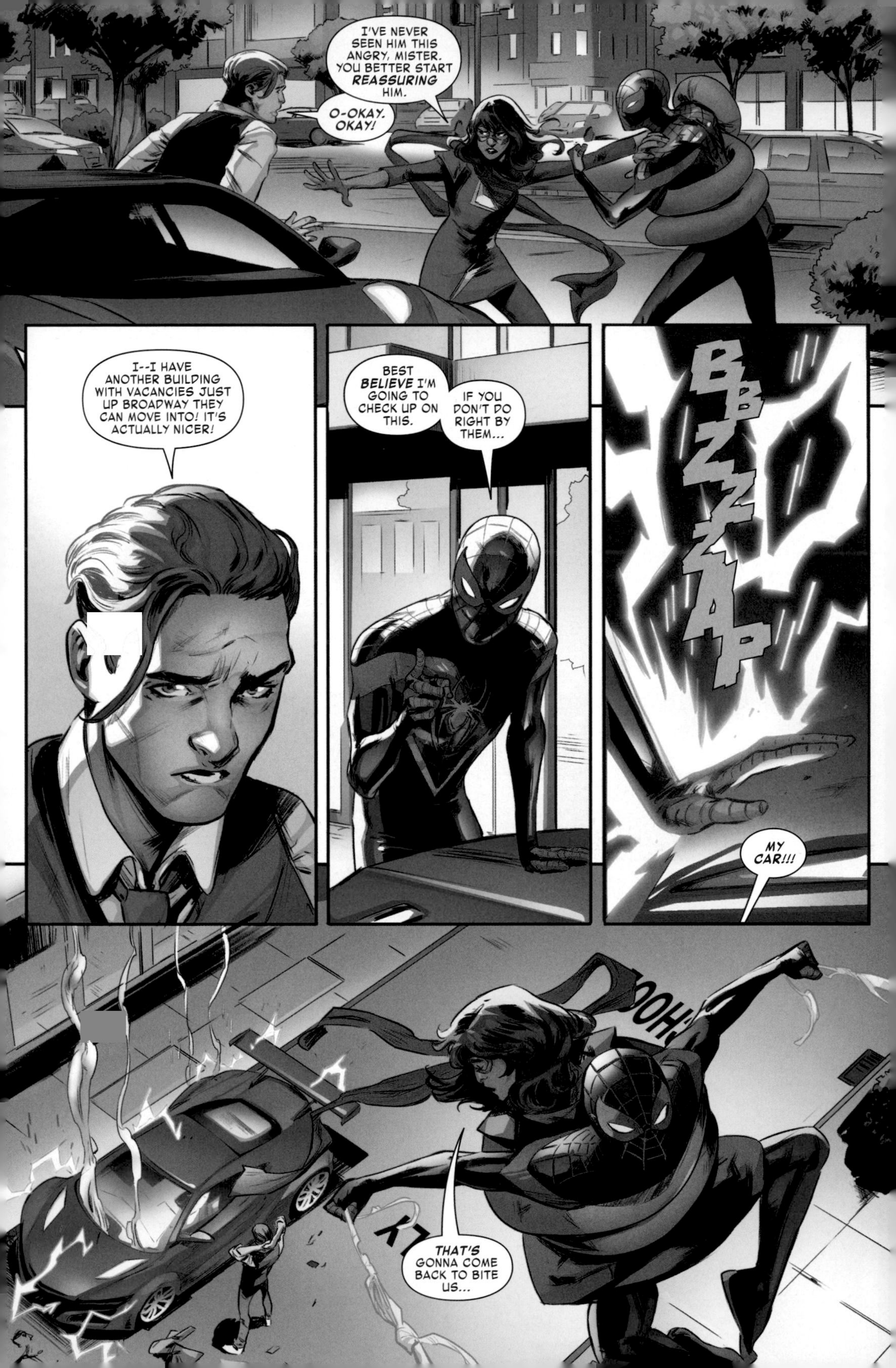
I'VE NEVER SEEN HIM THIS ANGRY, MISTER. YOU BETTER START *REASSURING* HIM.
O-OKAY. OKAY!
I--I HAVE ANOTHER BUILDING WITH VACANCIES JUST UP BROADWAY THEY CAN MOVE INTO! IT'S ACTUALLY NICER!
BEST *BELIEVE* I'M GOING TO CHECK UP ON THIS.
IF YOU DON'T DO RIGHT BY THEM...
BBZZZAP
MY CAR!!!
THAT'S GONNA COME BACK TO BITE US...

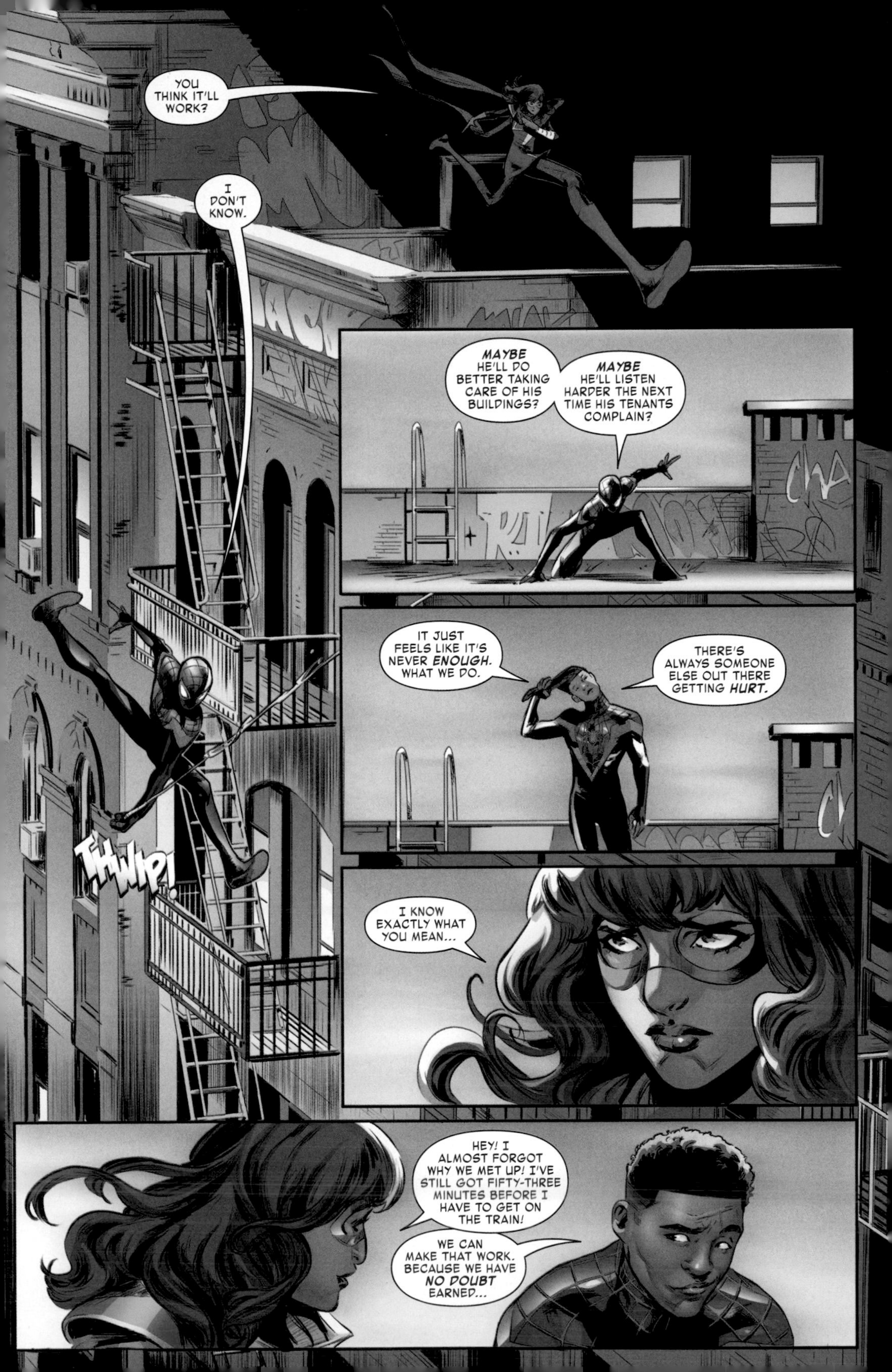
YOU THINK IT'LL WORK?
I DON'T KNOW.
THWIP!
MAYBE HE'LL DO BETTER TAKING CARE OF HIS BUILDINGS?
MAYBE HE'LL LISTEN HARDER THE NEXT TIME HIS TENANTS COMPLAIN?
IT JUST FEELS LIKE IT'S NEVER ENOUGH. WHAT WE DO.
THERE'S ALWAYS SOMEONE ELSE OUT THERE GETTING HURT.
I KNOW EXACTLY WHAT YOU MEAN...
HEY! I ALMOST FORGOT WHY WE MET UP! I'VE STILL GOT FIFTY-THREE MINUTES BEFORE I HAVE TO GET ON THE TRAIN!
WE CAN MAKE THAT WORK. BECAUSE WE HAVE NO DOUBT EARNED...

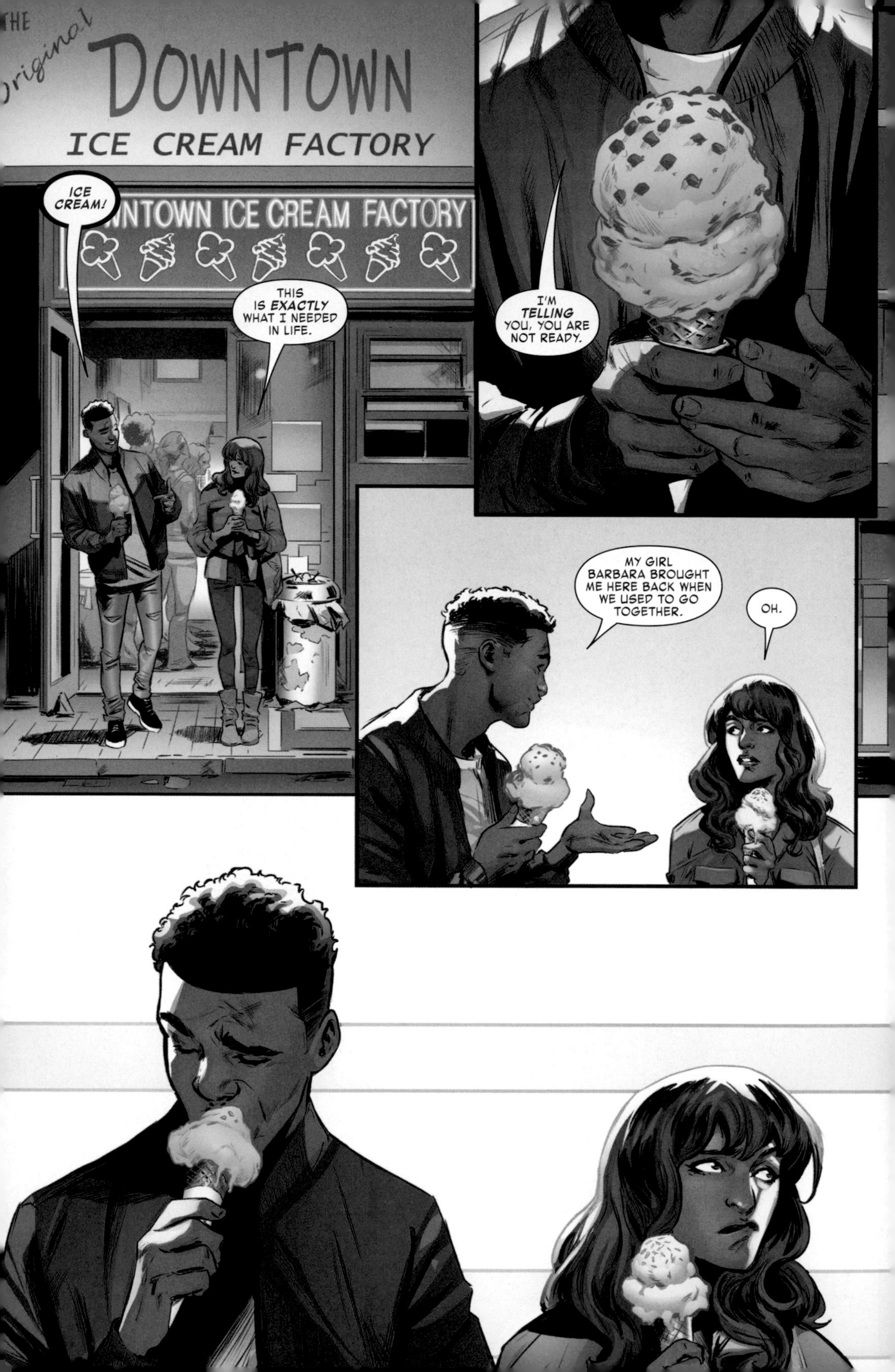
THE Original DOWNTOWN
ICE CREAM FACTORY
DOWNTOWN ICE CREAM FACTORY
ICE CREAM!
THIS IS EXACTLY WHAT I NEEDED IN LIFE.
I'M TELLING YOU, YOU ARE NOT READY.
MY GIRL BARBARA BROUGHT ME HERE BACK WHEN WE USED TO GO TOGETHER.
OH.

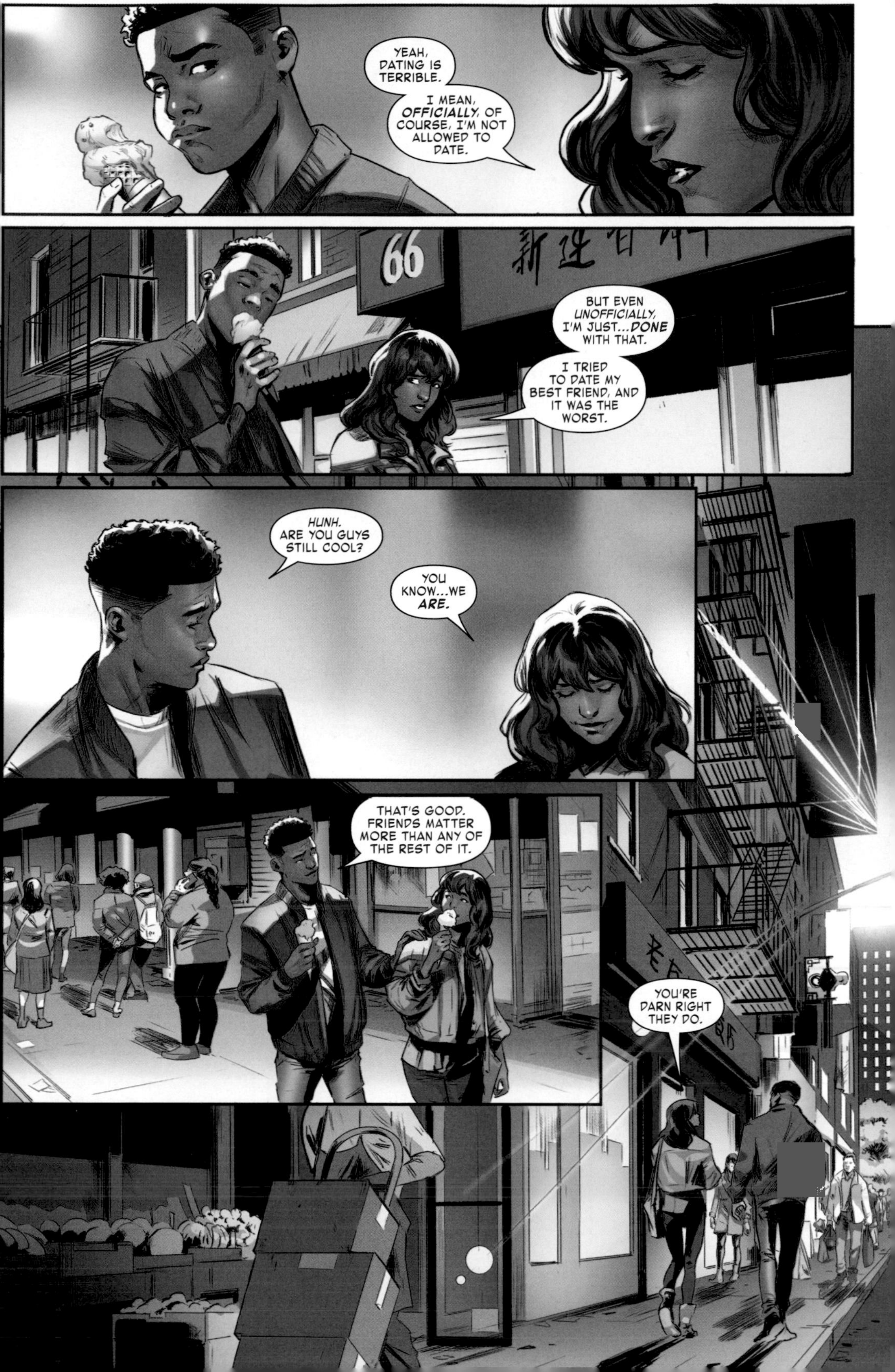
YEAH, DATING IS TERRIBLE.
I MEAN, *OFFICIALLY*, OF COURSE, I'M NOT ALLOWED TO DATE.
66
BUT EVEN *UNOFFICIALLY*, I'M JUST...*DONE* WITH THAT.
I TRIED TO DATE MY BEST FRIEND, AND IT WAS THE WORST.
HUNH. ARE YOU GUYS STILL COOL?
YOU KNOW...WE *ARE.*
THAT'S GOOD. FRIENDS MATTER MORE THAN ANY OF THE REST OF IT.
YOU'RE DARN RIGHT THEY DO.

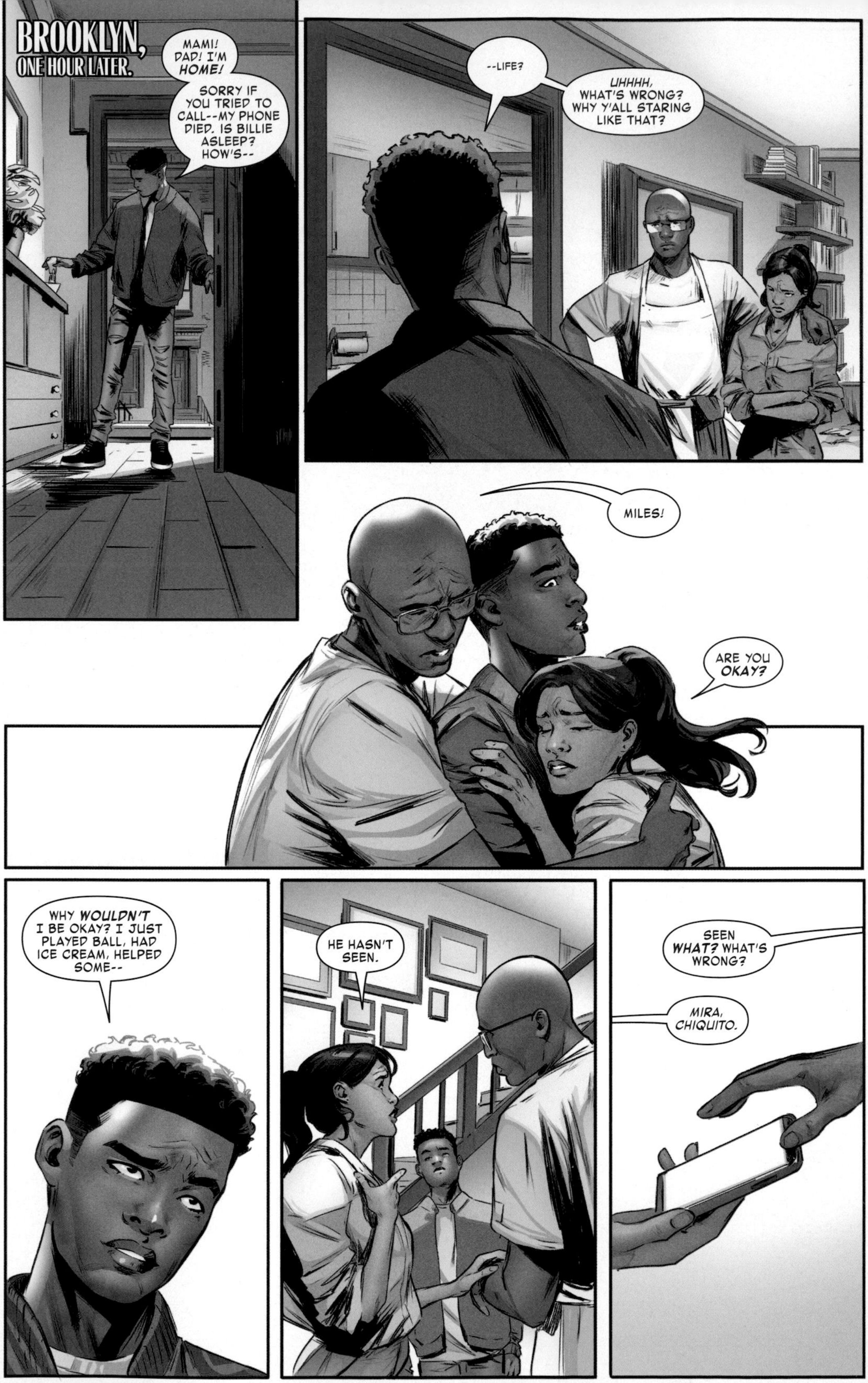
BROOKLYN, ONE HOUR LATER.
MAMI! DAD! I'M HOME!
SORRY IF YOU TRIED TO CALL--MY PHONE DIED. IS BILLIE ASLEEP? HOW'S--
--LIFE?
UHHHH, WHAT'S WRONG? WHY Y'ALL STARING LIKE THAT?
MILES!
ARE YOU OKAY?
WHY WOULDN'T I BE OKAY? I JUST PLAYED BALL, HAD ICE CREAM, HELPED SOME--
HE HASN'T SEEN.
SEEN WHAT? WHAT'S WRONG?
MIRA, CHIQUITO.

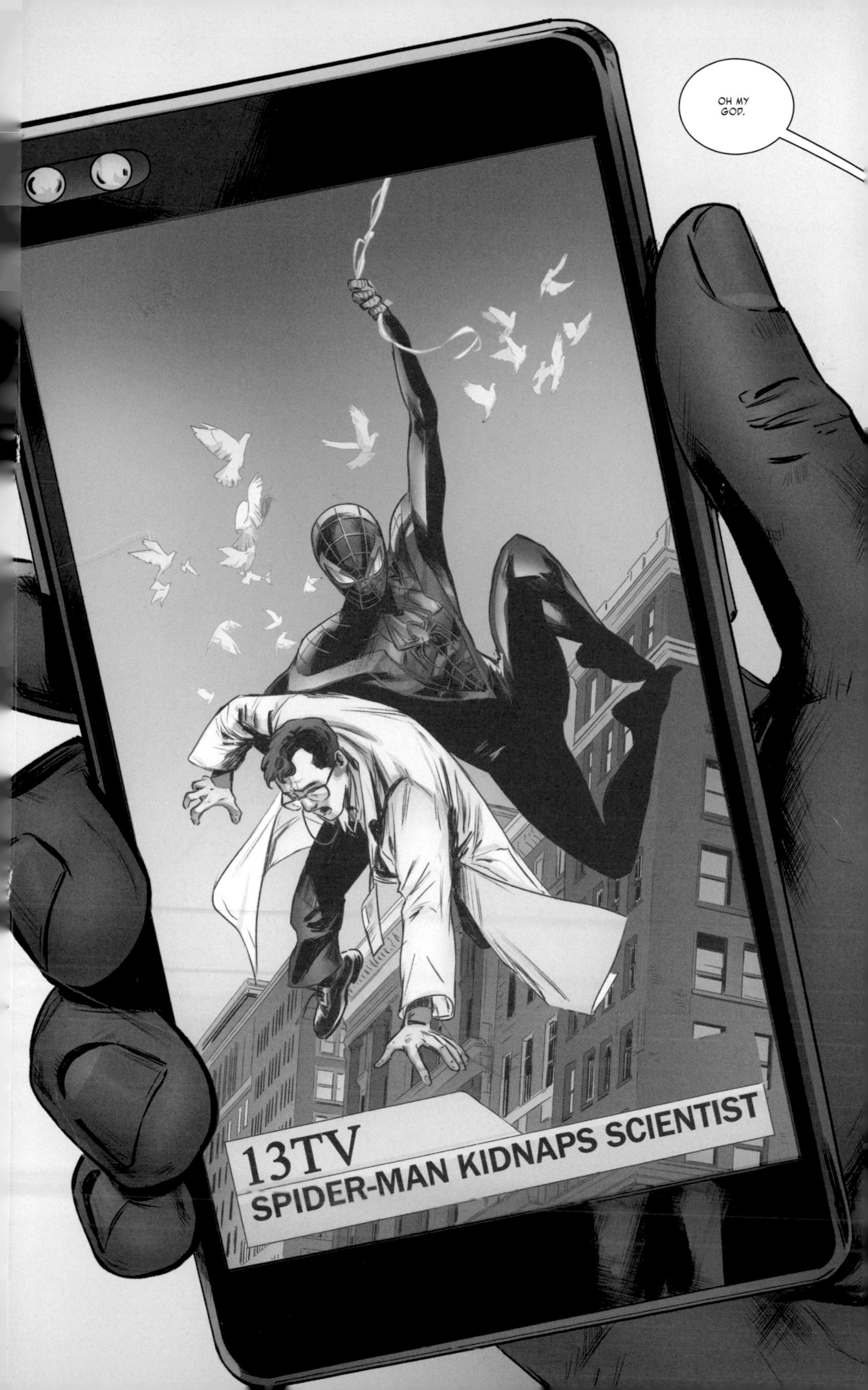
OH MY GOD.
13TV
SPIDER-MAN KIDNAPS SCIENTIST

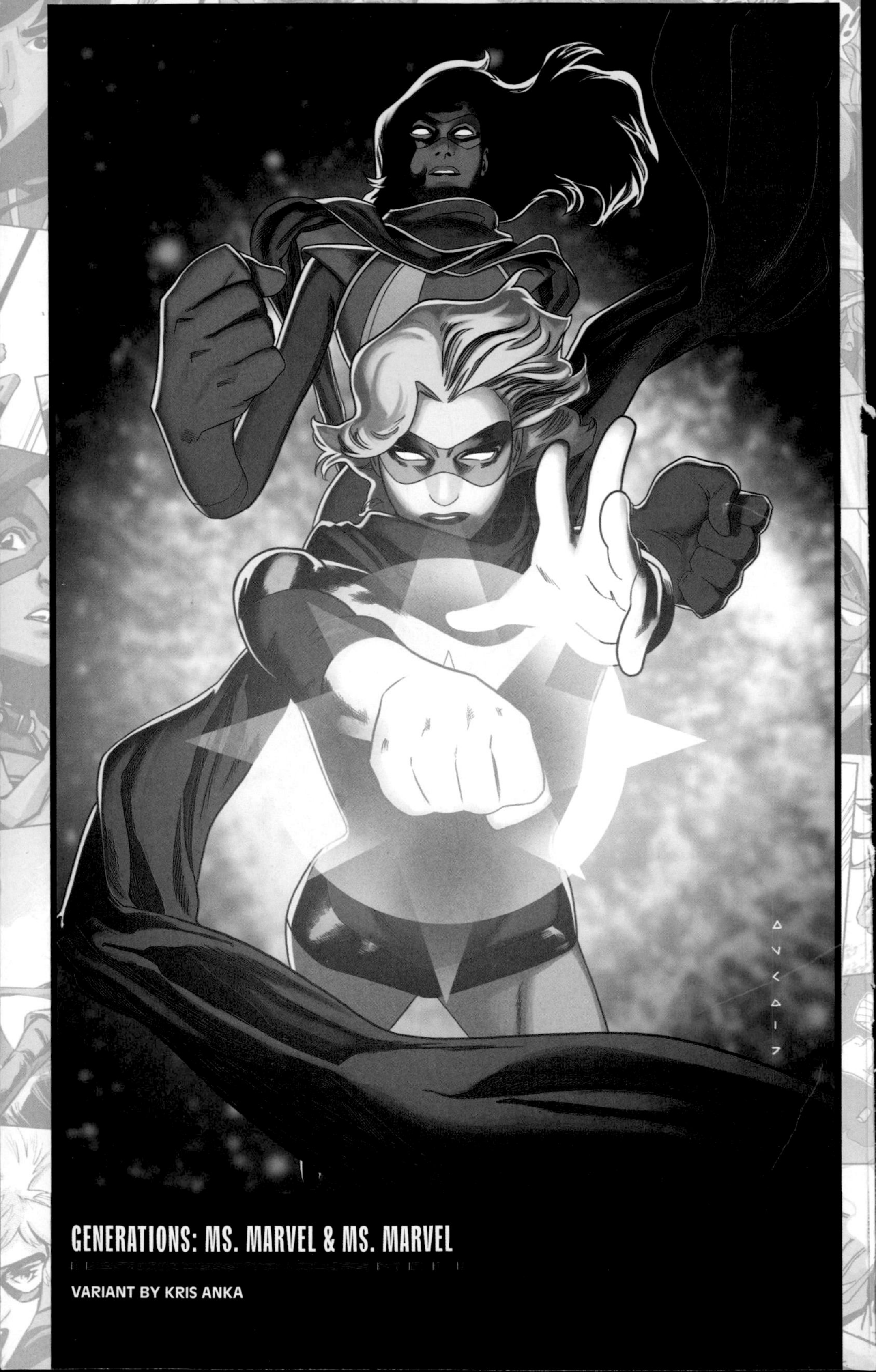

GENERATIONS: MS. MARVEL & MS. MARVEL

VARIANT BY KRIS ANKA